DESTINY:

THE SACRED CITY

Also by Andrew Lawrenson:

Legacy: Shadow Watch

Prophecy: The Dreamlands

DESTINY:

THE SACRED CITY

Book three of the Brotherhood of the Star trilogy.

By Andrew Lawrenson

Published by Pyrian Publishing

Destiny: The Sacred City

ISBN 978-1-910980-06-4 (Kindle)
ISBN 978-1-910980-07-1 (Paperback)
ISBN 978-1-910980-08-8 (Hardback)

Published by Pyrian Publishing
info@pyrian.co.uk

4 6 8 10 9 7 5 3

For Jasmine & Max

"There had been aeons when other Things ruled on the
earth, and They had had great cities. Remains of Them, he
said the deathless Chinamen had told him, were still be
found as Cyclopean stones on islands in the Pacific. They all
died vast epochs of time before men came, but there were
arts which could revive Them when the stars had come
round again to the right positions in the cycle of eternity."

– H.P. Lovecraft, "The Call of Cthulhu"

"Ph'nglui mglw'nafh Cthulhu R'lyeh wgah'nagl fhtagn.
In his house at R'lyeh dead Cthulhu waits dreaming."

– H.P. Lovecraft, "The Call of Cthulhu"

Prologue.

Jack and Jennifer Knight looked at each other across the dark room. Jennifer took a hesitant step towards her husband, stepping out of the shadows and into the flickering torchlight.

'I understand now,' she said in a quiet and emotionless voice. 'I can see how this has to end.'

Jack looked at her as she slowly raised her hand; in it she held an old revolver.

'Jennifer, what are you doing?' His voice was wavering and unsteady, the concern clearly audible in his tone.

'Only what needs to be done for our son.' In contrast to her husband, her voice was calm and even.

Jack took a step forwards and then stopped as she raised the gun higher. 'It doesn't need to be like this,' he pleaded gently. 'We can find another way.'

Jennifer could see a tear in his eye, and she shook her head slowly, looking down at his feet to avoid his gaze. 'This is the only way out for him, I can see that now. I wish there was another way, but...' She stopped, letting the words trail off into silence.

Jack dropped to his knees before her, his tears now starting to flow freely. 'At least look me in the eyes one last time.'

Jennifer lifted her head slightly, so she was looking directly at him, their eyes meeting again across the room.

'I love you,' he said softly.

'I know,' she replied almost inaudibly, as she lifted the gun and took aim. 'That's what makes this so hard.'

'Please don't,' he implored her, his eyes wet and his hands clasped together in supplication.

With a tear in her eye and a lump in her throat, she took a deep breath. For a moment, Jack thought she wasn't going to go through with it, and then she closed her eyes.

'I love you, and I'm sorry,' she whispered as she pulled the trigger. There was a deafening crack as the sound of the gunshot echoed in the small chamber, and then the soft thump of a body hitting the floor.

Chapter 1.

October 12th, 2016. St Ives, Cornwall, England.
6 months earlier.

Jack Knight opened the cottage door and stepped out of the wind and rain, into the shelter of the house. The aroma of home cooking was wafting through the warm air: a chocolate sponge cake if he wasn't mistaken. He took off his wet coat, hanging it on a peg next to the front door to dry before removing his muddy boots and placing them on an old newspaper left by the door for just that purpose. Only once he had shed his wet and muddy clothes did he stroll into the kitchen, where he found Jennifer opening the oven door and sliding out a cake tin.

He stepped behind her, grasping her gently by the waist and giving her a quick kiss on the back of the neck. 'Guess who?'

'I'm kind of in the middle of something, Jack,' she replied, shuffling over to the counter where she rested the cake tin on a heat-proof mat. 'Are you keeping an eye on the time?' she added.

'I've got an hour yet 'til I need to pick Bill up from the nursery,' he replied. 'Plenty of time.'

'Good. You can go and sort out the camera in the back garden then. It's been a week since it last worked.'

'I know, I know,' he replied with a sigh.

'Look, I realize there's never been any sign of them, but...'

'I know. Tomorrow might be the day they catch up with us, find us. They day they try and...' He didn't finish the sentence; it was something that didn't need to be said, something that had lurked at the back of their minds for the last three and a half years – every parent's worst nightmare.

Ever since their wedding day, the same day that Jennifer had realized she was pregnant, they had been on their guard, waiting for the Brotherhood of the Star to return. The cult's leader, Randolph, believed that their son, Bill, was to be a future leader of the Brotherhood, and that the boy's destiny was to be with them. There was no way that Jack and Jennifer were going to let that happen, and they had gone to great lengths to try and prevent it.

They had left the family home that they had inherited in Dartmoor, boarding it up and paying a large fee to a specialist company who would guard and maintain the property in their absence. They had liquidated many of their other assets, cashing in some of their savings, and moved down to Cornwall where they now lived in a rented cottage – paid for in cash and under an assumed name.

They tried to live as anonymously as they could manage, leaving as few clues as possible as to where they could be found. All contact with old friends and family had been severed. They had no credit cards, paid for everything in cash, and all communications were with anonymous pay-as-you-go mobiles, which they replaced every few months. Even their internet usage was kept as anonymous as possible; each had several email accounts opened in fictional names and only ever used at open wi-fi hotspots.

Jack went back to their living room and opened one of the drawers in the desk, digging through the pamphlets and sheets of paper within. He was looking for the manual that had come with the CCTV cameras that they had installed around the property: silent sentries keeping watch for incoming intruders. After a few moments he found it – a few scrappy sheets of photo-copied A4 paper folded and stapled together, written in the usual Engrish associated with cheap Asian goods. He had just opened the manual and started to look through it when he felt a vibration in his pocket and then heard his mobile phone ring. He slipped his hand into his pocket and pulled out the phone; the screen showed that it was Bill's nursery calling.

'Hello?' he said, as he hurriedly swiped the screen to accept the call.

'Is that Mr Smith?' The voice was that of an elderly woman, which he thought he recognized as the headmistress of the local nursery and infants school.

'Yes,' said Jack. They had been living under the names of Jack and Jennifer Smith; something as common and anonymous as possible.

'This is Miss Erikson,' she continued, 'the headmistress here at Willow Primary.'

Jack's heart started beating faster; he could feel it pounding in his head. The nursery wasn't due to end for almost an hour yet. He reasoned that if it was important enough to call and not just wait until the end of the school day, it had to be serious.

'What is it?' he snapped. 'Is there a problem with Bill?'

'There has been an incident here, yes,' she replied. Jack tried to analyse the tone of her voice for urgency but wasn't getting anything. 'If you and your wife are able to come in as soon as you can–'

'What is it?' interrupted Jack. 'What's happened?'

'It's not something I can discuss over the phone, Mr Smith. As I said, if you and your wife could please come–'

'We'll be there in five minutes,' he said, disconnecting the call. 'Jenn!' he shouted. 'Drop whatever you're doing. We need to leave right now.'

❋ ❋ ❋

Four and a half minutes later, their car screeched to a halt outside the school, Jack ignoring the double-yellow lines painted by the side of the road. Just inside the school gates, they could see two police cars parked in the staff car park.

'Shit, shit, shit,' cursed Jack as he and Jennifer opened their doors and hurriedly climbed out of the car. Then he relaxed slightly; he could see other parents leaving the school buildings and taking their children home with them; not just from the nursery but from the infant and junior schools too. 'Maybe it's not just about Bill,' he called to Jennifer over the roof of the car. 'Maybe it's something affecting the whole school – a small fire, or some other kind of incident?'

Jennifer wasn't listening though; she had already set off towards the reception. Jack sprinted after her, but slowed as they were intercepted by Mr

McLeish, a middle-aged man with a beard and thick glasses, the deputy headmaster of the junior school.

'Mr and Mrs Smith,' he said, holding up his hands to stop them. Jack thought he looked uneasy; it was a side of the man he hadn't seen before, and it started to make him feel uncomfortable again. 'Good of you to come so soon,' he said, lowering his arms. 'If you could just come this way...' He indicated off towards the main school building.

'What is it?' challenged Jennifer.

'If you could just come this way,' he repeated anxiously, turning and heading rapidly back towards the main building. Jack noticed that he was nervously fiddling with the wedding ring on his finger as he went. Something was definitely up.

Jack and Jennifer followed him quickly and silently, and were ushered into the head mistress's office. It was a small room with few decorations save for some framed qualifications on the wall. Miss Erikson, the headmistress, was sat behind her desk, and a uniformed police officer was standing at the side of the room, holding his hands behind his back and looking out of the window onto the playing fields. As they entered, he turned to face them, noticeably standing up straighter.

'What is it?' asked Jennifer. 'Will someone *please* tell us what the hell is going on? Where's Bill?'

Miss Erikson stood up, started to extend a hand and then stopped as she saw the expression on Jennifer's face. 'I'm afraid that's why we've called you in,' she said timidly. 'There's no easy way to say this... but Bill has gone missing.'

'What do you mean *missing?*' demanded Jack.

'Just that,' said Miss Erikson. 'He disappeared from his class this afternoon, and I'm afraid we can't find him.'

'Surely he can't just have wandered out,' exclaimed Jennifer. 'Has someone taken him?'

The police officer stepped forwards. He was a uniformed officer whom Jack thought he recognized; it may have been from a school fête where they had brought along a police car for the children to sit in. He seemed nervous here, little beads of sweat visible on his forehead. 'At the moment, there's no sign of any foul play, and no reason to suspect anything sinister. I'm sure he'll turn up soon enough.'

Jack and Jennifer looked at each other. They were finding it hard to reach the same conclusion, but they were aware of factors that he was not, factors they could not easily explain.

'If you could please take a seat,' said Miss Erikson, gesturing towards two chairs in front of her desk. Jack and Jennifer reluctantly stepped forwards, sitting down in the seats.

'From what we can tell so far,' said Miss Erikson, 'the children were having nap time when their teacher, Mrs Purdie, stepped out of the room to get some art supplies from the stationary cupboard. She was only out of the room for thirty seconds and when she returned, Bill was gone.'

'Are you sure it was only thirty seconds?' enquired Jennifer.

'We're fortunate enough to have a CCTV camera facing down that corridor, and we can see that she was gone for less than a minute, and that during that time no one else entered or left through the door.'

'Then someone must have come in through another door...' started Jennifer.

'The only other door in the classroom is a fire exit, and it's alarmed,' replied Miss Erikson. We also have a camera recording the playground it opens onto. We've both reviewed that footage too,' she said, casting a glance towards the police officer, 'and can see that no one comes or goes.'

'Then what the hell's happened?' demanded Jack.

'Our current hypothesis is that Bill has chosen to hide, for reasons unknown,' added the police officer, stepping over. 'Maybe he was scared of one of the other children and wanted to hide; maybe it's all some kind of prank.'

'Bill wouldn't do that sort of thing,' said Jennifer.

'Nevertheless, that does seem to be the most likely explanation,' said the headmistress. 'Are you aware of any other children bullying or taunting Bill recently?'

'Isn't that something that you and your staff should know?' snapped Jennifer.

'Please, Mrs Smith,' she said, just about managing to maintain a professional tone. 'Of course I've spoken to his teacher, and she's not aware of anything, but sometimes bullying can be quite subtle. He hasn't spoken to you about anything like that?'

'No, nothing like that,' said Jennifer, trying to restrain her temper. 'He got on well with the other children.'

'And none of the other kids saw anything?' asked Jack.

'No,' replied Miss Erikson. 'As I said, it was their naptime, and many of them were asleep – or at least had their eyes shut. At the moment, several members of my staff and a couple of police officers are conducting a thorough search of the school. We're sending the other children home to make the task easier – making sure, of course, that Bill doesn't leave with any of them.'

'We expect to find him before long as part of the search,' added the police officer, 'but if not, we plan to talk to each of the children in Bill's class, to double check what they may have seen.'

'If you are able to join with the search, that could help immensely,' added Miss Erikson. If he *is* scared and hiding somewhere, the sound of your voices may help to bring him out.'

They all spent the rest of the afternoon repeatedly searching the school. Every nook and cranny was investigated; every locked room was opened and checked. They even opened the water tank in the roof above the kitchens, before reluctantly admitting failure and expanding the search into the rest of the town.

Sniffer dogs were brought in. Every one of the students and staff in the school were questioned, and every second of CCTV footage was examined and then re-examined. No one could explain how Bill had disappeared from the school in the middle of the day, let alone identify any suspects. Jack and Jennifer gave a press conference at the request of the police, but they knew it would be useless. They didn't yet know how, but they were both convinced that Randolph and the Brotherhood were behind Bill's disappearance.

It was exactly a week after Bill's abduction, and Jack and Jennifer were both in the kitchen, the sounds of a mid-afternoon radio show drifting through from another room. Jack was emptying the dishwasher, putting the crockery away into the cupboards and Jennifer was standing by the sink, gazing absently out of the window at their garden.

Jack had just put the last of the plates away when his mobile began to ring, skidding across the smooth stone surface of the kitchen worktop as it vibrated. He snatched at it, swiping it from the worktop and looking at the screen. Precious few people had this number; they had made sure any enquiries went through the police to cut down on crank calls.

The phone was displaying a number he didn't recognize and he frantically swiped the screen to answer. 'Yes?' he barked into it.

'Jack Knight?' It was the voice of a middle-aged woman who sounded vaguely familiar.

'Yes. Who is this?' he demanded. It hadn't escaped his attention that whoever this was, they knew his real name.

'Detective Sergeant Cross. I heard about your... predicament.'

Jack relaxed slightly, his shoulders slumping. 'Hello there,' he said, his tone softening. 'How can I help you?'

'Actually, I was wondering whether I could help you.'

'What do you mean?' he asked.

'I saw the details of your son's disappearance – I didn't realize it was you two at first, but then, when I saw your pictures...' She cleared her throat. 'Tell me Jack, do you think that this is... well... that same group of people again?' She didn't need to mention the Brotherhood by name; they both knew who she was talking about.

'I haven't got any proof, but yes I do. We both do.'

'Look... I've called to say that if there's anything I can do to help, you let me know. *Anything*. This is my personal phone I'm calling from – you can call me back any time, night or day. I may not be able to investigate officially, but... I've still got resources I can call upon.'

'I see. Why the offer, if you don't mind me asking?'

Cross sighed. 'If this *is* the same lot, then this is personal. Not as personal as for you, obviously, but...' The line went quiet as she thought for a moment. 'Can we meet?'

'Err... sure,' said Jack. 'Where?'

'There's a pub in Oakhampton, the Broken Drum. Can you do eight o'clock tomorrow?'

Jack glanced back at Jennifer, who was looking at him quizzically, wondering who he was speaking to. 'Yeah, that should be fine,' he replied. 'Any problems, I'll call you back on this number.' He thought for a second, remembering the start of the conversation. 'Did you say Detective *Sergeant* Cross?' he asked. 'Didn't you used to be Detective *Inspector*?'

Cross sighed. 'It's a long story. I'll explain everything tomorrow.'

Chapter 2.

October 20th, 2016. Oakhampton, England.

Jack and Jennifer stepped out of the cold autumn air and into the warmth of the Broken Drum. The décor was that of a traditional country village pub; dark timber beams and exposed stonework, with horse brasses and other tack mounted on the walls. The lights were low, with folk music that neither of them recognized quietly playing from behind the bar. Jack didn't think there was anyone in here who wasn't at least forty.

Jack quickly scanned the interior and immediately recognized Detective Cross sitting at a table in the rear corner. It looked like the years hadn't been kind to her; there was now a noticeable amount of grey in her hair, and her face looked considerably more weather-beaten than when they had last met. She was hunched over a newspaper with a pen in one hand. As they approached, they could see she was doing the cryptic crossword.

Cross looked up at them. 'Five letters, Pigment physician. Starts with a D?'

Jack thought for a moment. 'Drink?' he suggested.

'I'll have a coke if you're offering,' said Cross with a grin, placing the pen down on the table.

Jack smiled and headed for the bar to order a round, while Jennifer broke the ice with some small talk. Once they had exchanged pleasantries, their conversation immediately turned to more important matters.

'When I heard about this case, and then your involvement in it, something immediately struck me,' said Cross.

'What's that?' asked Jennifer.

'Well, I presume you remember what happened last time I got dragged into a case involving you?' said Cross.

'If I remember correctly, you said that you were investigating the man who had attacked me, when you came across the scene of a massacre and arrested someone called Randolph,' said Jack. He and Jennifer exchanged glances at the use of the name, but if Cross noticed, she didn't say anything for now.

'That's right,' said Cross. 'I saw some weird things that night. *Terrifying* things.' Jack and Jennifer exchanged another glance with each other, and this time Cross did notice. 'I suspect weird and terrifying might be all too commonplace for you?' she suggested.

Jennifer let a small smile appear on her lips, and nodded for Cross to continue.

'What struck me about Bill's disappearance was how it occurred – the way he just disappeared in broad daylight. Almost a classic locked-room mystery – which is exactly what happened to Randolph after I'd arrested him. That was *literally* a locked-room mystery. He went missing from within a locked police cell, with no trace of him to be found and no evidence of how he went about his escape. Again, like the school, there were CCTV cameras recording outside his cell that showed no sign of anyone entering or exiting through the door.' She sighed and took a sip of her drink. 'The two can't be unconnected, surely?'

Jack took a deep breath, and glanced at Jennifer, who gave him a brief nod to continue. 'Before I start,' he said, 'How does the Statute of Limitations work?'

Cross chuckled. 'I think you've been watching too much American TV – it doesn't really exist on this side of the pond for anything serious. But, unless you've been going round killing innocent parties, I don't think you've got too much to worry about – I'm strictly here tonight in an unofficial capacity – as a friend, not a police officer.'

Jack nodded. 'Good to know.' He thought for a moment and was about to say something when he stopped. 'If we're going to think of you as a friend, I'm not sure you've ever told us your first name?'

Cross sighed. 'It's Betty.' When she saw the looks on their faces she added, 'Not my parent's finest decision, I know. There's a reason why I normally just use *Detective*. Please feel free just to call me Cross. Most people do.'

'Well,' said Jack, 'we may know more about your Randolph than we led you to believe.'

'How so?'

'He's the leader of the cultists that we became involved with.'

'The Brotherhood of the Star?' checked Cross.

'That's the one,' confirmed Jack. 'He wasn't the leader originally – that was another man named Silas. He died that night at the Necropolis – but Randolph wanted to take over after he was gone. Shortly after I returned from Edinburgh, I was approached by another member of the Brotherhood – he told me that Randolph wanted to meet with me, that he had a proposition.'

'He presumably wasn't the one who tried to kill you?'

'No, this was the one who saved me from him.'

'Okay. So what did he want?'

'Randolph suggested a deal to me. An alliance, if you like.'

'He wanted to work with you?' asked Cross. She sounded dubious.

'Let me try and explain,' said Jack, taking another sip of his drink. 'As Randolph explained it, the founder of the Brotherhood was believed to be a prophet, and had made various predictions. Some of these were specifically about Jennifer and me. This was all several hundred years ago, by the way.'

'And you believed this?' said Cross, with noticeable incredulity.

'He showed us a painting, clearly painted long ago, which showed Jack and correctly described events that had happened only recently,' added Jennifer. When Cross raised an eyebrow she added, 'The events in the Necropolis, specifically.'

'Okay, so he managed to convince you that these prophecies could be plausible. What happened next – where did you meet? I'm assuming you met?'

Jack nodded. 'This is going to sound quite hard to believe.'

'Try me,' said Cross with a slight tilt of the shoulders. 'I'm less sceptical than I used to be.' She took another sip of her drink.

'It was in another world,' started Jack. Cross almost spat her drink out and coughed violently. When she had finished, Jack continued. 'It was a world much like this one, but more primitive and fantastical, accessed through your dreams.'

'A dreamland, if you like,' added Jennifer.

'And what happened there?' enquired Cross.

Jack briefly recounted their experiences there, describing up to the point of finding Randolph and journeying to the Shrine of Aloysius. He decided not to mention the incident involving his possession — it would only create more questions, and he wasn't sure it was directly relevant to what was going on now. 'When we found the resting place of Aloysius, we also found a legacy he had left behind, this kind of metal orb covered in runes and engravings. This was what Randolph had been after.'

Cross nodded slowly as Jack described the orb. 'That sounds a lot like what he was after at La Marre's house — the scene of the massacre where I found him.'

Jack nodded back in agreement. 'Once he had that, he left us. One of his colleagues rendezvoused with him, and... Well, what I haven't told you is that there are these rings that allow you to take items with you when you leave the dreamlands. Randolph gave us one in order to return with a book of prophecies that he had given us.'

'So... a magic ring?' asked Cross.

'I know it's hard to believe,' said Jennifer. 'I wouldn't believe a word of it if I hadn't lived through it myself.' Cross gestured for Jack to continue.

'One of his colleagues also had such a ring. She wrapped her arms tightly around him before they both disappeared before our eyes — presumably returning to the waking world. I don't know for certain, but I suspect that's when he disappeared from your cell — I'm guessing he awoke with his partner.'

'I suppose that makes sense,' said Cross. 'As much as any of this makes sense, anyway. I'm still not sure what this has to do with your son, though.'

'According to the prophecies Randolph gave us, Aloysius believed that our child would be raised by the Brotherhood and lead them into greatness. In Randolph's eyes, Bill belonged to them and should be raised by them.'

'Hence, the whole moving away, starting a new life,' said Cross.

'Exactly,' said Jack. 'I should probably also add that Aloysius predicted that Bill would return and kill Jennifer when he came of age.'

Cross turned to face Jennifer. 'And do *you* believe this?'

'Personally, I refuse to believe that my son's destiny is pre-defined and laid out before him,' she said with a stoic look on her face. 'I choose to believe in free will. I will, however, concede that *Randolph* believes it. And that's what makes it an issue.'

Cross nodded slowly, sitting in silent contemplation and staring into space. 'So do you think they used the same trick to snatch Bill?' she asked a few moments later. 'The end result sounds awfully similar.'

Jack grimaced and shrugged his shoulders. 'It's plausible, but it presumably only worked with Randolph because he was able to travel to the dreamlands. We could only go there with...' He shook his head as if not quite believing it himself, '...an ancient ritual.'

'A magic spell?' said Cross. She simply gave a small smile; she had obviously become a believer. 'And presumably you've never done anything like that with Bill.'

'No,' replied Jennifer, shaking her head. 'We've never even tried again ourselves since that night.' She didn't add that since Jack had died there, they believed it to be impossible for him to return.

'Okay, so maybe not that exact same scenario – but it's too similar to just be a coincidence,' said Cross.

'Agreed,' said Jack.

'Agreed,' added Jennifer.

'So what now?' asked Cross.

'I don't know,' said Jack. 'The police are looking for him, and they've got his description circulated at ports and airports, but... I'm not sure Randolph uses those much. The Brotherhood seem to have a knack for staying hidden when they don't want to be found.'

Jennifer nodded. 'Back when they kidnapped me, they managed to get me from America back to Edinburgh, but I'm still not sure how. I was asleep at times, possibly sedated... but I'm fairly sure they didn't use a commercial aircraft – and not enough time had passed to suggest a boat.'

Cross took a sip of her drink and nodded in silent contemplation. 'I suppose the Brotherhood's involvement is good news in a way,' she eventually said.

'*Good* news?' said Jack. '*How* exactly?'

'You said that the Brotherhood wanted to raise Bill to be their leader. That means they've got no intention of hurting or killing him.'

'They do presumably intend to brainwash him into their cult though,' added Jennifer.

'True, but with proper help that should be easier to recover from than physical or sexual abuse,' said Cross. It also means that we've got a bit more time to work this all out. That kind of indoctrination takes months or years. Not that you don't want him back as soon as possible,' she added quickly, when she saw the look on Jennifer's face.

'No, we understand,' replied Jennifer.

Silence descended over the table as they all considered what to do next. Jack finally broke the silence. 'You said you'd explain why you're now a Sergeant rather than Inspector.'

Cross cleared her throat and took another sip of her drink. 'After Randolph disappeared from his cell, I was furious. I wanted to find out *everything* I could about what had happened. About everything that had happened that night. It wasn't my case officially, but I put all my spare time into investigating it – until my superiors found out.'

'Then what happened?' asked Jack.

'As far as I can tell, someone from high up wanted the case closed as quickly and quietly as possible. It was declared that the massacre was gang-related – a gang confrontation gone wrong. I'm guessing it's the only way they could gloss over that many deaths.'

'And you're pretty certain it wasn't?'

'I worked in the Met for a few years before moving over to this corner of the country. I've seen my fair share of gang-related killings in my time – they weren't even close to what I saw that evening. They said that trained attack dogs must have caused a lot of the carnage, but I've seen dog attacks before. This was a step above what even a whole pack of dogs could have done. And gang warfare in a sleepy country village? There was also the same...' She hesitated, trying to think of the right word, '...occult trappings,' she eventually concluded. 'Both crime scenes had what looked like altars, each with the sign of a goat's head surrounded by trees, and a statue of this goat-woman thing.'

Jack and Jennifer looked at each other. 'That doesn't sound familiar,' said Jack.

'According to the official report, that was meant to be a gang symbol. When I started to undertake my own research, however, I uncovered links to an underground cult called *The Thousand Young*.'

'*The Thousand Young*?' replied Jennifer. 'That was the ancient society that the founder of the Brotherhood first joined before breaking away to start his own.'

Cross nodded in agreement. 'Gangland fighting also wouldn't explain what I saw behind the house.'

Jack leaned closer. 'What was it you saw?'

Cross took another deep breath. 'Something struck me, knocked me to the ground. The blow to my head knocked me out for a minute. When I awoke, I saw Randolph standing in front of two creatures. Huge creatures that I think he was conversing with, but not in any language I recognized – or that sounded even vaguely human.'

'What did they look like?' asked Jennifer, her eyes wide with curiosity.

'It's hard to say for certain,' replied Cross. 'It was pitch black, with no lights and thick cloud cover, and they were darkly coloured. I could only really make out their general shape and size – which was huge – although I got a slightly better view of their silhouette when they flew away.'

'How did they explain that as gang-related?' chuckled Jack.

'I was the only one who ever saw them, and I never put it in any official report,' said Cross, with a look of sheepish embarrassment on her face. 'It would have been career suicide – despite the fact that it was true.'

'Well, we believe you, if it makes you feel any better,' said Jack. 'We've both seen enough to know that there's more to this world than most people think. I'd just hoped we'd left that all behind.'

'Anyway,' said Cross. 'I continued investigating – not that I discovered much. There was one time when I thought I was on to something, thought I may have tracked down a member of the Brotherhood. I followed him back to an abandoned warehouse that didn't look as abandoned as it should have been. There were people busy inside and sentries keeping a watch on the outside. I retreated and called in official backup, but when we came back that night, it was empty, deserted. There were signs of recent activity but it had been swept clean: no sign of any crimes, no clues, no evidence.'

'Did you ever find out if he was from the Brotherhood?' asked Jennifer.

'No. I never saw him again. And once my superiors became aware of my extra-curricular activities, they warned me to stop. They said it was a waste of official resources and that there was no place in the force for personal vendettas. But I couldn't. I had to know exactly what had happened, what those things were. When I carried on, they ended up busting me for insubordination. I was demoted, warned that if I continued I would be fired. I'm too old to start another career, and can't afford to lose my pension.

Someone upstairs really didn't want me poking my nose in.'

'So you stopped looking?'

'Stopped *actively* looking. I still keep an eye out for anything that might be related, but there was nothing... until the disappearance of your son.'

'So you can't help officially,' said Jennifer.

'No,' replied Cross with a grimace and a shake of the head. 'Strictly off the books, but I'll do what I can unofficially. If you ever need a favour, if there's anything you think I can help with, just let me know.'

'Can you suggest anything *we* can do?' asked Jennifer.

'Well... if what you say is true... maybe you ought to go back to these dreamlands, see if you can find any trace of Bill there? It's got to be a long shot, but what else can you do? Knowing you two, I don't think you're the type to sit around waiting.'

Jack and Jennifer exchanged glances and a small smile.

'Is there anything you want from us?' asked Jack.

'What else can you tell me about the Brotherhood?' asked Cross.

'They believe in a pantheon of ancient gods,' began Jack, 'who walked on the Earth long before mankind arrived. There are cults like theirs going back thousands of years, each shrouded in secrecy. The main god that the Brotherhood worships has been imprisoned, and can only be released when the stars are right. That was part of their ritual at the Necropolis – an attempt to release him.'

'What do you mean by "the stars are right"?' asked Cross.

'As I understand it, various stars need to be aligned in the heavens for them to be able to release their god from his imprisonment.'

'Some kind of cosmic time-lock?'

'Something like that. From what we can gather, it only seems to come around very infrequently.'

Cross glanced at her watch. 'I need to get going soon,' she said. 'I'm sorry I couldn't help more, but I at least wanted you to know that someone else really knows what's going on and has your back.'

'It's appreciated,' said Jack.

'I'll continue to investigate unofficially,' added Cross, 'and will let you know if I find anything.'

'And we'll let you know if anything changes,' said Jennifer. 'We'll make sure we keep in touch.'

Chapter 3.

October 23rd, 2016. Ash House, Dartmoor, England.

The police search for Bill was continuing but already decreasing in effort from the original frantic searches. The first forty-eight hours after a disappearance were always the most critical. It had now been over ten days, and there had been no sightings, no clues and no leads. There had been no contact demanding a ransom, and while the police would continue their investigation indefinitely, their honest opinion was that if the boy were still alive he could be anywhere by now, probably in a different country. They were told that it would take a very lucky break to turn the case around, and they should brace themselves for the worst.

Jack and Jennifer decided to return to Ash House. They told the police that they wanted to escape the spotlight of the media, they wanted some time to themselves to come to terms with what had happened. In reality, there was just no point hiding anymore, and there was equipment stored there that they would need in their own search for Bill. They brought in a removal company to clear the bulk of their goods from the rented cottage, and returned to Dartmoor with several bags stuffed into the back of their car.

By the time they had unpacked and turned the water and heating back on again, it was evening, the darkness settling over the house. They set themselves to their business, Jack retrieving the *Liber Somniorum* and dream incantations from the basement, while Jennifer retrieved the ring that Randolph had given them; she had left it in a locked drawer in her bedside cabinet.

They still had the clothes and equipment from when they had last returned from the dreamlands, stored in a suitcase in the attic, and Jennifer retrieved them, kitting herself out in the old-fashioned garb.

'Should I try and come too?' asked Jack. 'I mean, we don't think it'll work, but we've only got Randolph's word for that, haven't we?'

Jennifer hesitated for a moment. 'I don't suppose it could hurt, could it?'

'I wouldn't have thought so.'

An hour later, they were both lying in bed side by side, the sheet of incantations under the pillow, as they drifted off to sleep.

Jennifer awoke standing in a dark hall, four flaming torches attached to pillars providing what little light there was. She recognized this as the same place they had arrived the first time they visited these lands, but this time she was alone; as expected, Jack had not been able to join her. The last time she had arrived, she had managed to materialize just outside her intended destination, but that had been a long time ago.

With a resigned sigh, she lifted a torch from a pillar and started to descend the long wide staircase. The sudden change into total darkness was less of a shock this time, as was her arrival outside, finding herself standing in the bright sunlight.

She put the torch down and scanned her surroundings. It was just as she had remembered it, the clear blue sky above the barren landscape, with the rusty red desert laid out before her. As she gazed out across the desert, she could just make out the buildings that she now knew were the town of Aladoth – her destination, where she hoped their friend Armindel would once again be able to help her.

She set off across the sterile wilderness with an optimistic step, but as she drew nearer to the town, she could tell all was not as it once was. The oasis outside the walls of the structure was dry and barren, and the walls themselves were crumbling and worn.

As she reached the edge of the town there was now only an empty space where once there had stood an immaculate set of wooden gates. Looking through, she could see that this was now a ghost town. The buildings stood in ruins, the population gone. Even the animals – the cats and birds that had once called this place home – were no longer present.

She wandered down the deserted streets towards the house were Armindel had lived, but she knew it would be in vain. All that remained was an empty husk of a building, a battered shell of worn and crumbling stone. This all looked to her like it must have happened a long time ago. From her time frame, it had only been a few years since she had last visited, but this looked like it had happened decades ago. Then she remembered that this wasn't inconsistent with her understanding of how time worked here.

If she had any chance of finding Bill here – if he even was here – she was going to need another plan.

Chapter 4.

April 6th, 2017. White Private Investigations, Exeter.

Peter White was dozing behind the desk in his office when there was a knock on the door. He jerked upright and shook his head to try and rouse himself. A glance at the clock on his wall told him he had been asleep for just over an hour.

'Come in?' he called hesitantly.

The door opened to reveal a middle-aged couple standing in the doorway. The lady stepped cautiously into the room, as if hesitant about what she might find within. Her partner followed a couple of steps behind her. She looked to be in her late forties and thin-set, her blond hair cut into a bob. The man looked slightly younger, but sported day-old stubble, giving him a slightly unkempt look. As he stood up to greet them, Peter noticed that he was wearing mismatched socks: one black, one dark blue.

'Please take a seat,' offered Peter, gesturing towards the two chairs sitting in front of his desk. The lady stepped forwards, taking a look around the office before lowering herself gently into the chair, followed shortly by her husband. The office was dark, the drawn shades blocking our most of the daylight and only a small desk lamp providing illumination. Peter thought about turning the main lights on and then decided against it; he'd had to let

"

the cleaning lady go due to cash-flow issues, and didn't want to highlight the dust and dirt that now frequented most surfaces. Instead, he opted for drawing back the blinds, letting a small amount of light from the dying sun in through the window.

'So, what can I help you with?' he asked, as he sat himself back behind the desk and made a show of tidying some papers and placing them into a desk drawer; they were mainly overdue bills.

'We're not sure if you can help or not,' said the gentleman. 'We've never used a private detective before.'

'Not many people have,' replied Peter. *Something my accountant would whole-heartedly agree with*, he silently added to himself. 'But if there's any kind of matter you need someone to look into, then I'm sure I can help.'

'It's about our son,' the man added nervously.

'Kids, eh?' said Peter with a conspiratorial grin. 'Has he got himself into some kind of trouble, or do you only suspect something and would like me to find out what it is?'

'No,' said the lady with a slight sniff. 'He's dead.'

Shit, thought Peter. *My first potential client in a week and I've managed to put my foot in it within the first sixty seconds.*

'I'm so sorry,' he added quickly. 'My most sincere condolences for your loss.' When no one spoke for a few moments, he added. 'So, how do you think I can help?'

'Our son, David, died a couple of weeks ago while at university,' said the man. 'He fell from the window of his university accommodation. The police and coroner ruled it a suicide, but...' He let the words hang, staring into space for a moment.

'You don't agree?' suggested Peter.

'No. He was happy with his life; his course was going well, everything was fine.'

'Did he have a girlfriend?'

'No, but he hadn't just broken up with anyone either.'

No one you know about, thought Peter. 'So you'd like me to investigate, see if I can find another reason for his death. Find out if it truly was suicide, or something else.'

'Yes,' replied the lady. 'We've spoken with the university. His room is still untouched since the police investigation and they're happy for you to take a look. We haven't removed anything – although the police may have – and we can provide you with any other information you might require.'

'Do you have his computer or phone? There may be information on there about what was going on in his life.'

'Yes,' she said. 'The police took them for their investigation, but they've returned them to us. We can arrange to have them delivered to you.'

'Very good. If you choose to use my services, I charge a fixed rate of forty pounds per hour, plus reasonable expenses – travel, accommodation where necessary, that kind of thing.'

'Yes, yes, that's fine. The money's not an issue,' replied the man.

Damn, thought Peter. I should have gone for fifty.

The man reached into his jacket pocket and drew out an envelope. 'This contains the details of where David was staying and contact information for the university, as well as a letter authorizing you to investigate on our behalf. We'll ring them and let them know they should be expecting you, so there shouldn't be any issue there.'

'Very good,' said Peter, taking the envelope and placing it neatly on his desk. He would open it later when they had gone; best not to look too eager.

'I'll arrange for David's laptop and phone to be couriered over tomorrow for you,' the man added. He drew out his wallet. Peter wondered whether he was about to give him a cash advance, but instead he took out a business card, handing it over to Peter. 'If you need anything, call me any time, day or night.' Peter looked at the card: *Duncan Packham, CEO of Packham Enterprises.* The business name was unfamiliar to him; it could have been a multimillion-pound business or a one-man shop. He'd have to assume for now that he could pay, though.

'Very good,' said Peter again. 'I'll let you know the minute I find out anything of interest.'

Chapter 5.

April 7th, 2017. Ash House, Dartmoor, England.

Jennifer awoke with a start, her body twitching compulsively as her eyes snapped open.

'Are you okay?' asked Jack from where he lay next to her. He was holding a book in one hand, a cheap paperback novel.

Jennifer took a second to adjust to where she was. The light of the rising sun was just starting to creep in between a gap in the curtains, casting long shadows over the room.

'I think so,' she said slowly. 'I just had the weirdest dream.'

Jack put down his book, laying it face down on the small table next to his bed so as not to lose his place.

'What happened?' he asked with genuine curiosity. He assumed this would have been an ordinary dream. In the months since Bill had disappeared, Jennifer had taken to visiting the dreamlands several times a week in addition to their more terrestrial searches, trying in vain to find any trace of either him or Randolph. Last night hadn't been one of those attempts.

Jennifer shook her head gently, as if trying to shake a memory free. 'It was odd,' she said, closing her eyes to try and aid her recall. 'I was walking down this hallway, a dark stone corridor, but everything was much bigger than normal. It was as if I was sneaking through some giant's castle.'

'Like in Jack and the Beanstalk,' said Jack, thinking of the story. It had been one of Bill's favourite bedtime books. 'You didn't see any talking harps or golden eggs?'

Jennifer shook her head and swallowed. Jack wasn't sure, but he though he saw a slight shiver run over her.

'No,' she replied. 'But there was an odd feeling to everything. As I wandered down the corridor there were several old wooden doors, arched, with metal reinforcements. As I passed them, I could hear conversations behind some of them, but I couldn't understand what was being said.'

'Couldn't make them out, or were they in a foreign language?'

'I don't think it's possible to dream in a language you don't know,' she said. She closed her eyes and thought for a minute, trying to recall the fragile memories; it was already growing much harder. 'I think it was English, and I could hear the words; I just didn't understand most of them. I don't suppose that makes a lot of sense.'

'It's a dream. It doesn't have to make sense,' said Jack, leaning over and picking up his book again. It didn't sound as interesting as he had hoped. 'That'll just be your subconscious not bothering to fill in the details.'

'There was a word I kept hearing.' She stared into the distance as she tried to recall it. It was something like *kindcord*. Maybe *king corpse*? Do you think it means anything?'

'It's just a dream,' he said in what he hoped was a soothing tone. It came out sounding more patronizing. 'It *was* just a normal dream, wasn't it?'

Jennifer hesitated. 'I guess so, yes. It definitely wasn't the dreamlands. I just... I haven't had a normal dream that felt that vivid for ages.'

'Well then. Sometimes a dream is just a dream.'

'Maybe...' she replied uncertainly, then rubbed her eyes and smiled. She sat up, stretching her arms as she yawned, before rolling over and climbing out of bed.

She opened the bedroom door and stepped out onto the landing. She was heading downstairs to the kitchen, but stopped next to Bill's bedroom and opened the door. Bill hadn't slept in this room since he was an infant; they'd moved away a long time ago when he was still very little, but Jennifer had insisted on unpacking Bill's things and recreating his bedroom just as he had left it in Cornwall. This wasn't about trying to create a shrine to remember him by – more a statement that she was determined to get him back and resume where they had left off, no matter what it took.

She went over and sat down on the bed. Next to her was a bookshelf and she plucked the Ladybird copy of Jack and the Beanstalk from it, flicking through the pages, half of them writing, the others full-page illustrations. Maybe it was just a normal dream, she considered. Bill had obviously been on her mind, and she did associate this book with him, with his bedtime.

She closed the book with a snap, slotting it back into the hole on the shelf, and stood up. The coffee wasn't going to make itself.

Chapter 6.

April 8th, 2017. Dartmoor University Student Halls, England.

Peter White looked at the corridor that stood before him. It was clean and well maintained, with beige painted walls and a tough brown carpet on the floor. It was also surprisingly quiet for this time of night; there was the distant sound of music and the occasional slam of a door, but it was much less rowdy than he would have expected.

He slowly walked along the corridor until he stopped outside room 308. There was no doubt that this was David Packham's room; there were still traces of police crime-scene tape stuck to the door frame.

He reached into his pocket and pulled out the key that the university security had given him. It slipped easily into the lock and he twisted it. There was a quiet click, and the door swung inwards, revealing a dark room beyond.

Peter stepped inside and flicked the switch on the wall to turn the lights on. A dim glow from an energy-saving light bulb illuminated the room and its stark furnishings: a bed with a plain blue duvet and pillow, a desk with various books, pens and papers, a wardrobe and a chest of drawers. There were several music posters on the walls, and an old acoustic guitar sat on a stand in the corner of the room.

He turned and shut the door behind him. Before doing anything else, he drew his phone out from his inside pocket and started the camera. It was unlikely that there was much in the room that *hadn't* been disturbed by the police or university staff, but a process is a process. He carefully took photos of the room from the doorway, and then stepped further inside, taking photos of everything that lay in the room: the clothes in the wardrobe, the items on the desk, the contents of the drawers. You never knew what little detail might be relevant later on.

He stepped to the side of the desk and opened the main window. The cool evening breeze wafted into the room, replacing the stale and stuffy air from inside. He opened the window wide and lent out to get a good look. *This was where he jumped*, he thought as he peered around. He was three stories up. It was a reasonable distance, and while not guaranteed to be fatal if you fell, the odds wouldn't be good for you surviving, as David had found out.

Once he had pulled the window to, just leaving it open a crack to air the room, he turned to look at the items on the desk a cheap lamp, a pen holder full of pens and pencils, a wireless access point, several pads of paper and a stack of books. He examined the titles, taking another photograph of them; they all related to art and artists from the last few hundred years.

There weren't any large electrical items, but then he remembered that no one of David's age would have TVs or stereos anymore – they'd just use their laptop or phone – both of which the police had taken. He'd scoured through both of them when he'd received them from David's parents. They'd contained only what you'd expect from a man of his age: games, messages from friends, lots of music, some porn; nothing untoward or suspicious.

Next, he turned his attention to the contents of the desk, opening its drawer and taking a quick look through; more pens, a pair of sunglasses, a concert ticket, a packet of condoms – unopened. He glanced at the concert ticket – it was for a rock band playing at the university a few days ago – several days *after* he had died.

He knelt down and looked under the bed; nothing but dust. This wasn't turning into the most interesting of crime scenes. He sat down on the bed, tapping his fingers on the mattress next to him and looking around for inspiration.

He noticed the guitar in the corner of the room again and went over to pick it up. He had a quick peek inside the hollow body, and when he was satisfied that it was empty gave the strings a quick strum. It was still in tune and he briefly considered playing a quick tune, but then discounted it. It had been quite a few years since he last played, and he wasn't sure the neighbours would appreciate it at this time in the evening. It also struck him as a pretty unprofessional thing to do, so he ended up just placing it gently back onto its stand.

Instead, he headed back to the desk, picking up the top pad of paper and flicking through the pages idly, looking for anything that jumped out at him. It was all just pages of notes from his lectures, dotted with the occasional doodle.

Just as he was placing the pad back on the desk and reaching for one of the books, the quiet silence of the evening was broken by a blood curdling scream from somewhere up above him. He hesitated momentarily as he wondered what the hell was going on, but then there was another. This was no half-hearted yell of annoyance or playful shriek. This was the scream of someone terrified to the very depths of their soul. He sprinted to the doorway, yanking the door open. Stepping into the hallway he looked left and right for stairs. To his left, he could see the stairwell he had taken to get here, which carried on to the upper floors. He ran towards it, throwing the door open and leaping up the stairs two at a time.

When he reached the next floor, he paused, wondering whether to continue upwards. Then he saw that he was on the correct floor. Students were charging towards him. They were panicking, trying to get away from something in a hurry. He ran down the corridor against the flow, dodging the young women who ran past him, until he stopped before an open doorway. Lying just inside the room was a woman in her early twenties. Her hands were pressed against her stomach, blood seeping from between her fingers.

Standing above her was another woman of about the same age, but this was no normal student. There was a wild, crazed look in her eyes.

'Get away from me!' she screamed, not towards Peter or the girl on the floor, but seemingly to empty space. In her right hand, she held a knife. From a quick glance, it looked like a small kitchen knife: not designed for combat, but still quite effective as a weapon. As if on cue, she slashed frantically at empty air with it.

Peter cast a quick glance at the girl on the floor; it looked like she was bleeding heavily – he would have to do this fast. He stepped into the room, closing the distance between himself and the woman with the knife. As he approached, she whipped around to face him, and he could see the sweat on her face, the madness in her eyes. It looked to him like she was on some kind of drugs; if so, this was one hell of a bad trip. She ran towards him, slashing the knife backwards and forwards, but she was obviously no expert. As she brought her right arm down, Peter brought up his left, grabbing her by the forearm. He twisted her arm backwards, hard, and she dropped the knife, crying out in pain. He followed through by swinging his right arm around, his fist connecting with the side of her head. She collapsed, falling to the floor like a rag doll.

He looked around quickly, spied a lengthy charging cable on the desk and ripped it from the charger. He rolled the unconscious woman over, tying her hands behind her back with the white plastic cable; it would do for now. Then he kicked the knife over into the corner of the room, away from her. He didn't think it would come to it, but he didn't want his fingerprints on the weapon.

The attacker taken care of for now, he knelt down next to the bleeding girl.

'You'll be okay,' he said in a calm and reassuring tone. He looked around for something to help stop the bleeding and picked up a navy-blue sweatshirt from the floor, pressing it hard against the wound. 'Let me have a look,' he asked, still in a soothing voice, trying not to convey any fear. The girl slowly removed her hands as he applied more pressure, then he quickly removed the cloth, carefully trying to look at the wound as quickly as possible. It was nasty, but not too deep. He didn't think it would be fatal, just as long as she received some medical assistance.

'Just keep pressure on this,' he said to the girl, placing her hands back on top of the cloth. 'I know it looks bad, but I think you're going to be just fine.' He'd seen quite a few stab wounds in his time, and this one wasn't even in the top ten. Hell, he'd even been stabbed himself, nearly fatally.

He drew his phone from his pocket again, dialling 999 to request police and an ambulance, even though he was pretty sure someone must have already done so. When he had finished, he was about to put his phone away when he stopped. Instead, he opened the camera and panned around the room, taking several dozen shots; of the attacker, the victim and the room itself. It was always best to have as much evidence as you could, and he seemed to have found himself two crime scenes for the price of one.

Chapter 7.

Peter was sitting in a bedroom just across the hall from where the attack had taken place; the police had commandeered this room to try and minimize disruption to the crime scene. Whoever normally lived in the room was nowhere to be seen. Peter guessed that most of the students on this floor – hell, most of the students in this building – probably wouldn't be staying here tonight if they had anywhere else they could go.

He was trying to wipe the last of the blood off his hands with a damp towel when a familiar face appeared in the doorway. It was Detective Cross.

'Well, isn't this a blast from the past,' she said casually as she strode into the room.

'Good to see you too,' chuckled Peter.

'It sounds like you did a good job tonight,' she said. 'Saved the life of that student, by all accounts.'

Peter shrugged, as if this was an everyday occurrence.

'What were you doing here?' she asked. The question was phrased as a casual remark rather than as part of a formal interrogation.

'I was on the floor below, investigating another student's suicide,' he replied. 'Happened a couple of weeks ago, the parents wanted me to look into it and see if it was anything more sinister.'

Cross nodded silently, as if recalling this. 'So... an attempted murder and a suicide within a couple of weeks,' she pondered.

'Or maybe two murders,' replied Peter with a mischievous grin. 'I haven't finished my investigation yet. In fact, I've barely started.'

'Either way... Is university life that much harder than it used to be, or are they putting something in the water supply?'

'It does seem rather coincidental,' said Peter, and then shrugged. 'But you know... coincidences do happen.'

Cross took out a notebook from her jacket pocket, and flicked through a couple of pages, looking at something written there. 'Have you been seen to by the officer in charge?'

Peter nodded. 'I've given a brief statement. I'm coming in tomorrow to give a formal one.'

'And the paramedics?'

'Yeah. I'm fine. Any concerns about the psychological stress of the event disappeared when I told them about my military background.'

Cross gave a slow nod. 'Okay then. I'm sure you can go if you need to.'

Peter stood up. 'Can I have a look at the crime scene again before I go? Just in case it's in any way related to my case?'

Cross hesitated for a second, and then gave a smile. 'Sure, as we go back a way, why not. But only from the threshold. Your DNA will be all over the crime scene already, but there are still rules.'

Peter walked back over to the room where the attack had occurred and stood in the doorway.

A couple of crime-scene technical experts wearing full-body coveralls and face masks were on their hands and knees, examining the floor around where the attack had taken place.

'Don't worry about him – he's with me,' said Cross, and Peter took out his phone and leaned in through the doorway. It all looked as he re-membered it, but he still took a few more photos, taking his time this time, carefully making sure he took everything in. His hands were steadier than before; hopefully any photos would be less blurred.

'Have you seen Jack and Jennifer Knight recently?' he asked casually as he took the photos, thinking back to the last time he and Cross had seen each other.

'A few months ago,' she said.

'Didn't they have a kid?' he asked. 'How's he doing?'

Cross took a deep breath and sighed. Then she stepped closer to Peter, talking now in hushed tones. 'He's gone missing. We think the Brotherhood was behind it.'

'Shit,' he exclaimed under his breath. 'How?'

'He went missing from his nursery in the middle of the day. No one's been able to explain it.'

'That's some seriously bad news,' he reflected as he put his phone away again. 'If there's anything I can do to help, just let me know.'

Chapter 8.

April 9th, 2017. Ash House, Dartmoor, England.

Jennifer woke up and opened her eyes. As she looked up, she noticed that the ceiling above her was different. Unlike the ceiling of her bedroom which had decorative Artex swirls, this was a dropped ceiling made up of large white tiles. Some of them were made of an opaque plastic with a dull white light glowing behind them.

She slowly turned and looked around. She was lying in a large metal bed with clean white starched sheets. Seven other beds were placed evenly around the room, its walls clean, white and empty apart from a few plug sockets and a large mirror on one wall. Some kind of machine was sitting on a metal trolley next to the bed, but its screen was black, the power switched off. Was this a hospital? Had she been in some kind of accident?

She climbed down from the bed, which seemed further from the floor than expected, and stepped towards the only exit. The door seemed unusually tall and stood ajar.

There was something wrong here, she could feel it. She felt as if there was something lurking, watching her, *studying* her. She tried to move faster, but as she moved towards the doorway, it was as if she was wading through water – everything seemed overly slow and cumbersome.

She stopped at the door, grasping up at the handle, and pulled it towards her. It opened into a vast long corridor, the ceiling towering high above her. No lights were on in here, and the dark shadows made her wary. Several closed doors, all of a similar size, were present on either side, but at the other end another door stood ajar, light spilling out into the otherwise dark corridor.

Slowly, she shuffled towards the door, feeling irresistibly drawn towards it. She reached up, grabbing the handle, and pulled it. The door swung quietly open, and she slipped into the room on the other side. At the far end of the room, she could sense a group of men sat around a table, talking. She could hear the sounds of bottles clinking and could tell that some of the men were drinking – the voices were loud and angry, which made her feel unusually nervous.

She tiptoed across the floor, staying in the shadows and out of the men's sight, towards where a large white-board was hung on the wall. It was covered in a mess of writing, jumbled up words and letters. Pictures were stuck to the side of the board, images of faces and places that she didn't recognize. Words were written underneath them. Words that she felt that she ought to be able to read but, for whatever reason, could not.

Suddenly, fear gripped her as she turned and saw a man standing facing her. He was gigantic, towering over her.

'What you are doing in here?' he snarled in a booming voice. 'You're not supposed to be in here!'

She turned to get away from him, and caught her reflection in a window on the other side of the room. Only it wasn't her face looking back at her.

With a jolt, Jennifer sat upright in bed, her breathing rapid and shallow. 'It's Bill,' she cried out, shaking Jack from his slumber. 'It's Bill!'

Five minutes later, they were both downstairs in the kitchen. Jennifer was sitting at the table, still in her dressing gown, and Jack had just made two cups of strong black coffee. He walked back over to Jennifer, passing her the mug and then pulling up a chair opposite.

Jennifer took a deep breath, inhaling the rich aroma before she took a sip. She loved the taste of coffee, but always found the smell even more intoxicating.

'So you think you were seeing... what?' asked Jack, breaking her out of her reverie. 'A dream of Bill's? Were you seeing through his eyes?'

'I... I just don't know,' she stammered. 'Now I've woken up properly, it all sounds so stupid. But just at that instant – I was convinced.'

'We've been through too many lucid or prophetic dreams to just discount this.'

Jennifer nodded. 'I can't just ignore this.'

'But how? How is this happening?'

Jennifer shrugged and shook her head. 'I'm not even sure *what's* happening.'

'So what can you remember? If this *is* something that's happened to Bill, did you see anything to help us work out where he is?'

Jennifer shook her head and inhaled another deep breath from her coffee. 'There was some kind of notice board,' she said. 'It was covered with words and pictures, but I just couldn't make them out clearly.'

Jack thought for a second. 'That other dream you had a few days ago. Was that set in the same place?'

'No,' said Jennifer almost instantly. 'The first place felt old, almost medieval. This second place seemed modern, almost hi-tech. They both had the same sense of scale though – I think that was because I was seeing them from Bill's perspective.'

'Was there anything else in common between them? What about that word you couldn't place in the first dream? *Kin-cord*, or *king-corpse*?'

Jennifer took a longer pause this time, but then started to nod. 'Yes,' she murmured. 'I think that may have been one of the bits of writing on the notice board.'

'Did it start with a K or a C?'

Jennifer thought for a moment. 'A K.'

'Are you sure?'

'No. This is all hazy – and it could just be wishful thinking. But what else have we got to go on?'

'Not much,' admitted Jack.

'So what now?'

'Why don't you go have a shower and freshen up, and I'll do some research and see what I can find.'

✳ ✳ ✳

'Okay, I've been trying to find any references to kin-cord or something similar,' said Jack, when Jennifer finally came back into his study. She was still wearing her dressing gown, but now had her hair up in a towel. 'I've come up with a few possibilities,' he said beckoning her over, and she came and stood behind him, leaning over his shoulder as he sat as his desk. He could smell the faint aroma of her coconut shampoo.

'The first is a place called Kincopse in central France,' said Jack. 'It's a small village, quite old.'

He switched to a page in his browser and Jennifer leant further over his shoulder, peering closely at the pictures; it was a website about the village, quite an amateurish affair. Some of the photos were overlooking the village from the outskirts, while some were of the town centre.

'Does any of that look familiar to you?' asked Jack. He scrolled down the page to show further pictures of the town: the town square, town hall, church.

'I'm afraid not,' she said.

'Okay, how about the next one,' said Peter.

Jack clicked on the next link, and browser changed to a company website. 'This is Kin Corp, a small company in Scotland that researches family histories, family trees...'

Jennifer shook her head. 'No...' she murmured.

Jack clicked and the laptop screen changed again, this time to show several countryside pictures. There were a few photographs of nondescript concrete buildings and their surroundings. 'There's not too many pictures of this one,' said Peter. 'It used to be an old stone quarry, but since it was re-purposed by the MOD, its exact nature has been classified. The current theory is that it was a nuclear bunker and arms store. It was mothballed over twenty years ago now, but there still isn't a lot of information about it.'

'What's it called?' asked Jennifer as she looked at the pictures.

'It's now referred to as Tarsham Bunker, but was originally Kincord Quarry. What do you think?'

Jennifer sighed and shook her head again. 'No. Sorry.'

'Okay, try the next one,' said Jack. 'This one's an old mental hospital — abandoned for many years now. Kincord Sanatorium.'

'That's it!' exclaimed Jennifer as she looked at the pictures that flashed up in front of her.

'Are you sure?' asked Jack.

'Not one hundred per cent,' she replied. 'But now that I've seen it – the shape of that building, just the look and feel of the place – it feels right.'

'What the hell do they want with an abandoned sanatorium?' asked Jack.

'Maybe somewhere to hide something?' offered Jennifer. 'Or where something is hidden?'

'Maybe somewhere for them to hide out?' suggested Jack.

'Whatever the reason, we need to go,' said Jennifer, standing up straight. 'If there's any chance Bill's there, I'm not waiting. I can't afford to let him slip through our fingers – we're going right now.'

Chapter 9.

Kincord Sanatorium, the New Forest, England.

Jack drew the car to a halt a hundred yards down the road from the aging sanatorium, pulling off the tarmac and onto a patch of dirt and gravel. The sun was starting to set and the road was quiet; they hadn't seen another car for several minutes.

The sanatorium was a huge gothic building, standing alone in the middle of the countryside; Jack assumed that not many locals had liked the idea of inmates as neighbours. A short stone wall topped with tall iron railings encircled the building and its grounds, which were surrounded on three sides by a dense forest. On the opposite side of the road were farmer's fields, and beyond those, more woods.

Jack and Jennifer withdrew torches from the back of the car, pocketing them before heading towards the tall front gates on foot. They stood firmly closed, the long driveway behind them snaking all the way up to the front of the building.

When passing from a distance, the building had looked impressive in the afternoon sun, but as they drew closer the true story become more apparent; most of the windows on the ground floor were boarded up, and very little glass remained in the frames of the ones higher up. The tiled roof was sagging in places and completely collapsed in others; pieces of fallen masonry littered the grounds in front of the building.

As they reached the gates, they saw that they were not just shut but padlocked. Jack felt the padlock and chain in his hands; solid, heavy and rusty.

'We're not getting in this way,' he muttered to Jennifer.

She was standing ten feet to his right, looking at a large board that had been mounted on the wall. It was covered in warning notices.

'Have you brought your hard hat?' she chuckled. 'It also says that trespassers will be prosecuted.'

'Like that's ever stopped you before,' replied Jack. 'Let's look for a way in round the side.'

It didn't take them long to find a section of the wall where the brickwork had crumbled. It was off to the side of the grounds, half hidden by trees and bushes, and left just enough room for them to squeeze in under the railings.

Once inside, they found themselves in what would have once been a car park; although there were no vehicles, they could make out faint white lines on the few parts of the asphalt not covered in grass and weeds. Small piles of beer cans and empty wine bottles were scattered by the walls, suggesting that local kids had probably found this way in before them.

They had started to walk slowly towards the front of the building when Jack stopped, holding his arm out in front of Jennifer to stop her too.

'Over there,' he whispered, squatting down behind a ragged bush and gesticulating towards a small portacabin near the front of the main building.

Jennifer crouched down next to him. 'What?' she replied in hushed tones. 'What am I meant to be looking at?'

'That building. In the shadows... Is that someone in there?' muttered Jack quietly.

Jennifer squinted for a moment or two before replying. The squat rectangular structure was in bad condition, possibly worse than the main building. Its windows were gone, and it looked like some of the roofing was missing too. Amateur graffiti covered the side nearest to them, declaring that the Fallout Kidz had been here before them. The inside was dark, but through an empty window frame, Jennifer thought she could just make out the shape of a man deep in the shadows. He was sitting in a chair, lying forwards against a table.

'It's hard to tell, but I think you're right,' she said. 'What now... do we go the other way round?'

Jack said nothing for a good thirty seconds, staring intently. Then he stood up. 'He hasn't moved at all since we've been here. Either he's a really good sentry, he's asleep, or...'

'Or what?'

'I'm going to go and have a look.'

'For God's sake, be careful,' she hissed at him.

Jack crept slowly towards the small building, shifting from bush to bush for cover. It didn't take him long to reach the edge of building, and then he slowly inched along the wall.

Jennifer held her breath as she watched him draw closer and closer to the window through which they had seen the man. He stopped and then peered inside before leaning all the way in through the empty frame. Then he pulled himself back out, turned and waved his arm to beckon her. She casually jogged over to join him. She slowed as she approached, and then stopped when she could see the man more clearly.

'Is he dead?' she asked.

Jack nodded. 'And the body isn't cold yet, so it can't have happened too long ago.'

'You mean they're still here?'

Jack shrugged. 'There's a good chance, I suppose.' He looked at the corpse again. 'Do you reckon he's one of them?'

Jennifer stepped closer to get a better look. The body was dressed in black: black leather boots, combat fatigues and a thick woollen turtleneck sweater. There was a chunky signet ring on his left hand and a small stud in each of his ear lobes. 'He's not dressed like a security guard or groundsman, so possibly...'

'So then who killed him?' asked Jack.

Jennifer paused for a moment and then started walking around side of the cabin.

'Where are you going?' hissed Jack.

'To get some answers,' replied Jennifer, stopping by the door and grabbing the handle. When she turned it, the door swung open and she stepped inside.

Jack followed her through to find her standing over the body. He was sitting in a chair; his arms were slumped onto the desk before him and his head was resting face down on them. A large crimson stain had soaked through the back of his sweater, a pool of blood congealing on the floor under the chair.

Jennifer picked up a short metal bar from the debris on the floor and poked the body; unsurprisingly, it didn't move. Then, with her arm extended, standing as far back as she could, she placed the bar under his neck and lifted it up. With a grunt of effort, she managed to lift his head; it rose up and then flopped back, hanging at a horrible angle.

'Looks like his neck's been broken as well as being stabbed in the back,' grimaced Jack. 'Whoever did this wasn't messing about.'

'Look in his pockets,' urged Jennifer, 'for any identification.'

'Are you kidding?' replied Jack, staring at the blood-soaked corpse before him.

Jennifer just stared back, gesticulating as if to indicate that they weren't mucking around here. Jack reluctantly reached over, patting the corpse's trouser pockets.

'Nothing,' he replied.

'Okay,' said Jennifer. 'Let's continue.'

'Are you sure,' said Jack. 'Whoever did this is obviously prepared to kill. Shouldn't we call the police first?'

'And say what? How would we explain our presence here without implicating ourselves? The police have never exactly been a great help to us.'

'Well... what about Cross? She could help.'

'Her force isn't responsible for this area... and it would take her too long to get here. With every passing second, Bill could be getting further away.'

'We don't even know he's here!'

'No, but we can be fairly certain that there's someone here who could lead us to him. Or there was. We need to get going, Jack.'

Jack shrugged and nodded as he grudgingly accepted this. 'Okay, but for God's sake, let's just be careful. I'm getting too old for this shit.'

'That's something we can both agree on,' said Jennifer. 'Come on.'

Together, they left the smaller building and headed towards the front door of the asylum. As they drew closer to the building, they spotted an empty window, one without glass that had lost its boarding. Jack crept along the wall and took a quick peek through the opening. The inside looked like it might have once been an office, but it was hard to be sure. It was unoccupied, however, and so he climbed through, followed closely by Jennifer.

With most of the windows boarded up, the inside was dark, and they drew out their torches. A few pieces of wood, what might have once been shelves or cupboards, were still attached to one wall but were badly rotted. The plaster on the walls was crumbling away, revealing disintegrating wooden boards beneath, and the floor was littered with chunks of stone and rotted wood and cloth. There was a strong smell of mould and decay in the air. A single empty doorway led out of the room, and they left through it.

It opened into a long corridor stretching to their left and right. Its floor was bare stone, covered in rocks, dirt and wooden debris. Opposite were empty window frames opening onto an inner garden and allowing in some more light. Several doorways stood on either side, their doors missing. Halfway down, a solitary metal wheelchair lay on its side, the upmost wheel curved and bent. Further along, there was a large hole in the ceiling where part of it had collapsed.

'How long ago did you say this place was abandoned?' asked Jennifer.

'About thirty years ago – in the eighties,' replied Jack. He was peering through another of the doorways. This room could have been a dormitory; several iron bed frames stood on the floor in different states of disrepair. There were piles of rotting materials scattered around that might once have been sheets or bedding.

'Let's keep moving,' urged Jennifer. 'We're on the clock here.'

They carried on down the corridor, looking through the doorways as they passed. All the rooms were in a similar state of decay, and none of them contained anything of any obvious interest.

It didn't take long to reach the end of the corridor, where they found a staircase. Inside, there were wooden stairs heading up and down. It looked decidedly rickety; the wood looked warped and rotten, the banister in the middle mostly gone.

'Shall we?' suggested Jack.

'Up or down?'

Jack was about to suggest heading upstairs when he heard a noise echoing from far away, a deep clanking sound of metal on metal. 'Was that from downstairs?' he whispered to Jennifer. She nodded back by way of reply. 'I guess it's down then,' he confirmed.

The stairs descended to a landing a floor below, where it then bent back on itself, continuing down to the basement. Jack took a few hesitant steps down the stairs; the wood was damp and slippery, creaking as he trod on it. He stopped, standing still as he felt the wood underneath him bending and flexing.

'Is it okay?' called Jennifer.

'I think so,' replied Jack as he started his descent again. He moved cautiously from step to step until he reached the far landing. He turned, looking back up at her.

'It's fine, it's just a bit–' he started, when the floorboards underneath him disintegrated. His reply was cut short and he plunged down through the newly formed hole. He grabbed out as he fell, letting out a cry as his arms hit the floor and temporarily halted his fall. He looked up at Jennifer, only his upper torso visible above the rotting floorboards, his legs flailing helplessly beneath him, desperately trying to get purchase on something and failing. He could feel himself slipping, but just managed to get his fingertips into the gap between two uneven floorboards.

Then, first with a groan and then an almighty crash, the stairs between him and Jennifer began to collapse. It started with the steps closest to Jack and then rippled up the staircase as the structure gave way.

'Shit!' cursed Jack as his fingers gave way, and he finally slipped through the hole onto the floor below. Luckily, the floor was less than a single storey beneath him, and he landed unevenly on the remains of the staircase below, the rotten wood softening his fall. He tumbled over onto his hands and knees.

Jennifer frantically shone her torch around the wreckage lying at the bottom of the stairwell, and found Jack picking himself up from the floor. 'Are you okay?' she called.

Jack took a few seconds to reply. 'I think so,' he replied between deep breaths. 'That winded me a bit, and my leg is aching... but yeah, I think I'm going to live.'

'Well... what now?'

Jack turned his torch on, and when nothing happened, gave it a bang against the wall. It flickered back into life and he glanced around. He was standing two storeys beneath Jennifer now, next to huge piles of shattered and broken wood. On the wall to his right, he could make out a doorway behind several planks.

'There's a doorway down here,' he called back. 'I'll keep looking. You try and find another way down.'

'Okay.'

'And try to be careful,' he added.

'Don't worry. I've no intention of repeating what you've just done. Just be careful yourself.'

She watched in the torchlight as he clambered over the wooden wreckage, stopping to remove some of the boards that were blocking the door. After removing a few, the debris still covered the bottom half of the doorway, but he managed to crouch down and squeeze though the gap into whatever lay beyond.

Chapter 10.

After leaving the stairwell, Jack found himself in a short corridor that ended in another door; these were the first they had seen within in the building. He set off towards it, but as he drew close, he stopped. There were signs of recent damage around the door frame. The wood was cracked, and splinters were still visible on the floor. Someone had forced the door open.

He tiptoed towards it and then stopped, putting his ear against the door. In the distance, he thought he could just make out voices and the sound of something being dragged across the floor. He took a deep breath to steady his nerves and then pulled the door open ever so slightly.

On the other side, there was another corridor, but this one was longer. It was in better shape than the corridors at ground level; doors were still attached to their frames, and the plaster was still on the walls. There were even light bulbs hanging from the ceiling, although they weren't switched on. The bulbs had been connected to electrical cables, which were draped along the walls; someone had been wiring up their own electricity down here.

Moving as quietly as he could, with his torch pointed down to the floor, Jack progressed along the corridor, stopping at the first open doorway.

He leaned in and pointed the torch towards the corner of the room, revealing an empty desk and chair. As he panned the light across the room, he jumped as the torch illuminated a corpse lying in the other corner. It was wearing a cheap grey suit, now ruined by the pool of blood from the large gash in his neck. As Jack stared at it, something on the body glittered in the torchlight, drawing his attention.

He drew in closer, squatting down next to the corpse to take a look. His left arm was lying across his stomach, and on his ring finger was a chunky signet ring, just like the corpse in the portacabin outside. It was half covered in blood, but by the way it glittered in the torchlight, Jack thought it was probably gold. He patted the corpse's pockets. Like the previous body, there was no wallet or sign of identification, but they did contain a handkerchief. He pulled it out, using it to take hold of the ring and pull it from the corpse's finger. He gave it a wipe, trying to remove some of the blood.

The ring had a flat bezel with a pattern of shapes engraved onto it. He held it close in front of his face and squinted in the torchlight. It looked like three overlapping ovals with a circle in the middle. He realized it was a representation of an atom, memories of long-ago chemistry lessons coming back to him. *No*, he thought to himself as he wiped more of the blood away, *not a circle in the middle but an eye.* And the ovals were stylized; they looked like creepers... or tentacles.

He shoved the ring into his pocket. He had no idea what it represented, but it was the first clue he had found that might help them work out what had happened down here.

Standing up, he continued to look around the room, scanning through the darkness with his torch. There were more desks and chairs around the walls, but no clue as to their purpose. Against the far wall there was a smashed table, and as he looked closer, he could see blood on the floor. There had obviously been a fight.

Jack retreated back to the corridor and advanced slowly until he reached the next door. This one was open just a crack, the room beyond dark and silent. He gave the door a gentle nudge with one hand. It swung inwards with an audible squeak, revealing a dark office. Jack was surprised to see that the room was in a good condition, or at least the furnishings were. Two wooden desks stood on either side of the room, modern office chairs parked in front of both of them. Each desk had a camping lantern sitting unilluminated on it, as well as several sheets of paper.

Jack walked to the desk on the left and picked up the papers, scanning through them. They were all in a language he didn't recognize, possibly Russian or some other Eastern European language, and seemed to contain lists of numbers and dates. He shuffled through the rest of the pile quickly and then placed them back on the table; they were all just as incomprehensible to him.

On the other desk were sheets of paper that were slightly more understandable; maps of central London, as well as photographs of several buildings. He had no idea what any of this meant, what any of this was doing here. And still no clues about Bill.

He glanced at his watch; he needed to get a move on. He headed back to the corridor and then crept up to the end. He slowed as he approached the far door, which stood ajar, a thin sliver of pale light leaking through. In the distance, he could hear voices again; they sounded rushed and impatient. Someone was giving the order to hurry up.

Jack turned his torch off and cautiously pushed the door open.

The room on the other side was large and open-plan. He waited for a few moments to see if anyone had noticed him, and when there were no shouts or signs of movement, he turned his torch back on and quickly scanned the room. Barrels and crates were strewn around the corners of the room, and at regular intervals, irregularly shaped pillars were holding up the crumbling roof. There were several closed doors set within the far walls, and against the wall to his left was a large metal structure that he guessed might once have been a furnace.

Half a dozen tables were placed around the room, each surrounded by three or four chairs. As with the furniture in the other rooms, they looked like recent additions, standing out in contrast to the crumbling and dilapidated building. Sitting on the tables were the remnants of recent occupation: bottles and food cartons, books and magazines. A pack of playing cards was scattered across one, some of the cards fallen to the floor.

Lying face down on the floor between him and the tables was a body; it wasn't moving. Jack cautiously inched over to it before nudging it with his feet. When there was no reaction, he knelt down and rolled the body over. It was an adult male, possibly in his forties, the hair and beard dark with just a hint of grey. He checked the body's pockets, which once again were empty, and was just about to move on when he noticed something around the man's neck.

He grabbed the man's shirt and ripped it open, revealing a coin hanging from his neck. No, not a coin, he realized, some kind of talisman on a leather thong. It was made from a dark grey metal, the symbol of a five-pointed star etched into one face. *Finally, some proof of the Brotherhood's involvement*, he thought, although he again had no idea of its purpose. He turned it over, and saw that the other side was etched with vaguely familiar runes and sigils. He hesitated for a moment, pondering on the best place to keep it safe, before slipping it over his head so that it now hung under his own shirt. The metal felt oddly warm against his skin.

He stood up again, advancing towards the middle of the room. Sitting in a chair facing him was another corpse, its head tilted back with a dark bullet hole in the centre of its forehead. Jack shone the torch around the room and picked out three more bodies lying in the shadows. As he continued to scan his surroundings, he noticed several dark footprints on the floor, stretching away to a door on the far side of the room. It took him a moment to realize that these were trails of blood from one of the corpses, spread across the floor by whoever was responsible.

More shouts burst out suddenly from behind the door with the bloody footprints, and Jack froze.

'Come on!' somebody was shouting. Jack stood perfectly still and listened. 'We haven't got time,' he continued. He sounded urgent, frantic. 'We need to get out of here right now!'

'But what about...?' asked another voice.

'Leave him. There's no time. It won't matter soon anyway.'

Shit, thought Jack. He'd made quite a racket when the stairs had collapsed. It sounded like whoever had caused all of this bloodshed was leaving, and in a hurry.

He started towards the far exit, but as his torchlight lit up one of the pillars before him, he stopped suddenly. Their irregular shape made sense to him now. The pillar had several rectangular packages wrapped around it, held in place by black duct tape. The packages were unlabelled, but he'd watched enough movies to recognize what they were: C4 explosives, each with wires running out of them into another black box. He shone his torch around the large room at the other pillars; each was the same.

With a sinking sense of dread in his stomach, he realized why the voices were been in such a hurry to leave. He grabbed his phone and stared at it;

remarkably, he still had one bar of signal. As he raced towards the far exit, he frantically tapped the icon on the screen to dial Jennifer. She picked it up after only two rings.

'Jack–' she started.

'Get out. Get out now!' he shouted.

'What?'

'There's a bomb. The whole place is going up any second now.'

'What...' was the only reply he heard. The signal was breaking up. He hoped she could make him out clearly enough to understand.

'Just go. Go now. I've got a plan.' Wherever the others were heading to, he would have to go too. He had no choice; he couldn't go back up the ruined staircase, and judging by the others' urgency, he wouldn't have time to look for another way out. He had no other option – even if it meant capture. Staying here was certain death.

'But...'

'Go!' he shouted, hanging up the phone to stop her arguing any longer.

Jack flung the door open and looked at another corridor on the other side. Several doors stood closed on either side, but at the far end was something far stranger. A glowing white doorway stood before him, maybe a hundred feet away. He sprinted towards it, and as he closed the distance, he could see that this doorway was in fact a collection of lines and curves drawn on the wall. The lines were embellished all around with signs and sigils, all of which were glowing with an unnatural light.

He was a few steps away and still running at full speed, when the doorway started to flicker, momentarily changing from the eerie glowing light to a dull white colour and back again.

As the world seemed to explode in a cacophony of heat and noise around him, Jack threw himself towards the shimmering portal.

Chapter 11.

Jennifer grabbed hold of the window frame as she jumped, pulling herself through the window. She stumbled as she landed, but got back to her feet, sprinting away from the building. She heard the explosion at the same time as she felt the blast pushing her from behind, throwing her through the air and into the ground.

Even from where she lay on the grass, she could feel the heat of the giant fireball as it ripped through the ancient structure, scattering remains all around. She lay on the floor, her ears ringing, too shocked and dazed to move, as chunks of masonry continued to rain down around her.

Once the air had cleared of falling debris, she rolled over, staring at what little remained of the sanatorium. The main building was gone. What hadn't exploded out had collapsed back in on itself afterwards, flattening the structure. The wings either side were barely any better, the remaining walls wavering precariously.

'Oh God,' she muttered to herself. 'Jack...'

She staggered back towards the building, weaving left and right, unable to keep to a straight line. She was looking for any signs of life, but there was none to be found. Anyone who had been in there had surely stood no chance, and there was no sign of Jack anywhere outside.

She collapsed to her knees. She had come here looking to save her child, but now had lost the only other person in the world who truly meant something to her. She was the one who had insisted they come here straight away without backup, and now Jack had paid the price. It was all her fault.

Slowly, she picked herself up and tried to get her bearings. There was a new hole in the wall by the road where it had been struck by flying masonry and she staggered towards it. She was surprised to discover that she was walking with a limp. She looked down at her leg in a daze, but couldn't see any blood. She couldn't remember being hit by anything, but her head was still spinning, her memory hazy. When the adrenaline wore off, she was sure she would be aching all over.

As she climbed through the ragged hole in the wall, she pulled her phone out of her pocket. The screen was cracked from when she had been thrown to the floor, but fortunately it still appeared to be working. Dragging herself unsteadily back towards the car, she found that her legs were growing weaker and shakier with every step. As she walked, she picked a number from her contacts and waited while it rang.

She could just hear a faint voice say 'Hello?' as if from a distance, before she realized she was still deaf from the explosion.

'Detective Cross?' she called out rather too loudly. 'It's Jennifer Knight here. Remember you said to call if we ever needed a favour? I'm afraid I've done something incredibly stupid.'

She briefly explained to Cross what had happened, who in turn gave her some advice – firstly not to go anywhere as she was in no state to drive and might need medical attention. The last thing she needed now was to drive off the road and into a tree. She told Cross her location and then hung up the phone. As she slipped it back into her pocket, she looked around; she was almost back at her car, but had no memory of walking most of the way there. Her head was spinning, as if she had had too many glasses of wine and then stood up quickly. She fished her keys clumsily from her pocket and unlocked the car, climbing into the driver's seat and collapsing. Her keys fell to the floor, dropped by fingers that were now shaking uncontrollably as the adrenaline started to wear off.

She placed her phone in her lap, putting it on speakerphone and dialling 999. Her hands were shaking so badly that it took her three attempts. She explained briefly where she was, telling them that she had been driving along the road when there had been a huge explosion from an abandoned building. The shock and panic had caused her to drive off the road, banging her head in the process. She confirmed her location and details and then hung up the phone, knocking it to the floor as she did so. She didn't try to pick it up.

Along with the shaking, tears had begun to flow now, steady and unstoppable as the enormity of what had happened began to sink in. They'd both had scares about losing the other before, but she didn't see any way he could have survived that explosion. Jack was gone.

Chapter 12.

Jack landed face down on the floor, dry dust kicking up into his face. It made him want to cough, but he held it in, wary of drawing any attention to himself. He felt drowsy and disoriented, a dull ache throbbing between his temples, and as he lifted himself up he felt as if the room was spinning.

He counted to ten, waiting for the dizziness to die down before he pulled himself to his knees, taking his first proper glance around at his surroundings. He was standing in a circular room, almost thirty feet across. Twelve stone doorways were set around the edge of the room, but there were no doors between them, only a solid stone wall. On nine of these, someone had drawn the shape of a door. Some were drawn with thick painted lines, others only scrawled in chalk, but all were intricate and finely decorated with embellishments – words and shapes carefully drawn around the outside of the frame.

To his right stood one such doorway, its lines a bright white, the doorway between them glowing a dull snow-white colour. Above this was written a word he didn't recognize: *Palilicium*. Turning, he could see the doorway he had stepped through was also glowing. Both were dimming however, and their light was the only thing illuminating this room.

There wasn't much time to make a decision. He didn't want to be trapped here, wherever *here* was, in the dark and alone, waiting for someone to find him. He took a couple of quick paces across the room and stepped through the glowing doorway with a small jump.

As he passed through, he was hit with an intense feeling of exhaustion, his body suddenly tired and drained, his drowsiness increasing. The pain in his head briefly intensified, causing him to wince and close his eyes. Then it died away again almost as quickly, ending as a dull throb.

Jack opened his eyes to see that he was now in a large white-stone room. It looked like a temple, with two sets of wooden benches facing an altar, which was itself raised on a dais. A domed roof sat above him, and to his right, off behind the benches, were a set of double doors, one of which stood open. The light in here was dim, illuminated only by two torches set either side of the doors, but he didn't think there was anyone else in here with him. Somewhere beyond the open door, he could just make out some voices, too quiet to understand. As he took a step forwards, he was overcome with a powerful feeling of dizziness and disorientation, like being drunk and suffering from a hangover at the same time – not a good combination. He was feeling nauseous, his heart pounding and his chest tight. He lent forwards, resting his hands on his thighs. He tried to take some deep breaths, but found it hard to catch his breath. The air seemed thin, as well as having a slightly acrid taste. Where the hell was he?

He stood there, leaning forwards for a few seconds to get his breath back. Slowly, the dizziness and disorientation faded away; the tiredness in his body did not.

He turned to look behind him to see only a stone wall, a rough outline of a door marked out with dark paint, again decorated with signs and sigils around the edge. He slid his phone out of his pocket and checked it had survived the crash landing on the floor. It looked okay, and he turned it on. The top of the screen showed no signal; not a huge surprise as he seemed to be within a solid stone structure. He opened the camera app and quickly took a couple of pictures of the doorway, cursing silently as the flash illuminated the room. Luckily, there was no one around to notice. He didn't know quite how he had got here, wherever here actually was, but he was sure those markings had something to do with it. These doorways seemed to be a gateway between different locations, the previous room a nexus between them.

Once it became apparent that he was in no imminent danger, he relaxed slightly and started to take a more detailed look at his surroundings. There were two statues on the altar, one on either end, and he took a couple of steps towards them to get a better look.

The statue on the left was two feet tall, carved from a green stone and depicting some kind of monster, something from an ancient nightmare. It stood tall and upright, large wings extending behind its back and long tentacles writhing from the front of its bulbous head. Carvings in an unknown language surrounded the creature, carved into the stone on which it sat. Jack didn't recognize the writing but felt as if he should, as if he had seen these letters somewhere before. Maybe he had, years before, but that memory had faded now.

The statue on the other end of the altar was a similar creature, endowed with the same tentacles and wings, but this one was squatting on a stone block, its wings tucked up behind it. The stone block was again covered with the same symbols.

They were intriguing, but Jack wasn't sure how they could be of any use. He needed to get going before anyone came in and discovered him. He crept up to the open door and peered through. It opened into a corridor almost fifty feet long. There was a closed door on either side half way along, and at the end it opened into a large area that was brightly lit compared with where he was now.

He set off quietly down the corridor – quickly at first, then slowing to a crawl as he neared the end; the voices he had heard before were growing louder as he drew closer. As he inched his way along the passage, there was no cover, nowhere to hide, but as he neared the room at the end, its contents became clearer. He could see some large stone pillars, as well as several large leafy plants in ceramic pots, a possible source of concealment.

He tiptoed to the end of the corridor and listened. The voices seemed to be some distance away now and growing fainter. He chanced a look around the corner and was rewarded with the site of a large airy room, empty of any people. In the centre were four circular stone pillars set around a pool of still water. The pool was surrounded by many of the potted plants. He looked at the spiky emerald leaves hanging from the plants; he had never fancied himself as much of a botanist, but they weren't recognizable as any plant he was familiar with.

To his left and right, corridors retreated away from this room, while opposite, obscured by the plants, he could just make out a pair of glass doors opening onto a balcony, a pale red light seeping through from outside.

He cautiously made his way across the room, going around the pool and using the plants as cover. The water was clear and still, and he could see a mosaic on the floor of the pool, a tessellated pattern of red and white stars that seemed to waver before his eyes despite the stillness of the water. He stopped by the water's edge as he passed, crouching down and dipping his hands into it. He wiped his face with the cool liquid, washing away some of the dirt and dust that had accumulated there. He was still feeling short of breath, but at least the sense of nausea was now gradually fading.

He backed slowly towards the double doors, pulling one open and slipping quietly onto the balcony. As he turned to look at the vista before him, he froze, momentarily unable to comprehend what lay before his eyes.

He was standing on a second-floor balcony, looking across a rocky and mountainous landscape, but it was what he saw in the sky that struck him dumb. A huge red sun sat above the horizon, impossibly large. For a second he thought that it must be a trick of the light or an optical illusion, but as he turned his eyes further to the right, he could clearly see two moons hanging high in the sky.

Wherever he was, he was no longer on Earth.

Chapter 13.

Kincord Sanatorium, the New Forest, England.

When Detective Cross arrived at the scene almost two hours later, the area was swarming with emergency services.

Dusk had fallen and the area was now awash with blue lights, as well as several spotlights illuminating the ruins where rescue workers were searching the edges of the wreckage. Police had closed the road and fire crews were still attempting to make the area safe before they could begin a painstaking search for anyone who might have been in the building. With the state of the ruins, and the fact that it had been abandoned for so long, they weren't expecting to find anyone, but they couldn't discount the possibility that there might have been vagrants living there or curious children exploring, somebody who could have caused the explosion.

Cross found Jennifer sitting on the bonnet of her car, wrapped in a blanket and drinking from a plastic cup, its contents visibly steaming in the cool night air.

'The paramedics have checked me out,' she said, slightly too loudly. 'A bit of short-term hearing loss, that kind of thing.' She looked around to make sure no one else was in hearing range. 'I told them I was driving past when the place exploded. Slammed on the brakes, drove my car off the road in surprise, and banged my head on the steering wheel.'

Cross nodded. 'And Jack?'

Jennifer looked back towards the ruins of the sanatorium. 'He was inside.'

'And they haven't found anything?'

Jennifer gulped. 'I'm not sure what they may have found, but they certainly haven't found any survivors yet.' She closed her eyes, and when she opened them again, Cross could see she was crying.

Cross sat down next to her, putting an arm around her shoulder and drawing a white handkerchief from her pocket. She passed it to her and Jennifer dabbed at her eyes. 'Can you tell me what happened?' she asked.

Jennifer nodded and began to recount her story: the clues from her dreams, the body in the portacabin, the collapsing staircase. And then the phone call from Jack, just moments before the place had exploded.

Cross listened to it all quietly, not taking any notes; this wasn't a formal interview and she didn't want to create any incriminating evidence. When Jennifer had finished, Cross stood up.

'I'm going to go and talk to whoever's in command here, find out what the score is. Will you be okay for a moment?'

Jennifer nodded, and watched as Cross left her, journeying from one policeman to another until she found who she was after. They chatted for a short while, before she turned and headed back.

'Okay,' said Cross. 'The police here don't have much idea what happened yet; they're thinking maybe a gas leak, something along those lines. An old hospital like that might have had anything stored in the basement – chemicals, gas cylinders, who knows what? By the sounds of it, the portacabin you mentioned is now sitting under part of the west wing, so I don't think they'll find your friend there for a little while yet.'

Jennifer nodded. 'So what now?'

'You're free to leave, if you're up for driving... or I can give you a lift. I've vouched for you with the local police.'

'What about when they find Jack's body in there? Won't that be hard to explain?'

'Possibly,' grimaced Cross, and then shrugged. 'We'll cross that bridge when we come to it, I suppose.' She took Jennifer's hands in hers. 'It's possible, depending on how close he was to the centre of the explosion, that they might never find his body...' She hesitated for a moment. 'Or it might be unrecognizable,' she added. She wondered if Jennifer might start crying again, but instead she just swallowed and then looked up at her again. 'Are you sure he couldn't have got out?'

Jennifer thought for a second. 'He didn't come out behind me... but...'

'But what?'

'When he called me, it was hard to make out what he was saying – he kept breaking up – but I think he might have said he had a plan.'

'But you don't know what that was?'

'No. But we heard sounds. There may have been others down there... If they were the ones who set off the explosion–'

'–then they must have had a way out!'

'But how?' asked Jennifer.

'A tunnel?'

'I suppose that might make sense,' said Jennifer slowly. 'But any chance of following them is gone now. And we've got no way of knowing whether Jack made it out – or even if he did, whether he's now safe.'

'No.'

'And I'm still no closer to finding Bill.'

Chapter 14.

Jack crouched down in the corner of the balcony, trying to make sense of what was hanging in the sky above him. He knew that he'd been transported to somewhere else, but he'd never imagined it could have been to another planet.

He wondered whether this could be the dreamlands again, but then quickly concluded that it wasn't. Firstly, he didn't believe he could return since his death there, and secondly he still had his phone, contradicting all their experiences of what normally happened to technology there.

He briefly considered how on earth he was going to get back home, and concluded it would probably have to be the same way he got here – hitching a ride. The return journey might be significantly trickier though; he would just have to take this one step at a time.

While he was here though, he might as well see if he could find any trace of Bill, or any clue as to what the Brotherhood were up to.

He slipped back through the doors and into the building, heading for the nearest corridor, towards where he thought the men he had followed here had gone. Up ahead, he could see a couple of doors, one on either side, before it turned a corner and continued out of view.

Slowly, he inched his way along the passageway until he neared the two doors, plain wooden panels set into solid stone frames. The door on the left was ajar, a sliver of pale light just visible between the door and its frame. He stopped and listened at the threshold; he could just make out voices talking in the room beyond.

'Have you secured the goods?' asked an elderly male voice. Jack wasn't sure, but he thought it sounded like Randolph.

'Yes, Master,' replied a younger voice, keen and eager. 'They're being stored right now, just as you ordered.'

'Good. They must be kept separate for now.'

'If I could, Master, I'm still not sure about this plan.' This was a third voice, vaguely familiar. Jack took only a few seconds to place it: Sebastian. This was the man whom Randolph had sent to arrange a meeting with Jack and had ended up saving his life from a more hostile member of the Brotherhood. 'We've been at peace with the others for so long,' he continued, '...or at least maintained a cold war. These actions seem destined to plunge us into a bitter conflict on several fronts. Surely–'

'–I told you before... that does not matter. We are approaching our endgame now. Time is against us and we need to act decisively – we only have a small window of opportunity. If all goes to plan, then in a week's time none of them will be interested in us anymore. They will all have more pressing concerns. As will you, if we don't retrieve the last set.'

'But you won't tell me...?'

'Only those who need to know have been told the full details. But all will become clear shortly, I promise. Tell me, what of our other plans?'

'I've checked on our guest in Kheth. He's safe and secure.' Jack's ears pricked up at this – did they mean Bill? He would qualify as a guest, he supposed. He just didn't know where Kheth was.

'As to the others, our spies are in place and observing. We believe the orbs are on site. We're just waiting for confirmation.' *Orbs again*, thought Jack. Were these more of the same orbs Randolph had been searching for the last time they had met?

'Work at the dig site is also progressing – we're certain now that we're at the right place.'

'Excellent. Inform me the moment there are any updates,' said Randolph. 'Until then, leave me.'

'As you wish,' replied the others, followed by the sounds of footsteps.

'*Shit!*' cursed Jack under his breath as he realized they were heading straight for him. He looked left and right but either end of the corridor was at least thirty feet away. He looked at the door opposite and darted towards it. He prayed that there was no one on the other side, but it was possible detection there versus certain discovery if he stayed.

He grasped the iron handle and twisted it. With a sigh of relief it turned, the door opening to reveal a dark room beyond. He slipped inside, pulling the door to, just as the other opened. He left it open just a crack, fearing that the sound of it closing might attract their attention, as well as wanting to keep an eye on the proceedings.

He saw two men emerge from the doorway dressed in black robes. Their hoods were down and, as he had suspected, one was clearly Sebastian; the other was a man he didn't recognize. They turned and walked away silently, heading away from his arrival point and further into the complex.

Jack breathed a sigh of relief and then turned to look at the room he now stood in. It was clearly some kind of store room. The walls, as well as the space in between, were covered in shelves, all of which were full of crates and barrels. He stepped over to the shelf nearest the door, its contents the most clearly illuminated by the light from the corridor. On the shelf were several wooden crates with *U.S. Government Property, Commercial Resale is Unlawful* stamped on the side. Fearing the worst, Jack cautiously lifted the lid on a crate from the lowest shelf. Inside were dozens of brown plastic packages. Jack pulled one out and held it up to the light. On it was stamped:

Meal, Ready to Eat, Individual
Menu no 17. Beef Teriyaki.

Military rations? thought Jack in amazement.

The boxes on the next shelf along were unlabelled. Jack grabbed a box and ripped the packing tape off the top. Reaching inside, he pulled out a package labelled *Military-Grade Light Sticks.* He pulled one out, cracked it and shook it; a pale blue glow illuminated the area around him.

Useful, he thought to himself, stuffing a couple more into his pockets.

By the glow of the light he resumed searching the room. He found water, kerosene, bleach, more dried food, toilet paper, basic medical supplies and several fully stocked tool-boxes. He was surprised at just how many supplies they had stockpiled here, but there was nothing sinister, nothing to indicate what their current plans might be.

There were no other exits from the room and he headed back to the door, opening it a crack and checking for signs of activity. It was quiet outside, with no sign of any movement, so he closed the door behind him and carried on down the corridor. When he peered around the corner, he could see another two doors, both of which stood shut. He crept along until he was level with them, and then tried the door on the left. The handle refused to turn as he twisted it; it was obviously locked. The door on the right opened into another dark store room: more crates and barrels, more supplies.

Jack closed the door again, shuffling along the corridor until it turned another corner. Here the corridor split, one passageway leading to steps downwards, the other continuing on, several doors alternating on either side.

It's a little too quiet here, thought Jack. *Where is everyone?* Not that he had much cause for complaint, he supposed – it was better than the alternative.

He wandered up to the next door, which stood ajar. He poked his head inside and saw what looked like barracks. The room was currently unoccupied and Jack stepped inside. Bunk beds lined the walls, foot lockers on the floor before them. The room was plain, with white plaster walls and smooth wooden floorboards. There were no windows, but there was a small skylight in the ceiling made of frosted glass, and several oil lamps along the wall. It was all very utilitarian, with no signs of leisure or recreation.

Then he spotted a large bundle of black material lying on one of the beds. He picked it up in his hands and nodded to himself as he saw it was what he had hoped: a thick black robe, complete with hood. Hurriedly, he slipped it on over his head, covering him from head to toe. He hoped the disguise would conceal his true identity if someone were to spot him.

Next he tried the foot lockers, but they were all locked, each sporting a small metal combination padlock. He tried a couple of random numbers, but soon gave up; he didn't have time for this. Instead, he returned to the corridor and his search of the building.

Underneath the black robes, Jack now felt less conspicuous, and advanced down the corridor with increased confidence. It was still quiet inside the structure, but as he continued, he began to hear the sounds of a crowd off in the distance.

As he reached the end of the passage, it turned to the right, opening up onto a balcony and a set of stone stairs leading down to street level. Outside, across a street, he could see a village – no, a small town, built in the shadows of a rocky mountain range. He was facing a town square, a large open area with a grassy lawn and fountain in the centre. Hundreds of people were busily going about their business, some dressed in robes like the ones he now wore, some in dark combat fatigues, others just in casual clothes. Among the many people, however, there was not a single child to be seen.

All the people appeared to be busy, striding purposefully from one building to another, many carrying boxes or crates. At the far side of the square, he could see a tall building with a spire that sat high in the sky, towering over the other buildings. Jack guessed that this wasn't a normal church; rather than a cross, the stone front of the building was embossed with a huge red star. This was more likely to be a temple to whatever ancient gods these people worshipped. A large arched doorway stood open at the front of the building, a steady stream of people coming in and out.

Jack briefly considered heading down the steps and exploring the town, but then decided against it. He needed to find out what he could about Bill and the Brotherhood's plans. His best bet for that was Randolph, and he was based here in this building. Jennifer would be wondering where he was too, wondering if he was even alive, and he didn't want to get too far from the gate that had brought him here – the gate that might be his only route back home. He needed to find whatever information he could and get the hell out of here before someone noticed him. Otherwise, he might never make it back.

He decided to return to the room where he had heard Randolph and Sebastian talking. If there were any answers here, that would seem like his best chance. If Randolph wasn't there anymore, he would search the room and see what he could find. And if he was... well, he'd just have to take it one step at a time.

He turned and walked back down the corridor the way he had come. As he approached a bend in the corridor, someone stepped around the corner, less than ten feet away and heading straight towards him. It was a woman in her late twenties or early thirties with short golden-brown hair. She was wearing the same black robes, but with her hood down, and as she looked up towards him, Jack could see that she had sparkling green eyes. There was no way he could avoid her without raising suspicions; he would just have to continue on past.

As he approached, he gave a brief nod from under his hood and a short grunt of acknowledgement. She returned the nod with a polite smile and continued past him, not paying him a second glance.

Jack breathed a sigh of relief and continued around the corner, not daring to look behind him in case it raised suspicions. He didn't stop until he reached his destination: the doorway behind which he had heard Randolph and Sebastian. The last time he was here it had stood ajar, but it was now firmly closed.

He listened attentively, straining to hear anything, but there was nothing to hear. He considered knocking, but then decided against it — what if Randolph answered, telling him to come in? With his disguise, he might be able to pass random people in the corridor, but Randolph would surely recognize him. Instead, he grasped the door handle, and turned it, twisting it as slowly as he could, trying to minimize any noise. To his relief, the door opened with only a small squeak, almost inaudible. He hesitated momentarily, but when no sounds were obvious from within, he pushed the door open further, slipping in through the gap and then quietly pushing the door shut behind him, again turning the handle as slowly and quietly as he could.

He found himself in a small room, dark and silent. He reached into his robes, fishing one of the light sticks from his pocket, shaking and then snapping it. A pale blue glow fell over the area, illuminating his surroundings.

He was standing in a reception or living room; a pair of basic couches sat either side of a low table, a bowl of fruit in the centre. On one side sat a book, about three inches by six. He picked it up, revealing it to be a leather-bound notebook — he held the light up to the pages and flicked through them, scanning the contents, but it was all in a foreign language, something he couldn't recognize. He placed the book back on the table, trying his best to reposition it exactly where it had been, and looked around the rest of the room.

On the walls in front of him and to his left were a couple of paintings, abstract patterns, their colours odd and muted in the pale blue light. To his right was an arched doorway leading through to another chamber, and he crossed the room, stepping through and holding the light up in front of him.

Bingo, thought Jack. This room had the appearance of a meeting room – or at least one where some planning had been carried out. On the far wall was a large map of the world, with several drawing pins inserted into it. Underneath this was a bureau, its surface empty. In the centre of the room was a square wooden table, a chair positioned on each side. A bundle of loose papers were sat on one corner, neatly piled one atop another. In the left-hand wall, a curtain was drawn across a doorway.

He leant over the table, holding the glow-stick above the sheets as he leafed through them. There appeared to be several different sets of papers all stacked together. The first few he looked at were sheets of complicated mathematics, various handwritten equations and workings scribbled all over them. The next set appeared to be different maps, all hand-drawn, as well as some odd graphs covered in a multitude of wavy lines. After this were two sheets containing computer-generated relief maps showing the contours of what looked like a hill or large mound from several angles. On the final sheet was a printout with several sets of numbers on it. Most were crossed out, but one set of numbers was circled in red ink: *47-9, 126-43*.

Jack hesitated for a second before he folded the papers in half and then stuffed them into the pockets of his robe. If he ever managed to get out of here, then he could try to work out what they were all about.

Next, he moved over to the world map, running the light over the surface. There were holes all over the map, as if pins had been placed in it and then removed, but there were only four pins still remaining – one was on the south coast of England, near to where you would find the New Forest. The next one was almost due north of there, its exact position difficult to determine with the scale of the map – maybe somewhere in Oxfordshire? One was placed in north-east Africa and the final pin was in the middle of the ocean. The location of the first pin could easily correspond to Kincord Sanatorium, but the other two meant nothing to him. He was considering taking the map from the wall when he remembered his phone. He pulled it out and took several photos, first of the entire map and then close-ups of the pin locations.

He thought of the papers he had stuffed into his pockets and pulled them back out again. It would be better if he could leave as few clues as possible that he had been here. He placed the papers back onto the table and carefully photographed them with his phone before returning them to a neat pile in the corner where he had found them.

Now was a good time to try and return. He'd found some clues as to what they must be working towards, even if he couldn't make too much sense of them at the moment. It was too risky staying here for much longer; the longer he stayed, the greater the chance of his discovery. Maybe the others could make sense of the information he had found, work out where Kheth was, where Bill was maybe being held.

Carefully, he tiptoed back to the hallway. He slipped the glow-stick into his trouser pocket; under the thick cloth of the robe, its glow was unnoticeable. He quietly opened the door and slipped back out into the corridor before confidently striding along it, back towards the room with the pool and the plants.

Through the glass doors, he could see that the sun was now setting, the light slowly growing dimmer before his eyes. He made his way back along the corridor to the temple where he had first arrived, the room now cloaked in dark shadows.

As he returned to the temple, he first checked to see if it was unoccupied, before heading back to the wall with the doorway inscribed on it. He tried running his fingers over the patterns and pressing against the stone; it felt solid and unyielding, cold to his touch. *Either this is a one-way system, or something is needed to activate it*, he thought silently to himself.

He looked around again, wondering what to do. There was a large gap behind the altar, deep in shadows from the torches on the other side of the room. He slid into the space, crouching down and hiding himself. With the dark robe he was wearing, he thought that he would be pretty well concealed. He could wait here for someone to activate the gateway again and then slip through behind them.

There was nothing he could do now but wait.

Jack had been crouching down behind the altar for what felt like hours, his back and legs aching from holding the same cramped pose. It was also dark and hot under his thick robes, and it felt like an awfully long time since he had last slept. The heat and boredom were just leading him to nod off when he jerked awake at the sound of approaching footsteps and low voices. He listened carefully; from the sound of it, it was either two or three people.

Hopefully they were here to activate the portal. Quietly, he slipped his phone from his pocket, hiding it in the folds of his robe as he unlocked it, masking its glow. From a quick glance at the screen, he could see the battery was almost empty – he hoped it would have enough power. From the shadows of his hiding place, he started recording a video; he couldn't see much hidden behind the altar, and it was too dark for the camera to pick up much anyway, but he hoped it would at least record the audio of whatever happened, whatever was required to open the gateway.

Jack crouched in the darkness, keeping as quiet and still as he could, while the footsteps grew closer and then stopped just feet from him, standing on the other side of the altar.

One of the men started muttering something in Latin, a low chant that echoed in the stone temple. Jack was holding out his phone, covering the screen with his hand and trying to record the man's voice as the chant grew louder, when there was a burst of bright light. Even from his hiding place behind the altar, Jack was certain that the light was emanating from the wall where he had arrived; they had activated the portal.

The chanting stopped, and then Jack heard footsteps, followed by silence. They had gone. This was his chance; he wouldn't have long before the gateway closed again. He slipped the phone into his pocket and stood up, ignoring the pain as he extended his legs, and stepped out from behind the podium. He stopped, startled, to see one of the men still standing in front of the glowing doorway, slowly turning to face him.

'What the...' muttered the man.

There was no time to think. Jack rushed the short distance towards him, desperate to get through the gateway before it closed. The man stood his ground, and as Jack approached the man swung a fist towards him, almost instinctively.

Jack tried to duck, and the fist missed his head but caught him with a glancing blow to the neck, knocking him sideways and sending him careening into a bench. He dropped to the floor, cursing as he collided with the wooden pew, but quickly scrambled back to his feet.

His opponent had repositioned himself between Jack and the glowing gateway. Jack hadn't noticed until now just how large he was – surely six foot six, and heavy set.

'Just who are you, little man?' said the hulking man, his voice sporting a strong Russian accent.

Jack took a couple of steps back to appraise his situation. The Russian was advancing on him, holding his hands out, ready to grab him. 'Come to Kasamir...' he growled, advancing slowly.

Jack cautiously took several steps backwards. Whatever he was going to do, he had to do it quickly. It looked like this would be his only chance to escape.

The Russian lunged clumsily at him, and Jack side stepped to avoid his hands. As the brute staggered forwards again, Jack took another step towards the altar and grabbed hold of the monstrous statue sitting on it. He swung it in a wide arc towards the man as he carried on past him. It made a horrible dull thud and cracked into several pieces as it hit the back of the man's head. He slumped forwards onto the floor.

Jack dropped the statue, the broken pieces clattering to the floor, and then without a second thought took a running leap through the doorway.

Jack found himself back in the circular antechamber again, one of the doorways to his right glowing brightly. He felt dizzy, his legs wobbling beneath him, but without wasting a single moment he staggered towards the glowing doorway, throwing himself through it.

There was a flash of light as Jack stumbled out of the doorway, falling to his hands and knees. He felt winded, like someone had kicked him in the gut, and he lay there for a moment, trying to get his bearings.

He was lying on a patch of damp grass, weeds and brambles all around him. There was a light breeze blowing in his face and a deep mossy odour in the air. The air felt good, rich and thick. He'd forgotten just how thin the air had been in wherever it was he had just come from. He could hear people moving through the undergrowth nearby and he lay still, taking deep breaths and listening to the noise. They seemed to be moving further away, unaware of his presence.

As he pulled himself to his feet, he saw that he was standing next to a small derelict building, the brick wall next to him the only side that was still vertical. There was a brief pulse of light, and then the glowing of the gateway subsided, leaving only faint markings on the wall. All around were trees and bushes; it felt like he was in the middle of a wood. There was no sign of whoever he had followed. They obviously hadn't been hanging around, and for that Jack felt grateful; he felt in no state for another fight.

He needed to get going, before Kasamir woke up and came looking for him. He seemed to be more affected by travel through these gateways than the others; he wondered if it was something you could grow accustomed to.

Behind the ruins of the building, he could see a tall hill, its steep face leading upwards. There was an overgrown path in the opposite direction and he followed it, soon finding himself on an old trail that didn't look well used. He didn't know where it led, but he didn't care. For now, anywhere would do – any sign of civilization.

He pulled out his phone as he started his trek, but it was unresponsive – the battery had finally given out. He carried on in silence, following what he hoped was still the path – in some places it was so overgrown it was hard to be sure – until he finally emerged from the woods. Before him stood a large field of thick grass, a flock of sheep grazing in one corner. Over the far side he could see a hedge, and beyond that, buildings. Civilization at last.

He trekked across the field, clambering over the style on the far side and into a winding country road. From there, it took him just a few minutes to reach the outskirts of a small village.

A small shop stood across from a large grass area – a village green that doubled as a cricket pitch. In front of the shop were several stands containing assorted fruits and vegetables, as well as a handful of newspapers.

Jack stepped into the shop. It was small but packed with all the modern essentials; food, drinks, magazines and sweets. There was a middle-aged man standing behind the counter, leaning over an open newspaper. He looked up as Jack approached.

'Hello, sir, can I help you?'

'Yes,' said Jack. 'I was wondering if you could tell me where I am?'

The shopkeeper looked at him as if this were the strangest question he'd ever been asked. 'You're standing in my shop, sir,' he replied after a few moments' thought.

'No, sorry – I mean, what village is this?' When the man gave him another curious look, he added, 'I seem to have gotten a bit lost. I took a wrong turn a while ago, and my phone battery has run out.'

'You're in Woodperry, sir.'

'Okay... and whereabouts is that? On a national scale?'

The shopkeeper looked as if he wasn't sure whether this was all some kind of joke at his expense. 'Oxfordshire,' he replied slowly, and then added, 'about three miles east of Oxford.'

Jack reached into his pocket, pulling out his wallet. It had a reasonable amount of cash in it. He walked over to the chilled drinks and picked up a bottle of water, returning to the counter and placing it there, before handing the man a crisp five-pound note. As the shopkeeper rang up the sale and handed him back his change, Jack asked the man if there were any local taxi firms.

'There are some cards in the window, sir, if you wish to give one of them a call.'

Jack shrugged. 'As I said, my phone's run out of charge. I don't suppose I could borrow yours?'

The shopkeeper thought for a moment. 'You said you took a wrong turn. Don't you have a car?'

'It broke down,' said Jack. 'Otherwise I would have carried on.'

'I can recommend a local garage if you like?'

'I'm in a bit of a hurry. I'll come back for it later.'

The shopkeeper gave him a suspicious glance and then just sighed, picking up a cordless phone, and sliding it across the counter to him. 'If you could just keep it brief, sir.'

'Of course,' said Jack, picking up the phone. There were several business cards for taxis in the window and he picked one at random, dialling its number. Then he stopped and hung up before dialling his home phone number instead. 'Sorry,' he mumbled apologetically to the shopkeeper. 'I need to make another call first. Here,' he said, sliding the change back across the counter to him. 'For the call.'

The phone rang several times before it was picked up. 'Hello?' came Jennifer's voice. She sounded wary, unsure who was calling.

'It's me,' said Jack.

'Jack!' she screamed, forcing him to move the handset away from his ear. 'You're alive!'

'I'm fine, I'm fine,' he reassured her. 'I can't really talk now,' he added, casting a glance to the shopkeeper who was still eyeing him curiously, 'but I'm all in one piece. I'll be back in a few hours. I'll explain everything then.'

He said his goodbyes and then hung up, dialling the taxi company again and booking a taxi to Oxford train station, promising a large tip if they didn't hang around.

Chapter 15.

Ash House, Dartmoor, England.

It was early evening when the taxi dropped Jack back at Ash House. He paid the taxi driver, and watched him drive slowly back to the main road before shuffling over to the front door. He fished his keys from his pocket and slipped them into the lock. He was exhausted and couldn't wait for a good long sleep in his own bed.

He had barely stepped through the front door when Jennifer shot from the living room, wrapping her arms around him and giving him a long kiss on the lips.

'It's so good to see you,' she sighed. 'You had me worried for a while.'

'Aw, you won't get rid of me that easily,' he replied with a little chuckle. 'Do you mind if I go and sit down? It's been a very long day,' he added thirty seconds later, when Jennifer was still wrapped tightly around him. She reluctantly released him, and they both adjourned to the living room, where an open bottle of red wine and two glasses were waiting on a table.

Jack flopped down onto the sofa, and plugged in his phone to charge. Jennifer passed him a glass of the wine and he took a long slow sip before resting the glass back on the coffee table.

'So what the hell happened to you?' asked Jennifer.

'Just before the explosion, I followed some people I'd heard – members of the Brotherhood – and ended up going through this gateway.'

'Gateway?'

'The Brotherhood are able to create some kind of gateway, or portal. A wormhole maybe, which allows you to travel from one place to another, potentially across huge distances. The one they – and then I – left through took me first to some kind of junction room, where there were multiple gateways to several different locations. I don't know where most of them went. The one I followed them through took me to what I can only describe as a new base of theirs. They seem to be setting up a small community there, gathering provisions and preparing for something.'

'Do you know where it was?' she asked.

'Well, that's the odd thing. I don't know where it was, I just know where it wasn't.'

'What?' she said, an expression of confusion spreading across her face.

'The place had a giant red sun and two moons. Wherever it was, it wasn't on this planet.'

'Are you trying to tell me that the Brotherhood are aliens?'

'No, I don't think it's anything like that. I think it's more a case of selling up shop and heading off-world. There were rooms full of supplies, rations, that kind of thing.'

'Well... maybe that's a good thing. Good riddance to them, I suppose.'

Jack shook his head. 'Not if they've got Bill with them. And *why* are they going? Is it in search of something, or to get away from something... to *avoid* something?'

'What are you thinking?' she asked.

'I don't know. I just don't think it's a good sign.'

'You're thinking of a forthcoming apocalypse?'

Jack shrugged. 'I don't know,' he repeated. 'I did find these, though. They looked important, but I don't know what they mean.'

Jack's phone now had enough charge to power up and he took another sip of wine as he waited patiently for it to start. When it was done he opened the photos he had taken of the papers and documents, handing the phone to Jennifer. She slowly looked at each picture in turn, a look of confusion and annoyance growing with each one.

'They don't mean anything to you either then,' asked Jack.

Jennifer shook her head, turning the phone on its side and then upside down to see if it made any more sense. It didn't.

'What about Bill?' she asked, passing the phone back to him.

'Not too much luck there either, I'm afraid. I saw no sign of him, or any children, in fact.' Jennifer audibly sighed as he said this. 'There was one thing, though,' added Jack. 'Randolph mentioned that they had a guest in some place called Kheth, though I'm not sure who that refers to, or where it is. It could be Bill.' He looked up and saw the expression on Jennifer's face. 'What is it?'

'Kheth. That name. I've heard it before.' There was a look of deep concentration on her face as she searched her memories, until she finally made the connection. 'The dreamlands,' she said. 'It's a place in the dreamlands, a small town. I've never been there, but I'm sure I've heard people talk about it.'

'Do you know where it is?'

'Only roughly. I'd need help to find it.'

'And do you think the *guest* refers to Bill?' asked Jack.

'It could do. He's certainly someone who's staying with them, but isn't one of them. And we know he's got a connection to the dreamlands. It's got to be worth a try. I'll leave as soon as I can. If it's him, we can't afford to let them get away again.'

'Is there anything I can do to help?'

'I don't think so. I think this is one for me. You might as well get some rest.'

Jennifer stood up and was about to head upstairs when her mobile rang. She fished it out of her pocket and looked at the screen. 'It's Cross,' she said as she swiped the screen to answer the call.

'Hi,' she said, and then stood there listening. 'Yeah, that should be fine,' she said a moment later. 'See you in the morning.'

She turned back to Jack. 'She's going to come over in the morning. She's got some new information, but nothing that can't wait until tomorrow. We can tell her what we've found too.'

'And hopefully, you may have found Bill by then,' said Jack with a smile.

'Maybe...' said Jennifer. 'Wish me luck!'

✻ ✻ ✻

Jennifer opened her eyes to find herself standing outside the dreamlands town of Drinen, just visible across a short expanse of desert. It was a town she had visited several times before, and from what she had heard on her previous expeditions, she thought that Kheth wasn't too far from here. She didn't know exactly where though. She hoped someone here would know the way, or else it might be a long walk to the next town.

The sun was sitting low in the sky, rose red in colour as it began its slow journey across the heavens, casting long shadows all around. The town of Drinen was little more than a small village: a few stores and an inn, a few places for a weary traveller to rest his head while passing through.

As she began her trek across the desert towards the buildings, she scanned the horizon before her, spotting a small body of water at the edge of the town. Like many others in these parts, the town had grown up around the water source, a scarce commodity in this part of the lands. A few tall trees and bushes were visible around the side of the lake, and she could just make out a small caravan of camels standing under the trees, weighed down with a large number of sacks and bags. This gave her some hope; if this was a trade caravan, then its owners were likely to know the area well.

She headed for a group of three men sitting on the floor by the water's edge. As she drew close, they stood up, brushing the sand from their clothes.

'Can I help ye?' asked the man in the centre. He appeared to be their leader, more confident and forthcoming than he others. He was larger too, standing a good four inches taller than either of his companions and was considerably better built.

'Maybe,' replied Jennifer. 'I'm looking for the town of Kheth. Maybe you know where it can be found?'

'Aye, maybe we do. What's a wee lass like you wanting to go there for?'

The man was dressed in flowing white robes and wore a turban, but spoke with an accent that was strongly reminiscent of Scottish. It was almost comical given his appearance and their location, as if you had found a tour guide for the Eifel tower who spoke in Cockney English. Jennifer didn't point this out; his sour expression made her think he wouldn't have a great sense of humour.

'There's a man there I've got an appointment to meet,' she said, before adding 'He's got something of mine.'

The man turned his head both ways to look at each of his companions in turn. They both gave lazy, non-committal shrugs.

'Aye, well, we're heading in that general direction. We've got some cargo we need to take to the docks at Rinar. We could maybe swing round, take a slight detour.'

'How long will it take to get there?'

The man sucked in air and gave a slight grimace. As he did so, Jennifer could see a row of crooked yellowed teeth. 'If we leave soon, we should get there just before nightfall. It'll be a bit of a circuitous route for us though. It will take us a bit longer than normal, to get our goods to the docks, like.'

Jennifer sighed. She knew what was required from her. Her bag was slung over her shoulder, full of various oddities that they'd found useful in their previous adventures here, including a large amount of money. She reached inside and drew out a shiny golden coin. It gleamed in the light and she could see from the look in the man's eyes that this had drawn his attention. 'This now, another when we arrive,' she offered.

The man didn't bother looking at his colleagues this time. 'Aye, that'll do I reckon. We'll take you to within sight of the town. You can do the last bit yourself. Deal?'

'Deal,' agreed Jennifer, stepping forwards to hand him the coin. He took it eagerly, and when she stepped back again it had already disappeared, secreted somewhere about his person.

'The beasts are fully loaded though, so you'll have to walk,' he said as he turned and started to walk towards the camels. 'I trust that's not a problem, hen?'

'No problem at all,' she replied. She noted that he'd taken her money before pointing this out. Maybe he was naturally evasive, or maybe he was hoping to negotiate for more money. She guessed the latter, but it didn't bother her. She was happy to walk.

'We're leaving in five minutes,' he said as he started to check the saddles and packs on the camels. 'If you want a drink, or anything else, I'd get it now.'

Jennifer had brought some water with her, stowed away in her bag, but she still took the opportunity to refresh herself. It would be a long day.

✳ ✳ ✳

It was a hard day's trek across the flat and empty desert. The three men took the lead in the caravan, guiding the animals across the barren sand. There were precious few landmarks along the way, the men seeming to intuitively know what direction to travel in. They'd presumably travelled this way on many occasions before.

Jennifer kept to herself for the majority of the journey. Every so often, one of the men would glance over their shoulders at her and then whisper something to their colleagues, occasionally eliciting a short burst of laughter in response. She hoped and assumed that they were just checking that she was keeping up, maybe cracking some jokes at her expense, but there was something about their looks that she didn't like; their glances sometimes lingering just a bit too long or a bit too hard.

It was nearing nightfall, the sun low in the sky again, when she turned to her left and spotted the outline of a town, the buildings silhouetted against the horizon.

'Is that Kheth?' she called out to the men.

They stopped, the shoulders of the leader sagging, as if expressing disappointment.

'Aye,' he muttered, turning to face her.

'Well, I guess I'll be leaving you then,' she said. She reached into her bag, looking through it to locate another coin. When she looked up again, the three men had closed the distance to her. They had moved quickly and silently, and the leader was now holding a long machete out in front of him.

'I don't think so, hen,'

'We had a deal.'

'Aye, but I reckon there's a much better deal to be had. I reckon there's more of those coins than you're willing to share with us three.' The other two were moving slowly to the sides, flanking her.

Jennifer reached into the bag again, pulling out her leather purse. She hefted it in her hands to show the weight of it. 'I don't need this shit,' she muttered. 'Here, you can have all this, if you just let me go in peace. Neither of us wants a fight.'

'Don't you presume what I want, lassie,' he spat. 'Besides, I reckon we can get a good deal more than that for a young woman like you. And *then* we can take your money anyways. It's just a shame that we're not going to able to have you walk yourself any further.'

So, they were slavers, in addition to whatever else they were peddling... or smuggling. 'Please, don't hurt me... I'll do anything you say,' she pleaded in mock desperation. If she could catch them unawares, the three of them could very quickly become two – a much fairer fight.

'Oh, I think we can manage both of those,' he chuckled, a sickening leer spreading across his face and revealing his crooked teeth again.

The man to her left reached to grab her arm. Jennifer was holding the pouch of money by the top, and she swung it like a cosh with all her might. Her aim was perfect, and the considerable weight of the coins collided with his temple. He fell backwards, collapsing to the floor as the bag split open, the coins spraying all over the desert floor.

The man to her right was unprepared for this and was distracted by the sight of the money spread over the sand. They had assumed that she was a defenceless woman. What they didn't know what that she had spent five years waiting for the Brotherhood to return and to try and take Bill, five years in which she had prepared herself. Of particular relevance to her situation now was a considerable amount of martial arts training, as well as more practical self-defence – how to make sure you survived an attack, with no consideration of rules or fair play.

Jennifer span around, dropping down and extending her leg. She swept the man's legs away from under him, and he collapsed to the ground, a look of surprise and shock on his face.

As she completed her sweep, Jennifer stood back up again. She kicked the man, bringing her foot against his head with as much force as she could muster; this was no time to hold back. Her boot connected with his jaw and a splash of crimson blood sprayed across the golden sand, along with one of his teeth.

The leader was looking hesitant now; this certainly wasn't going the way he expected, but it was too late for him to back out now. He cast a quick glance to either side; both of his accomplices were lying on the floor, neither of them moving.

'You're going to pay for that, you bitch,' he bellowed, and he advanced, waving the machete back and forth. She could tell by his posture and the way he brandished the weapon that he was no expert with it, but it was still a deadly weapon, even in the hands of an untrained thug. He stopped just out of range, hesitant to advance.

Jennifer needed to finish this quickly. She'd had the element of surprise before, but if the others started to come around, she could soon find herself outnumbered again. She poised herself on the balls of her feet, her legs ready for action. 'What are you afraid of?' she goaded him. 'Afraid a little girl is going to kick your arse?'

He raised the knife up, striding forwards with hatred in his eyes, and Jennifer pounced. She sprung forwards, her left arm grabbing his wrist where he held the knife. She twisted it around and down, the sudden pain causing him to open his hand, the knife silently falling into the soft sand. At the same time as she was holding his arm firmly with her left hand, she brought her right hand down with all the force she could muster, cleanly hitting his forearm. This was a blow she had practised countless times on blocks of wood and tiles, but never before on a living person. It was just as effective though. There was an audible crack, followed by a scream of pain from the man.

He dropped to his knees. 'You've broken my fuckin' arm, you bitch!' he screamed in pain and fury. 'I'll fuckin' kill you!'

Jennifer tutted back at him. 'You just don't learn, do you?' she replied softly.

He looked at up her, and then lunged to the side, trying to grab the machete from the floor with his left hand. Jennifer span around, stretching out her right leg in a wide arc as she went. There was a thump as her boot connected with the back of his head, and then a grunt from the man as he fell forwards into the sand. Then there was silence.

She looked down at the three unconscious men around her. She checked each one in turn. They were all still alive, breathing but unconscious. She picked up the machete from the floor and was wondering where to stash it when she saw the sheath on the man's belt. She quickly removed the belt, using it to tie his hands behind his back; it wasn't a great way to bind someone's arms, but with a broken arm he'd be limited in how much he could struggle.

When she had the machete securely sheathed to her own belt, she proceeded to gather up any coins that could easily be recovered from the floor. She didn't think she'd particularly need them herself, but she was damned if she was going to let these guys profit from the encounter when they woke up.

Next, she went to the camels. She inspected their packs, intrigued to see what the men had been transporting, but it was disappointingly mundane; spices, cloth, some antique oddities and curios. There was nothing here for her. She slapped the camels on their hind quarters, sending them off on their own. Maybe they could find themselves some better owners out here somewhere.

With a final check to make sure they wouldn't be coming around any time soon, Jennifer set off on the final leg of her journey, towards the town of Kheth on the horizon.

The darkness of night had truly fallen by the time she finally arrived at Kheth, the small town illuminated by torches and candles glowing in the windows of the buildings. She needed somewhere where she could gather information, as well as a place to spend the night. An inn that sat facing the small town square seemed the obvious choice. An old and weathered sign hanging out front proclaimed it to be *The Black Galley*. The picture under the name was of an old sailing ship, but travelling through the sky instead of the ocean. Jennifer took a deep breath to reassure herself and then stepped inside.

The interior of the inn was dark and smoky, both from the candles flickering on the tables and the various men smoking tobacco in the shadowy corners of the room. As she stepped inside, conversations seemed to die away momentarily as the inhabitants turned to see who had entered, but resumed again almost instantly. She obviously wasn't that interesting an interruption.

She stepped up to the bar, where an overweight man was wiping some glasses with a damp cloth. He appeared to be merely wiping the dirt around the glass rather than actually cleaning them.

She took out a small coin from her bag, and slid it across the bar towards him. 'Some wine, please,' she said to the barman.

He looked at her suspiciously, and then at the coin. Once he was certain that it was real, he reached behind him to take an unlabelled bottle from a shelf where dozens of similarly anonymous bottles sat. He twisted the cork from its neck and he placed it before her, shortly followed by a tall glass from under the bar.

'That'll do you?' he said.

Jennifer assumed it was a question. 'Fine,' she said, pouring herself a large glass of the honey-coloured liquid. It smelt sweet with a hint of citrus.

'I don't think I've seen you in here before,' he said when she had put her glass down again. 'Have you got business in these parts?'

'Just passing through,' she said casually. 'I'm looking for someone who may have passed through before me.'

'Oh?'

'A young boy, aged five,' she said, and then thought about the difference in timescales between here and the real world. 'Possibly older,' she added. 'You haven't seen anyone come through with a boy you don't recognize?'

'Can't say that I have,' said the barkeeper, 'but we don't get a lot of kids in here.' He continued to wipe the glass in his hands with the dirty towel.

'Okay, what about a room for the night?'

'Aye, that can be arranged,' he said with a nod.

Jennifer took another sip of the wine; it was surprisingly good.

'What about a man called Randolph?' she asked. At the sound of the name, the barkeeper stopped wiping his glass, putting it down on the counter. 'Serious-looking man,' she said. 'Long black hair.'

'I don't know anyone by that name,' he said sheepishly. 'And I think you ought to be going.'

'What about my room?'

'I was mistaken,' he said gruffly. 'We're fully booked.'

Jennifer leaned forwards towards the man. 'If you know where he is, you need to tell me.' She spoke slowly and calmly, but with a deliberate force. There was clearly some anxiety on the man's face. 'You may be scared of him,' she added slowly, whispering so that no one else would be able to hear, 'but if you're not going to tell me what you know, then you should be even more scared of me.'

The barman looked her in the eyes and realized she wasn't kidding. He swallowed. 'Okay,' he whispered. 'But you didn't hear it from me. I don't want no trouble.'

'Mum's the word,' she whispered back. When the barman just gave her a puzzled look, she added 'I mean... your secret's safe with me. Tell me what you know and I'll be gone. You'll never hear from me again.'

'Just to the north, atop the hill, is an old fort. You should be able to see it from the outskirts of the town. That's where you should go.'

'That's where I'll find Randolph?'

The barman shrugged. 'I've heard stories, rumours... some of which mention his name. It looks deserted... but appearances can be deceptive. Most folks from here just keep well clear of that place.'

'And those that don't?'

'They don't always come back. If I were you, I would turn around, go back the way you came while you still can.'

Jennifer took another large swig from her glass, draining the last of the wine. 'I'm afraid I can't do that,' she said, as she put her glass back on the counter. She slid another small coin across the counter towards him. 'For your trouble,' she added, standing up and walking towards the door. As she pulled it open, she cast a glance over her shoulder. The barman had resumed wiping his glasses, and the coin was nowhere to be seen. It was as if she had never been there.

From the edge of the town she could indeed see a small stone building sitting atop a hill to the north, its outline silhouetted against the night sky. She would have preferred to do this by the light of the morning, but she already felt as if she had outstayed her welcome in this town. No time like the present, she supposed. She was grateful that it was at least a cloudless night, with the large moon glowing brightly in the heavens and providing enough illumination for her to see her way.

She set off at a brisk pace across the town before leaving its outskirts and heading off across a rocky wasteland. She started to slow as she approached the hill and the ground gradually changed first from rock to dirt and then to scraps of grass.

The building was a small circular tower, built from huge stone blocks and clearly quite old. From a distance, it looked like a ruin, but as she drew close she could see that this was merely illusory. It was in fact quite strong and secure; chunks of stone lay around the base, and the edges of the roof were uneven, but the core structure was solid and complete.

As the barman had hinted, the building looked dark and deserted. The large front door was locked fast, the windows barred and sealed shut from within. She paced around the building, looking for any way to get inside, but soon realized there was going to be no easy access. She looked up at the roof of the building, two stories up with uneven crenelated edges. Maybe if she could get up there, there would be some way in: a trap door or some other weakness. But try as she might, there seemed no easy way up there without ladders or grappling hooks, neither of which she had thought to bring with her.

She decided that she might just have to wait for someone to come, either someone on their way in, or someone on their way out. Behind the tower, the ground was less barren and there were several large bushes and shrubs scattered about, even a few small trees. She set off into them, looking for somewhere that would provide cover but might also offer some comfort; she might be there for a while.

She searched around the grounds for a suitable hiding place, trudging through the weeds and brambles. In the pale moonlight, everywhere looked the same: dirt, rock and brambles, none of it in the least bit hospitable. She was about to give up when she took a step around the base of a tree and heard something unusual. As she has taken a step, the sound hadn't been the usual soft footstep in the grass and dirt, but a muffled hollow tap.

She crouched down, pulling the foliage apart with her hands. Under a layer of weeds was a flat wooden surface. As she started to pull the plants away, a larger and larger piece of wood was revealed. No – not one but several pieces of wood. She grabbed the plants by the roots, ripping the rest of them from the ground by the handful, and then sweeping the dirt and gravel away with her hands.

When she had cleared the area, she stood up and looked down at the wooden square before her: a trap door, set into the floor. It stood not fifty feet from the edge of the tower. Surely the two must be connected – there were no other buildings anywhere near here. She knelt down and tried to run her fingers around the edge, trying to get enough purchase to lift up the door, but without any success.

She stood up again, looking around for inspiration, before she remembered the machete that was still sheathed at her waist; its sharp point made quick work of the dirt and muck wedged in the gap between the door and frame. When it was as clean as she could manage, she inserted the end of the knife into the narrow crack, carefully trying to lift the door up without snapping the metal blade.

It took a few attempts and a lot of swearing, but she eventually managed to get the wooden door to rise out of its frame, and she quickly slipped the toe of one boot underneath. She dropped the blade onto the ground, slipping her fingers into the gap, gripping the wood with both hands and heaving it up until it was lying vertically against the trunk of the tree.

She peered down into the darkness beneath. Some old wooden steps leading downwards were just about visible and then nothing, the rest lost in the murky gloom.

She took a few tentative steps down the stairs. The wooden boards were damp and squeaked as she put pressure on them, but they seemed to hold – at least for now. She crouched down and scanned what she could see of the room below, letting her eyes slowly adjust to the darkness. It looked like a passageway leading away from the steps, almost completely full of rubbish: broken boxes and furniture, smashed crockery and glass. She took another couple of steps down and then spied what she was after. Lying on the floor near the wall was a wooden torch, almost completely hidden under some shattered planks of wood.

She completed her journey to the bottom of the steps. The corridor disappeared away into inky darkness, the moonlight from above barely seeming to penetrate it. She crouched down and picked up the torch. It felt dry; hopefully, it was still usable. Rummaging around in her bag, she managed to find what she needed – her tinderbox – and she set about trying to light the torch. It took a few minutes and a few false starts, but when it finally burst into flames, the passageway lit up with flickering light.

The space around her looked like an old cellar, stuffed with years' worth of junk: wooden crates, broken barrels, and what looked like the remains of some old tables and chairs. There was smashed glass and pottery ground into the dirt and smashed bricks that looked like they were from the tower walls. There was also something down here that stank, a nauseous smell of death and decay. She decided to press on.

There was a narrow gap down the centre of the corridor between the piles of rubbish that had accumulated on either side, and Jennifer tiptoed carefully down it, trying not to knock into anything. She feared that if she did, the whole lot would come crashing down and either smother her or alert anyone nearby – or both. The building had looked deserted from the outside, but she knew that appearances could be deceptive.

At the end of the passageway was a sturdy wooden door, reinforced with metal bands. Jennifer inched closer and then stopped to press an ear against it. She could hear nothing but her own shallow breathing and the beat of her heart.

Holding the torch in her left hand, she grasped the thick metal ring of the door handle and hesitantly gave it a turn. She didn't really expect it to move, expecting the door to be locked and her journey to come to a brief end. To her surprise, it turned freely, if somewhat stiffly, in her hands.

The door opened an inch or two, and then stopped with a bang as it hit something. The room on the other side was dark, giving no clue as to what was blocking her exit.

She put her shoulder against the door, pushing slowly but firmly. Nothing moved. She tried again, pushing harder this time. Her effort was rewarded with a low groan and a squeal as something scraped along the stone floor. She kept pushing until the door was open a foot, and then she was able to slip sideways through the door, her left hand leading the way with the torch.

The room she was now in looked like an old study. The object behind the door had been a large oak table, now pushed out towards the centre of the room. Two large metal candlesticks stood on either end, a thick white candle in each, and in the centre a large leather-bound book lay open, the visible pages covered in handwritten notes. In the opposite wall was a closed wooden door, and the two other walls each contained large wooden bookcases from floor to ceiling. Jennifer walked over to the closest one, scanning through the books on its shelves. Just like the book on the desk, these were all leather-bound journals, their spines free of any writing or decoration. She plucked one at random from the shelf and looked at the cover; it was made of old leather and free of any name or title. She opened it and flicked through the pages. Every page was covered in small but neat handwriting. Although it wasn't in English – Latin would have been her best guess – from the format and headings of the pages it looked to her like some kind of diary or journal. She closed it and slipped it back upon the shelf where she had found it.

She pulled another book from the shelf, then another. They were all the same, at least as far as she could tell.

Nothing here appeared to have any connection to Bill, and she decided to move on. She moved over to the other door, the only exit from the room. Cautiously, she turned the round iron handle, and when it opened, slipped into the room on the other side.

She only had a chance to see the room briefly before a shape moved with speed beside her, someone stepping out from behind the door. From the corner of her eye, she just saw a blur of movement before a blow hit her on the back of the head and she fell forwards, stumbling onto the floor.

'You've picked the wrong fucking place to break into,' grumbled a deep voice. Then a foot swung through the air and collided with her head, and everything turned to black.

Chapter 16.

Jennifer awoke with a start. She was lying on a low bunk in a cell, her head throbbing. She could taste blood in her mouth and her vision was blurred. Slowly, she shook her head, gently rubbing the large bruise on her temple, and the blurring gradually subsided.

It was dark in here, the only light from a flickering torch on the other side of the room, mounted on the wall next to a winding staircase that led upwards. There was another cell next to hers, and a couple more on the other side of a narrow aisle. There was a stench in the air; the odour of sweat and filth.

She stood up, walking over to the door to her cell, which was constructed of thick iron bars. The wall connecting her cell to the one next door was made of the same solid metal; the other two walls were natural rock. She squatted down and examined the lock. It looked solid, good quality. Not that she had anything to pick it with anyway. As she stood back up again, she noticed movement from the cell opposite hers, something moving in the shadows.

'Who's there?' she called.

'I was wondering when you'd awake,' came a voice from the darkness. It was a strangely familiar voice, one she was sure she'd heard before but couldn't quite place.

'How long have I been unconscious?'

'It's hard to tell for sure. I've no way of keeping time, but I'm sure you've been down here for at least a few hours. I don't know how long you were out for before they brought you in though.'

Jennifer inched forwards, pressing into the bars of her cell, looking towards the cell that the voice was coming from, straining to see into its shadows. 'Who are you?' she called into the darkness.

A figure stood up and shuffled towards her. As he stepped out of the shadows, she gave a gasp as she saw his face. He was old, much older than when she had last seen that face, and he now sported a grey beard across his pallid white skin, but there was no mistaking him.

'But... you're dead!' she cried in disbelief.

Silas gave a brief shrug.

'I saw Jack shoot you...'

'All your adventures... All that you have experienced... And you still don't really understand, do you?'

'What...' she managed to mutter. She was struggling to make sense of it all.

'For *some* of us, death does not have the same finality as it does for others.'

'What do you mean?'

'Once you have fully experienced these lands, become at home here – become a *native* – then when your waking body dies you will have a chance to live on, a final life here in the dreamlands.'

Jennifer chuckled, despite herself. 'And you certainly look like you're making the best of it.'

'Alas, fortune has not smiled on me recently. I have been a prisoner here for some time now.'

'And where exactly *is* here? It this Randolph's hideout?'

'His secret retreat in the dreamlands. His private sanctuary.' He gave Jennifer a curious look. 'How do you know him?'

'Let's just say we've had a few disagreements since he took over from you.'

'I always knew Randolph wanted my job,' muttered Silas. 'I just didn't expect him to go to these lengths to keep it. He holds quite the grudge. I've been here for... quite a while now.'

'Then was he the one who hit me, brought me down here?' She hadn't had a chance to look at the face of the man who had attacked her.

Silas shook his head slowly. 'One of his henchmen – one of the locals. I haven't seen Randolph around here for a while now.'

Jennifer sat down on her bunk, making herself as comfortable as she could. She had a feeling that she might be here for a while. 'How long have you been here?' she asked.

Silas shrugged. 'Several years, I think. It's hard to be sure. But don't worry – I'm sure in your case, you'll be put out of your misery as soon as he's finished with you.'

Jennifer laughed. 'I think he has other plans for me.'

Silas laughed in return. 'Really? I wouldn't have thought you were his type.'

'No, not like that. It's a long story.'

'No – let me,' said Silas. 'It's all coming back to me now. Your fiancé was the prophesized one. I didn't realize at the time, not until I saw him fall from the sky. That makes you the mother of... let me see... I believe he was re-ferred to as the "nightmare child". The one who will lead the Brotherhood into greatness. Tell me, have you had the child yet?'

'You haven't seen him?' asked Jennifer, standing up and walking to the front of the cell, clasping the iron bars in her hands. 'A boy of about four? I was hoping to find him here. Randolph took him, and we understood that he was keeping a guest here...' She sighed, as the realization dawned on her. 'I suppose he must have been referring to you.'

'Alas, yes,' said Silas. 'Unfortunate for both of us.' He thought for a moment. 'And given who you are... destined to be killed by your own child... you believe Randolph won't kill you.'

'Not if he truly believes in these prophecies.'

'Yes, I see,' muttered Silas. 'Almost makes you immortal, doesn't it, knowing you can't die for several years yet?'

'I don't believe in your stupid prophecies,' she scoffed. 'I don't believe that the destiny of either of us is pre-determined.'

'Well, I think you and Randolph may have to agree to disagree on that matter. He believes quite strongly in the absolute truth of the prophecies.'

'And I don't suppose there's any way to change his mind.'

Silas merely shook his head.

'No, I suppose not. You can't argue sense into a madman, after all. What about you? What do you believe about all this?'

'I used to take it all with a pinch of salt. Oh, I believed that Aloysius had made the prophecies; I just didn't necessarily believe that they would come true. That all changed a bit when I saw your lover–'

'–Husband, now.'

'Until I saw your *husband* fall from the sky before me, as Aloysius had predicted. I must admit that did a fair bit to convert me to the cause. I had to re-evaluate my belief system after that. And after I died, of course.'

'So, what? You're immortal now?'

Silas chuckled again. 'Nothing of the sort. Just the opposite, in fact. Now that I have no waking body anymore, if I die here now, that's it. Game over.'

Jennifer smiled an evil grin. 'So, I can kill you myself, and exact my revenge for everything you've put us through.'

Silas held his hands up in mock surrender. 'Now, now, no need for that. In fact, I'm sure we could help one another.'

'Why would I *ever* help you?'

'Have you looked around recently? I very much doubt you're here of your own free will.'

'And you have a plan for escape?'

'Maybe,' he said coyly.

'If it's all the same to you, I'm sure I can find my own way out of here. And *then* come back to kill you.'

'Don't be like *that.*'

'You expect me to forgive you?'

'No, but I don't expect you to be pig-headed about it. We can work together, or you could spend the next ten years locked in a cold, cramped cell. Trust me – it's not a great lifestyle. I speak from experience.'

Jennifer went and sat back down on her bunk. She thought in silence for a few moments before standing up again. 'I don't need to escape,' she said. 'Unlike you, I'm only a temporary visitor here. As soon as my earthly self wakes, I'll simply disappear from here.'

'Ah,' said Silas with a sigh. 'I see.'

They both sat silently for a few more minutes until Silas broke the silence this time. 'You came here looking for your son. What if I could help you find him?'

'But how? You've been locked in here for God knows how long. You don't know where he is.'

'No, but there are lots of other things that I *do* know. About Randolph. About the Brotherhood.'

'And you're willing to turn sides? Betray the Brotherhood?'

'Look at me,' he said, gesturing to the cell in which he stood. 'Do I look like I'm on good terms with Randolph and the Brotherhood?'

Jennifer gave a grunt of acknowledgement. 'So, what? You help me with Bill – I help you escape. Is that what you're proposing?'

'It is.'

'But you don't know where my son is?'

'I'd love to able to say that I did. That really would be something worth trading, wouldn't it? But, alas, I don't. I've been here for quite a while now, and Randolph doesn't share many of his plans with me. He only comes here when he wants information.'

Jennifer though for a moment before asking, 'So what *do* you know of Randolph's current plans?'

'Not much, I must admit. He's up to something all right, but it's been a while since he's quizzed me about anything specific.'

Jennifer thought for a moment. 'He was after these ornate metal orbs – what do you know about them?'

Jennifer thought she saw Silas take a step towards her in his cell. 'Describe them to me,' he said.

'Metal sphere's about yea big,' she said, holding her hands a few inches apart. 'Covered in minute engravings.' Silas nodded silently. 'Tell me about them,' she added.

'If I do, will you help me escape?'

'I'll *consider* it.'

Randolph sat down on the floor and crossed his legs, sitting close to the aisle so that Jennifer could see him clearly.

'No one knows their exact origin,' he started, 'except that they are older than mankind, possibly older than this world. Their original name – or at least the oldest recorded name given to them by man – is the *Aztria*. Legend says that something of great power is sealed within them. Some say the spark of a dying sun; others a fragment of the blind god Azathoth, the nuclear chaos that reigns at the centre of the universe. There were four pairs of

Aztria, each with their own unique powers. Where they came from originally no one knows, but a long, long time ago, shortly after man first looked up into the skies and worshipped the gods that they saw there, they were handed down to mankind. They were bestowed to four different sects, four ancient groups each worshipping a different god. These factions have jealously guarded the *Aztria* for millennia, since before the dawn of recorded civilization.'

'What exactly are these powers they hold?'

'Each has slightly different powers. Some allow manipulation of people's minds; others allow a degree of foresight and precognition. All of them, however, have a localized effect on the surrounding time and space.'

'What does *that* mean?'

'According to my research, they can slow down the passage of time for those who own them, potentially distorting the space around them… *if* you can work out how to control them, of course.'

'So what would Randolph want with them?'

'I'm not sure.'

'Could we destroy them?'

'Not as far as I'm aware. The legends say they're impervious to any earthly force.'

'So what happens when Randolph gets his hands on them?'

'I suppose it depends which pair he was after. Do you know which ones he was trying to obtain?'

'I don't know. We think he has at least two pairs and is planning to take a third.'

'*What!* spat Silas, jumping to his feet.

'What? What is it?'

'That fool will destroy us all,' he growled.

'Why?' she cried. 'For God's sake, will you tell me what's going on!'

Silas shook his head in disbelief. 'As I said, the *Aztria* allow for the manipulation of space and time. Individually, each has a certain amount of power, but their power grows exponentially when combined. If he brought six together, or heaven forbid all eight…'

'What? What would happen?'

'Well, imagine if you will, creating a small sun somewhere on the surface of your planet. Or a small black hole.'

'You're *kidding*?'

'No one knows for certain, but there's a reason why they've always been kept apart, guarded by four separate groups.'

'So, what? He's planning to destroy the world? That does sound like his style, but surely that would be suicide... Oh, fuck.'

'What?' now it was Silas's turn to ask the questions.

'We think Randolph and the Brotherhood are forming some kind of colony on another world. Jack found some magical doorway that took him there.'

Silas nodded. 'They are known as *gates* – a way of transporting across potentially vast distances of space.' He thought for a moment and then shrugged. 'Well, I suppose it would make sense to move to another planet, if you're planning to destroy the current one.'

'Fuck!'

'Quite.'

'I need to get out of here,' she said. 'We need to stop him.'

'Agreed.'

'Really? I'd have thought that would be right up your street.'

'I don't want to destroy the world. I just don't believe it truly belongs to man – the ancient gods are its rightful owners. I just wanted to return them to the Earth to retake their true position over mankind. To have their world destroyed would not appease them.'

'Then why is Randolph doing this?'

'Maybe he doesn't understand their true power. He wouldn't be the first to be seduced by a force he doesn't understand and won't be able to control.'

'Or maybe he's just completely bat-shit crazy.'

'No. He will have some kind of plan. I just fear he has overestimated himself this time.'

'So, who has these orbs?' asked Jennifer. 'If we know where Randolph's going, maybe we can stop him.'

Silas stepped to the front of the cell and then sat down on the floor again, arranging himself into the lotus position. He sat in silent contemplation for a moment, gathering his thoughts.

'In pre-historic times, right at the dawn of this planet's civilization, the old gods walked free among us, their worshippers forming the world's first religions. The exact history of the *Aztria* is not well documented, as I said, but four of these groups are believed to have been granted possession of two orbs each, and have guarded them jealously ever since.

'The first cult worshipped the *Black Goat of the Woods*, the *Mother of a Thousand Young*. This was the cult that Aloysius first joined, the one he split off from to form the Brotherhood, taking one of the *Aztria* with him.'

Jennifer thought back to Cross's description of what she had come across. '*The thousand young*,' she muttered to herself, nodding slowly. 'We believe he's already got both of those – both the one Aloysius took as well as the one that this cult still had.'

'Okay,' said Silas. 'The next group have gone by several names over the centuries, but I know of them as the *Subjects of Yellow*.'

'Yellow?'

Silas nodded solemnly. 'They follow *He who shall not be named*, the *King in Yellow*.'

'Okay... and do you know where we might find these... *subjects*?'

Silas shook his head. 'They work in secret; I have not even heard any rumours of them for many years.'

'But when you did hear rumours... what did you hear?'

'The last time I'm certain they were around was in Paris at the end of the nineteenth century.'

'The nineteenth century? That's not much use.'

Silas shrugged to indicate that this wasn't his problem. 'There were rumours of their existence in New England in the early decades of the twentieth century. Whispers of secret temples to their god, hidden in the back streets of London in the 1980s.'

Jennifer sighed. 'Okay, let's put them to the side for a moment. Who's next?'

'*The Eternal Chaos*. They worship the blind idiot god Azathoth, who reigns in the centre of the universe. They are believers in chaos and anarchy.'

'And do you know where we can find them?'

'Not directly. But if you can find any organized groups of anarchists, professional sowers of chaos, chances are they won't be too far away.'

'Okay, I'll bear that in mind.'

'Well then, the final group called themselves *The Faceless*, worshippers of Nyarlathotep, messenger and servant of the outer gods, the *Chaos of a Thousand Forms*.'

'The what?' said Jennifer, shaking her head in confusion.

'Unlike many of the other gods, Nyarlathotep is frequently mentioned throughout history, as he can choose to take a form of his own pleasing. When he walks among men, he often takes the form of a tall black man. He ruled over ancient Egypt as the *Black Pharaoh*, and his presence has often been recorded just prior to disasters occurring.'

Jennifer now shook her head in disbelief. 'You describe them as if these gods are real.'

'My dear... they *are* real. Quite, quite, real, and more powerful than you can possibly imagine.'

Jennifer didn't believe a word of it, but she wasn't going to contradict him when he was providing quite so much information.

'And these *Faceless*. Do you know where *they* are?'

'Lost in the sands of time. They were an ancient cult. They disappeared from recorded history hundreds – possibly thousands – of years ago.'

Jennifer sighed. 'As far as we know, Randolph has the two orbs from *The Thousand Young*. We think he may have another couple from elsewhere, but we don't know which ones. So that leaves possibly two other sets – and we don't know whether he has any of those yet. Or any clue as to where they might be found.' Silas shrugged again.

She sat down on the floor of her cell again. 'I'm not sure I'm any better off than I was before I came here.'

Silas shook his head. 'You know your enemy better. You know what he is after. Even if you do not know where to find them at the moment... you at least now know what to look for.' Jennifer gave a small nod of the head to acknowledge that he was probably right. 'You may also have better resources to seek them out than I have.'

Jennifer considered this. Hundreds of years ago, even just a decade or two ago, secret organizations could hide with almost complete anonymity. But these days, with CCTV, facial recognition, massive police and security service databases... she reckoned it would be harder to stay completely hidden. Maybe Peter White and Detective Cross would have access to the resources needed to locate these groups.

Chapter 17.

April 10th, 2017. Ash House, Dartmoor, England.

Jennifer opened her eyes, woken by the cawing of crows from a tree outside their bedroom window. The clock by the side of her bed read 07:37. Jack was still asleep next to her, snoring softly. She was starving, and desperately needed something to eat, but she'd let him sleep for a little while longer before she woke him.

Jack came downstairs of his own accord half an hour later, roused by the noises from the kitchen and the aroma of coffee and bacon that had been wafting up the stairs.

He sat down at the kitchen table, still in his dressing gown, and Jennifer slid a bacon sandwich and freshly poured cup of coffee over the table towards him. He took the mug in his hands, taking a couple of sips of the steaming drink, letting the caffeine do its work.

When he looked suitably awake, Jennifer sat down opposite him and started to explain what had happened in the dreamlands: how Randolph's guest hadn't been Bill as they had hoped, but had still proved to be a unique and unexpected source of information.

'So how did you escape?' asked Jack, when Jennifer had fully described her encounter with Silas.

'Escape?'

'How did you get out of the cell?'

'I didn't. I just waited. Eventually I had to wake up here, and when I did... bye, bye, prison.'

'Then how long...?'

'About a week.'

'Jesus... are you okay?'

'It wasn't a fun time, I'll agree, but I'll live.'

'And Silas? Are you going back to free him?'

'Fuck him,' said Jennifer with unexpected savagery. 'After what he dragged us into and put us through, he can starve there for all I care.'

'Remind me never to truly piss you off,' said Jack, taking another sip of his coffee.

'So, how are we going to track down these groups?' asked Jennifer. 'You know what these secretive cults are like...'

'Secretive?'

'Exactly.'

'You think they really exist then, these other cults?' asked Jack.

Jennifer thought for a second. 'The Brotherhood exists. The cult of the Black Goat certainly seems to exist from what Cross has told us. He told me about them before I'd mentioned their name to him, and if they exist, why not the others?'

Jack nodded. 'And the gods that they worship?'

'That's another matter. He believes in them all right, and from what we've seen I'm sure there might be some element of truth to their existence. We've seen too much to completely discount them.'

'But whether they're actual gods...'

'...is very much up for debate,' she concluded.

❋ ❋ ❋

Jack and Jennifer were both in the living room when the doorbell rang. Jack looked at the clock on the wall; it was quarter-past eleven.

'That'll be Cross,' said Jack. When she had rung the previous night, she had arranged to come over at eleven o'clock; only running a quarter of an hour late was quite punctual for her. He stood up and went to the hallway to answer the door. As he opened it, he saw Detective Cross standing on the doorstep as expected, but he saw that she had also brought a friend with her. He had his back to the door and as he turned to reveal himself, a smile of recognition spread across Jack's face.

'Well, hello, old friend,' said Peter White, a wry grin on his face.

'Peter,' stuttered Jack. 'I wasn't expecting you... But where are my manners! Come in, both of you.' He held the door wide, and welcomed them both in, shaking their hands as they came.

When they had all gathered in the living room, Peter was the first to break the silence.

'Cross has told me something about your situation,' he said. 'And I thought maybe I could help. I can't dedicate all my time as I've got another case on at the moment – but in my spare time, if there's anything I can do...'

'I can't think of anyone I'd trust more,' said Jack. 'It's a great idea.'

'I can think of a better one,' said Jennifer. 'Forget this spare time nonsense. You're a private detective – we'll hire you.'

'You don't need to do that...'

'Nonsense,' said Jack. 'We're not short of cash, and if you can help in any way with Bill, it'll be money well spent. Whatever it costs, just send me the invoice and I'll make sure it gets paid.'

'I wish I had a few more clients like you,' chuckled Peter, and the others joined in, a warm feeling of friendship spreading around the room. 'So,' he continued when silence returned, 'Cross has given me an overview of what happened, but maybe you could just tell me again, in your own words.'

Jennifer re-told the story to Peter. How Randolph had told them that he believed their son belonged to the Brotherhood of the Star, and how they would raise him. How, after his birth, Jack and Jennifer had moved away, tried to keep quiet and inconspicuous, until Bill had gone missing from his nursery in broad daylight. They had no direct proof, but they were damned sure that the Brotherhood were behind his disappearance. In the six months since he had been taken, the police had made no progress – they still had no suspects, no idea of means or motive. Jennifer's previous visits to the dreamlands had been frequent but fruitless, as had their own investigations of places they associated with the Brotherhood, such as Bruadar Castle in Scotland and Randolph's old house in Lincolnshire. It had been as if the Brotherhood had just vanished off the face of the Earth. She finished off describing their adventures in Kincord Sanatorium, and Jack's lucky escape.

'I followed a couple of the Brotherhood out through some kind of doorway,' he said.

'I believe it's called a *gate*,' added Jennifer.

'I ended up... Well, you may not believe this, but it was on another planet,' continued Jack.

Peter's eyebrows went up at this. 'So they *had* vanished off the face of the Earth?'

'Some of them at least,' said Jack. They seem to have these doorways – these *gates*,' he corrected, with a nod towards Jennifer, 'that they can activate to travel from one place to another, potentially over huge distances if they can go to other worlds. Does that sound at all familiar to you?'

Peter thought for a moment and then shook his head. 'No. No, it doesn't.'

Jack retrieved his phone from his pocket and unlocked it, opening the photo gallery. He scrolled through until he found the pictures he had taken of the doorway he had travelled through, showing it to Peter.

Peter shook his head again. 'Sorry – still no idea.'

Jack pocketed the phone again. 'While I was there, I saw a few things.' He described the rooms full of stores, the town square and the temple. 'I also managed to find some things of interest,' he said. 'Let me go get them.'

'Do you have a recent photo of Bill?' asked Peter as Jack left to go to his study. Jennifer stood up and went over to a bureau, from which she removed a stack of papers. She took a handful from the top and passed them to Peter – fliers asking for any information about a missing child, with a large picture of Bill in the centre.

'That was recent when he went missing,' she said, 'but he'll have changed since – six months is a long time at that age.'

'Understood,' nodded Peter, slipping the sheet into his inside jacket pocket.

'Do you have any ideas?' asked Jennifer. 'Any idea how the Brotherhood could have taken Bill, or what they might want with him?'

'What about these gates of theirs?' asked Peter.

Jack grimaced and gave a small shrug. 'I don't think so. They give off this bright white light while they're active. Surely someone would have noticed that?'

'Or someone coming through and grabbing Bill,' added Jennifer.

Peter sat in silence for a moment, his fingers steepled, deep in contemplation. 'As I understand it, Bill was conceived in the dreamlands?'

'Yes,' nodded Jennifer. 'I didn't even think I was able to conceive... but I guess things worked out differently over there. Our bodies were noticeably younger – and healthier too, I suppose.'

Jack stepped back into the room holding several sheets of paper, which he handed to Peter. He took hold of them, placing them on his lap.

'In my admittedly limited experience, I've never heard of this happening before,' said Peter, thinking out loud. 'Maybe he has some kind of affinity with dreams and the dreamlands. While some people in the dreamlands are visitors from our world, others are natives, born and raised there their entire life. If Bill is a native, or somewhere in between – a hybrid if you like...' He let his thoughts trail away.

'So if he's... what? A native of the dreamlands?' said Jennifer, continuing his line of thought. 'You think he can travel there on his own?'

'I don't know,' admitted Peter. 'But it would go some way to explaining things. Did he ever have any particularly vivid or lucid dreams?'

'Not that he told us about,' said Jennifer. 'But he was only young... and how would you know that your dreams are different from anyone else's – especially at that age?'

Peter nodded. Then an expression of realization spread across Jack's face. 'We've never known how Bill was taken from his nursery in the middle of the day – but it was during nap time. We do know that Randolph – and others – are capable of pulling people back from the dreamlands into this reality with them. That's how we think he escaped from his police cell.' Cross gave a little shrug to acknowledge this. 'We never really considered it, as we'd never taken Bill with us to the dreamlands, never even told him anything about it...'

'I can see how that might be a difficult story to explain to him – how and where he was conceived,' said Cross.

'There's another recent development,' added Jack. Cross's eyebrow raised with curiosity. 'Jennifer has had a couple of dreams in which she thinks she's seen things through Bill's eyes. It could be nothing...'

'If he's special,' said Peter, 'and naturally sensitive to dreams... Children are also often especially close to their mother, and you, as I understand it, also have been quite a frequent traveller to the dreamlands recently?'

Jennifer nodded. 'We didn't know whether Randolph and the Brotherhood had taken him there to hide him. I've been there on dozens of occasions, trying to find any trace of him ever having been there... all to no avail.'

'So...' said Peter. 'It does look like Bill has some kind of special connection to the dreamlands — and to you, Jennifer. That might be how you were able to get these... *visions* in your dreams. Do you think you were experiencing his dreams, or his memories? Do you think that what you experienced was live, so to speak?'

'I'm really not sure,' said Jennifer. 'It had the feeling of something I was experiencing myself, for real, but it also had that surreal quality of dreams.'

'Okay,' said Peter. 'So it's possible — maybe even probable — that someone from the Brotherhood pulled him from the dreamlands, and that was how they managed to kidnap him in broad daylight. Quite how they do that, I don't know, but it's definitely one avenue to explore. We ought not to discount other possibilities though, including more... mundane explanations.'

'Agreed,' said Jack.

Peter turned to Cross. 'Are you able to get me the original crime-scene notes?'

'Officially... no. But I can get you a copy,' she replied.

'Good enough.'

Peter turned to the pages that Jack had given him, and leafed through them. 'What am I looking at here?'

Jack shrugged. 'I'm not sure, to be honest. Those are all photographs of documents I found in the Brotherhood's lair when I was... well, wherever the hell I was. I think they all belonged to Randolph and they looked important at the time. Does any of it mean anything to you?'

Peter took another longer look. 'Some of this is pretty advanced maths and physics — well above what I can understand. And some of this other stuff... my geography is pretty rusty. Or is it geology?' He looked over at Jack. 'You don't have any context for any of this stuff?'

'No,' said Jack, 'I'm afraid not.'

Peter thought for a second. 'My other case is over at the university — maybe I can show these to some of the people there, see if anyone can understand them. Hopefully some of the lecturers or professors there can make a bit more sense of it.'

'What about the numbers, and those places on the map?'

Peter shrugged. 'Those numbers could be almost anything.'

'A safe combination?' suggested Cross. 'Some kind of PIN or pass-code?'

'Maybe the solutions to some of those equations?' offered Jennifer.

'Without more context, it's going to be hard to know for sure,' said Jack.

Peter nodded. 'Now, the pins on the map... One of those is probably Kincord Sanatorium, but the others... I'll have a look, see if I can find anything interesting near those locations.'

'When I returned, I found myself a few miles east of Oxford, which is close to one of those pins,' said Jack. 'Something there has to be of interest to the Brotherhood.'

'Okay,' said Peter. 'Let's see what we can find of interest there, and the other location in Africa.'

'We've also got another couple of potential leads,' said Jack. 'Jennifer took another trip to the dreamlands last night. While she was there, she found someone who gave us the name of three other cults who are also meant to have some of these orbs.' He didn't mention Silas by name. He wasn't sure how much the others would trust any information if they knew it came from him. 'If Randolph is looking for them, then if we can find them first... maybe we can find him too. And from him, Bill.'

'Okay,' said Cross taking out a small pad of paper and a pen from her jacket pocket. 'What are these cults called?'

'The first group are the *Subjects of Yellow*,' said Jennifer. 'They follow someone called *The King in Yellow*, or *He who shall not be named*. The second are *The Eternal Chaos*, champions of chaos and anarchy who worship something called Azathoth, whatever he or it is. The final group are *The Faceless*. They worship *Nyarlathotep*, who can supposedly take on any form he likes.'

'Do you have any other information about them?'

'Not really, just the names. Everything else I was told... well it's all a bit out of date. Rumours of their whereabouts and existence decades ago.'

'Well, it's something I suppose,' said Cross, jotting down the names on her pad. 'I'll look through the police databases, and see what I can find.'

'What about you?' asked Jennifer. 'Have you got anywhere with your enquiries?'

'Just before we came over, I got a call about the explosion at the sanatorium,' replied Cross. They found the body in the portacabin, as well as a few more bodies in the wreckage of the basement. The explosion didn't do as good a job as I think it was meant to at removing any evidence. It looks like the asylum was being used as some kind of base of operations.'

'Who by?' asked Jennifer.

'They don't know yet,' said Cross. There was no formal ID on any of the bodies, and they were too burnt for fingerprints. They're trying to run DNA and dental records to attempt to identify them, but I wouldn't hold out too much hope for that. Do we think that they were one of these cults we're looking for?'

'I'd say there's a fair chance,' said Jennifer, 'but which — if any — of them, I don't know.'

'Hold on a second,' said Jack. He stood up and stepped quickly out of the room. When he returned a few seconds later, he was holding the ring and pendant he had taken off the bodies in the basement. First he showed the pendant to Peter and Cross. 'I took this off one of the bodies I found under the asylum,' he told them. 'This looks like something belonging to the Brotherhood. That star seems to be their emblem.'

Peter and Cross both nodded in agreement. Jack then passed the signet ring to Detective Cross, who gave it a close inspection before passing it on to Peter. 'That ring was taken from another man,' Jack informed them. 'That engraving on the bezel — that's not something I've seen before. Does it mean anything to either of you?'

Both of them shook their heads. 'I'm not aware of any cult using that logo,' said Peter. 'I can ask around though.'

'I can also make some discrete enquiries,' added Cross. She took out her phone, taking a couple of close-up photographs of the insignia, and then Peter did the same, before passing it back to Jack.

✻ ✻ ✻

The next day, Jack was sitting in his study. He was searching the internet, trying to find any significance to any of the clues they had found. So far, all of his searches had been fruitless.

He looked up from his laptop as his mobile began to vibrate, skipping along the desk in front of him. He picked it up and glanced at the screen; it was Detective Cross.

116

'Hi there,' he said as he answered the call. 'Any luck yet? I've not found anything.'

'There's been some progress with the examination of the asylum site.'

'Anything relevant to us?'

'If you remember, I told you that they'd found the body outside in the portacabin, as well as some more in the basement. There was no formal identification on any of them, but it turns out that the one outside was wearing a signet ring, just like the one you showed me.'

'I remember seeing one on him. I just didn't inspect it closely at the time.'

'Well, someone from Scotland Yard has identified the symbol on it with the help of some European agencies. Apparently it belongs to an Armenian group calling themselves...' She paused for a second, and coughed to clear her throat. '*Mijukayin k'aos,*' she said. 'The closest translation is *The Nuclear Chaos*. Nasty group of hard-line extremists from Eastern Europe and Russia, hard-core anarchists.'

'That sounds a lot like the *Endless Chaos* we're looking for. Silas said we'd find them wherever we find organized groups of anarchists – if that's not an oxymoron.'

'I agree. Most of the info about them is classified above my pay grade, but from what I understand, these were some pretty hard-core terrorists, intent on bringing down any kind of organized government and throwing the world into anarchy.'

Jack thought for a second. 'When I was in the basement, I saw some papers with what looked like Russian writing on them. That ties up with them being from Eastern Europe or Russia. So what were they doing in the basement of an abandoned asylum in England?'

'Your guess is as good as mine at the moment. If the security services have any idea what they were up to, they're not sharing it with the likes of me.'

'Well, if what we were told is true, the Brotherhood were presumably there to take the orbs – and took them out in order to achieve that.'

'Then it's entirely possible we owe them one, as odd as that sounds. I may not know why they were there, but I'm positive they were up to no good.'

✳ ✳ ✳

It was later in the evening when Jack received a phone call from Peter.

'I've got some new leads for you,' said Peter.

'Shoot,' said Jack.

'Firstly, I've done some digging on this *Endless Chaos* cult, helped by the info that Cross discovered about their Eastern European origins.'

'Okay...'

'According to some of my sources, there was a Russian Cult back in the eighties – back when it was still the USSR. They went by the name of *Navsegda Khaos* – the closest translation of which is *Forever Chaos*. They were said to worship a blind idiot god who sat at the centre of the universe. This god was supposedly capable of controlling space and time, but was also completely mindless. They believed he could wipe out humanity, not out of any malice or hatred, but just on a random whim.'

'That does sound like it could be the same cult.'

'The members were mostly nihilists and anarchists, many of them ex-Russian military. If they felt like their god wanted to wipe out mankind, maybe they thought they could give him a helping hand.'

'Okay,' said Jack, trying to collate his thoughts. 'This supports our theory that the group in the asylum were the *Endless Chaos*. In which case the Brotherhood were presumably there to take their orbs – by force, by the looks of it. We're not sure why the *Endless Chaos* were there, but I'm not sure that particularly matters. That's just one more opportunity lost.'

'Agreed,' said Peter.

'Okay, have you got anything else?'

'Yes,' said Peter. 'I think I may have tracked down what that pin stuck in the map of North Africa was referring to. Are you near your computer?'

'It's just in the other room,' said Jack, standing up and walking back to his study.

'I've sent you an email,' said Peter.

Jack opened the lid of his laptop and logged in, opening his email. He found Peter's message right at the top and opened it. 'Okay, found it,' said Jack.

'There should be a link in there – click on it,' said Peter.

Jack did so, and his browser started loading a web page. It was a website for an organization called NAAS – the North African Archaeological Society.

As he started to look through the page, Jennifer wandered into the room behind Jack, carrying a steaming cup of coffee. She leant over Jack's shoulder, peering at the screen.

'What's this about?' she asked.

'Peter's found a possible link to the location in North Africa,' said Jack. He put the phone down on the desk in front of him, and clicked on an icon. 'I've just put you on speakerphone,' said Jack. 'Jennifer's here with me.'

'Hi,' said Jennifer. 'What are we looking at here?'

'Hi, Jenn,' said Peter. 'Well, apparently, there have been some recent discoveries at a new dig site at a desert in Egypt, several miles west of Samalut.'

'What kind of discoveries?'

'I'm not sure. It's quite recent, and the archaeologists are keeping their cards close to their chests for now.'

'So it could be nothing,' suggested Jack.

'Possibly... But it's almost exactly where that pin on the map was. In addition, I've compared the location of the site to that hand-drawn map you found. If you take the river on the map to be the Nile, and account for some of the other terrain... It's not exact, but I think it's the same place.'

'That sounds like it could be worth a try,' said Jennifer.

Jack was silent for a moment and then suddenly jumped to his feet, as if his chair had been electrocuted. 'The dig site,' he said.

'What?' said Peter and Jennifer together.

'Sebastian told Randolph that work was progressing at a *dig site*. That can't be a coincidence.'

Jennifer stood up straight, drawing her own phone from her pocket. 'I'm booking us a flight right now. If the Brotherhood are still there, we need to get there before they leave. It's the only lead we've got to Bill.' She unlocked her phone, searching through her contacts for a number as he left the room. 'What's the nearest airport?' she called back as she started dialling the number.

'Cairo International,' called Peter.

'Anything else?' asked Jack.

'Not yet. But I'm still looking at the other leads.'

Jennifer popped her head back around the corner. 'Are you going to be coming as well, Peter?' she called out towards the phone on the desk.

'I'm not sure I can at the moment,' he said.

Jennifer returned to the phone in her hand. 'No, just two seats,' she said. There was a slight pause before adding 'Well, what about the day after tomorrow?'

'I've got some stuff I still need to look into here,' said Peter, 'I need to meet up with someone tomorrow, but you could probably do with some local help. I know a guide, Al-amir Alfarsi, based in Cairo. He's helped me before. Trustworthy man; helped me out of a couple of tight spots. I'll see if he's free, get him to meet you at the airport.'

'Okay,' said Jack. 'As soon as Jennifer's booked the tickets, I'll let you know when we're due to arrive.'

Chapter 18.

April 11th, 2017. Royal Devon and Exeter Hospital.

The morning visiting hour had just started when Peter White arrived at the recovery ward. He was there to see Cathy Hobbes, the student who had survived the stabbing in the university dorms. Peter was curious as to whether there could be any connection between her attack and David's suicide, and Detective Cross had pulled a couple of strings to arrange a meeting with her.

The hospital ward was half empty and quiet – a pleasant change from his previous stay – and he wandered over to her bed, which was situated halfway down the room.

Cathy was awake, sitting up in bed and reading a book – a well-worn paperback copy of *Wuthering Heights.*

'Hi, I believe you're expecting me?' asked Peter.

Cathy nodded. 'Take a seat.' As Peter pulled up a chair and sat down, she placed a slip of paper between the pages of her book and placed it gently on the table next to her bed. 'So, how can I help you, Detective White?'

Peter shook his head. 'You don't normally call private detectives *Detective,*' he said. 'Just call me Peter.'

'Okay, Peter,' she said with a smile.

'I must say, I was half surprised you agreed to see me. Most people don't like talking to private detectives – they worry about what skeletons in the closet we might be trying to uncover.'

'You *did* save my life. I kind of think I owe you one,' she replied with a grin. 'So how can I help? I wouldn't have thought there'd be much to investigate with my stabbing – the culprit was kind of obvious.'

Peter gave a slight grimace. 'I was actually at your dorm investigating the death of another student. He'd jumped to his death from his window.'

The smile on Cathy's face disappeared. 'Oh. David Packham,' she said.

'Did you know him?'

'No. I mean, I'd seen him around a few times, but never really said more than hello to him.'

'And your room-mate? Did she know him?'

'Melissa? Not as far as I'm aware.'

'What course was she studying?'

'English literature. I'm doing chemistry.'

Peter sighed. David Packham had been studying Fine Arts; they were unlikely to have any courses in common. This was starting to look like a dead end, but seeing as he was here, he decided to stay the course. 'Had Melissa started doing anything odd recently? Showing any odd behaviour? Had she started taking drugs?'

'Well, she took a bit of pot occasionally, but that was it as far as I know – nothing too serious.'

'Nothing else?'

Cathy thought for a second. 'Once a week or so, she'd get back very late or stay out all night.'

'Boyfriend?'

'No, not for a while. This was some research thing.'

'Research for a literature course?'

'It wasn't part of her degree. It was some kind of clinical research trial; they were paying money for research subjects, that kind of thing. She needed the extra money – who doesn't these days.'

Peter perked up slightly at that. 'What kind of research? Was it medical?' He wondered whether *they* were giving her any drugs.

'No, nothing like that. I think she said it was some kind of psychology study. She didn't talk much about it – it didn't seem particularly interesting –

probably why they had to pay people to participate.'

'But you don't know who was running it?'

'No, sorry.'

Peter thought for a moment. 'I never asked you... Why do *you* think she attacked you?'

Cathy shrugged. 'It was completely unexpected, completely out of character. We'd both gone to bed. When I fell asleep, she was still reading a book. I was woken by her screaming. I climbed out of bed, scared and wanting to know what was going on. As I approached her, she slashed at me with the knife.'

'Do you know where she got the knife?'

'It was one of hers, one of a set of kitchen knives. We tend to keep the decent kitchen stuff in our bedroom; otherwise it tends to go missing.'

Peter nodded to show he understood. 'And there was no warning before she went to bed? No signs of unusual behaviour?'

'No. I mean she seemed a little distracted, but nothing particularly unusual.'

'Do you know what book she was reading?'

'One of her course textbooks – I don't know which one.'

'Was there anything else about her behaviour leading up to that night? Anything that seemed normal at the time, but might seem odd in retrospect?'

'No,' she said with a small shake of the head.

'Think about it for a while... please.'

Cathy thought for a moment. 'Well... Melissa hadn't been sleeping too well for the last few nights. She was often still tired in the morning... but nothing that would cause homicidal rage.'

'And you don't know why she wasn't sleeping?'

'She didn't say, but she's got some big exams coming up. I assumed it was stress from that.'

'I see,' said Peter. He glanced at his watch and then got to his feet. 'I really ought to be going and leave you to your rest. I know how important that can be when you've had a serious injury. Thank you for your time.'

'And thanks again for saving me,' said Cathy with a wide smile.

As Peter turned to go, she called out after him again. He stopped and turned back to face her.

'Do you know what will happen to her?' asked Cathy.

'Melissa?' said Peter and Cathy nodded. 'I'm not sure, to be honest. From everything I've heard, my guess is that she won't be charged with attempted murder. There definitely seems to be grounds for a plea of insanity or diminished responsibility. It's likely that she'll be institutionalized for her own safety.'

'In an insane asylum?'

Peter grinned. 'They call them psychiatric hospitals these days. But wherever she goes, I wouldn't worry. I think she'll be incarcerated for a long time.'

Chapter 19.

Jack and Jennifer were in their bedroom packing when Jack's phone rang. It was Detective Cross, calling to update them.

'I've been busy all day hunting down any leads to those two groups,' she told them, 'searching our databases for anything that looks or sounds like it might be our guys.'

'Okay...' said Jack. 'What do you have?'

'Not much. Hints of this and that, nothing direct. For your first cult, the *Subjects in Yellow*, there was nothing in the police database for that name.'

'*But...*' said Jack, sensing that there was something else.

'Just over ten years ago, there was a murder and a couple of accidental deaths.'

'You think they're connected.'

'Maybe. There was a new theatre company trying to get off the ground in Oxfordshire. Budding new writer/director, fresh new faces just out of university trying to make names for themselves. The two main leads, who were a couple of several months, both died in a car crash. It was on a country road, late at night, no witnesses. There was no direct evidence of foul play.'

'I don't see...'

'I'm getting to it. The same night that occurred, the writer and director of our little troupe of actors was murdered in his flat. The place was ransacked. Theory at the time was that it was a burglary gone wrong.'

'Do you believe it?'

'If I was investigating at the time, I probably would have. The guy had no enemies, no one who would want him dead – a nobody really – and stuff was taken from his apartment as far as they could tell.'

'So what makes you think this had anything to do with our cult?'

'The stage show he was writing... he told the actors that it was inspired by this old play he found. It was an ancient thing, over a century old. He was trying to jazz it up, bring it into the twenty-first century. You know the kind of thing – create his own West Side Story from a Romeo and Juliet.'

'Okay...' said Jack hesitantly.

'The name of this play was *The King in Yellow.*'

Jack let out a low whistle. 'It *could* just be a coincidence.'

'Maybe. But to be murdered... And the book *and* his new stage play were never found at his flat. Given that his laptop was stolen, the stage play being missing wasn't totally unexpected, but what kind of burglar steals some mouldy old book. Unless they already know what it is, and what it's really worth.'

'And the two lead actors... killed because they knew too much.'

'Exactly. They'd only just started hiring other actors for some of the bit parts.'

'So you know who they were?'

'All the cast and crew were interviewed at the time – it's all in the records.'

'But it was all ten years ago... What can we hope to find now?'

'Probably nothing. But I thought I could go and have a quick chat with them – the ones I can find, anyway. With what we now know, maybe we can jog something in their memory?'

'Okay. What about the others? *The Faceless*?'

'Nothing yet, but I'll let you know straight away if anything comes up.'

Chapter 20.

April 12th, 2017. Dartmoor University, England.

Peter White had headed back to the university dorms where David Packham had committed suicide. He couldn't prove anything – yet – but he couldn't help but feel that whatever had happened to Melissa and Cathy must have had some connection to what had happened to David. It seemed unlikely that two such episodes in such a short timeframe could just be coincidence.

As he reached David's room, he pulled the key out of his pocket, inserting it into the lock and opening the door. It opened silently, revealing the dark room beyond.

The room appeared just as he had left it. He resumed his search, going into painstaking detail this time, looking through all his books for anything left between the pages or written in the margins. He looked under the mattress, behind bookshelves and under drawers, but found nothing of interest. He checked so see if the carpet came up easily anywhere; it did in one corner, but there was nothing hidden underneath, no loose floorboards. He went through the clothes in the wardrobe and drawers, checking every pocket for anything out of the ordinary, but again came away empty handed. Maybe the police had already removed anything of interest, but otherwise David seemed to have lived a pretty humdrum life.

He returned to David's course notes again, leafing through them. The recent ones all looked like lecture notes about various renaissance artists: Botticelli, Donatello, Raphael and others. In the margins, there were little sketches and doodles, the signs of a wandering mind. As time went on, the doodles became more and more prolific, as did little drawings in the margin. One shape returned time and time again, a single black eye, sketched in pen or pencil. It was small and inconsequential at first, but gradually grew larger and more prominent until the final page of the pad was completely filled with a single image. In this final depiction, the eye was intricately detailed and was clearly not a human eye, instead looking more reptilian. It gave Peter chills as he stared at it, and he placed the pad back onto the desk, taking a couple of photos with his phone. What the hell did this mean, if anything?

That was it for the room, he decided. Whatever secrets David had had, he must have taken them to his grave. Next up would be the neighbours – some brief interviews to see if anyone had noticed anything unusual.

He knocked on the door of the nearest room and was greeted by a young man wearing a black t-shirt, jeans and boots, with long black hair and several facial piercings. The t-shirt was covered in artistic squiggles and the name of a band that was too spiky and distorted to easily read. From his earphones, Peter could hear fast, loud music, some kind of heavy metal.

Peter motioned for him to take out his earphones. He did so reluctantly, and Peter showed him his ID, explaining why he was there.

'I was wondering if you saw anything unusual at all on the night Peter died?' he asked.

'Nah,' said the youth. 'He kept to himself mainly. Quite a quiet character.'

'You didn't see anything out of the ordinary in the days leading up to his death?'

Again he shook his head.

'You didn't hear anything on the night in question?'

'Nah.' He gestured to his earphones. 'I was listening to music all evening. Didn't know anything was up until the morning.'

'Did you ever see him taking drugs of any kind?'

'Don't think he was the type. Makes him the exception round here.'

'Well, thanks for your help,' said Peter with a sigh. 'I'll let you get back to your music.'

'If you want to know anything about him, you ought to talk to Dom.'

'Dom?'

'Dominic – lives in that room there.' He pointed to a doorway on the other side of the hallway, a few feet further down. 'I think he was his best mate here.' The earphones went back in again, and the youth started nodding his head to the music as he closed the door.

Peter turned and walked to the doorway, knocking loudly on it.

'Hang on,' came a low grumbling voice from within. Peter stood there idly, tapping his foot on the floor for almost a minute until the door opened slowly. It revealed a dark room, the curtains still drawn despite the hour. It was hard to see in the darkness, but the inside looked to be an utter mess. There were clothes all over the floor and dirty plates and mugs piled high on a table, waiting in vain for someone to clean them.

'Are you Dominic?' asked Peter.

The student standing before him shook his head slowly. 'Richard. His room-mate.'

'Do you know where he is?'

'Who wants to know?'

Peter pulled out his ID again and presented it to him. Richard peered quizzically at it, and then shrugged as if deciding it didn't really matter whether it was real or not. He grumbled something inaudible and then slowly shuffled over to the other side of the room to consult a wall planner that was stuck on the wall above a desk.

'Late night?' enquired Peter.

Richard ignored him. 'He's in lectures until noon. Renaissance art, room 203, in the Perryman building.' He shuffled back to the doorway. 'What's it about? Is he in trouble?'

Peter shook his head. 'I'm investigating the death of David Packham on behalf of his parents.' Richard nodded as if this wasn't unusual around here.

'Can you tell me what Dom looks like?' added Peter.

Richard let out a deep sigh, as if this was a completely unreasonable request. He turned and took a few steps back towards his bed, plucking a scrappy photograph from where it had been attached to the wall with tape.

He returned and handed it to Peter. It showed a pair of young men and women standing in a bar, drinks in hand. One of the men was Richard. 'Dom's the one on the left,' he muttered, and Peter nodded. He wasn't sure if

Richard was just showing him the photo or giving it to him, but he assumed the latter, slipping the photo into his jacket pocket. 'Thanks. Did you spend much time with David?'

Richard shook his head. 'Nah. Wasn't really my kind of guy. Only really knew him to say hi to. Dom's your man for any gossip.'

'Did you see or hear anything unusual on the night of his suicide?'

'Nah,

 man. I was out all night. Didn't get back until after the whole show was over.'

Peter nodded. The students around here didn't seem to be a particularly sociable lot. 'Okay, thanks. I'll let you get back to bed.'

Richard grunted something under his breath and lazily swung the door shut.

Chapter 21.

Exeter Police Station, England.

Detective Cross had spent the previous day going through all the original police reports for the *King in Yellow* case. According to the records, there had been six actors in their little troupe. The playwright's name was Oliver Wittman, and he was the oldest of the lot, twenty-four at the time. The others had been fresh out of university, eager young students, looking to kick-start their acting careers. Of the five others, the two leads, Dominic Cork and Julianne Sainz, had died in a car crash at the same time, leaving just three others to track down.

The police records listed their addresses and contact details at the time of the investigation; they had all been interviewed concerning the murder of Oliver Wittman, although no one had seriously suspected any of them of being involved.

Cross turned to her computer. She had direct access to plenty of police databases, and had cultivated many contacts over the years who had access to less official sources of information. It looked like she may not need them though. She quickly located details for two of the actors, William Mollock and Chris McIntire. Both had died a couple of years after Oliver's death, seemingly unrelated deaths. William Mollock had been killed in a road traffic accident – as a pedestrian – and Chris McIntire had committed suicide.

That left one remaining lead, Haley Lloyd, and fortunately she proved just as easy to track down. According to the electoral roll, she was still living at the same address as she had been all those years ago – a small flat in Wytham, a short distance outside of Oxford.

Cross looked at her watch. It wasn't even noon yet, plenty of time to get over there. She wondered about calling ahead, checking if she was in, but decided against it. Plenty of people would go out of their way not to meet with the police. It was harder when you were there in person, sticking your foot in the door.

'I'm going to be out for a while,' she said to her partner, Dave Brooks, as she stood up and picked up her coat. 'Cover for me, will you?'

Dave gave a non-committal grunt of acknowledgement from behind a mountain of paperwork on his desk. It didn't look like he was going any-where soon.

✳ ✳ ✳

The sun was just poking out from behind some clouds as Cross stood in front of Haley Lloyd's front door and knocked. She stepped back and waited, but no one answered. *Bugger*, she thought. *All this way and no one's home.*

She tried again, knocking louder this time, but as she stepped back she saw a twitch of lace curtain from one of the windows. *Someone* was home.

'Miss Lloyd?' she called. 'I'd like to speak to you, please.'

There was silence for a moment and then a quiet, meek voice. 'What do you want?'

Cross took a brief sigh, and decided to play it straight. 'I'm with the po-lice,' she said. 'You're not in any trouble, I promise. I just want to talk you about something that happened a long time ago.'

'Have you got a warrant?'

'No. As I said, you're not in any trouble. I'm not here to arrest you. I'd just like a quick word.' She stood there in silence for a good twenty seconds. 'Please, Miss Lloyd. I've come a long way to talk to you.'

Silence for another five seconds, and then finally there was a reply. 'If you're police, hold up your ID.'

Cross fished her warrant card out of her pocket, holding it up to the spyhole in the front door. A few seconds later, she heard the sound of a chain being removed from the door and it opened. A thin woman stood before her, her hair long and unkempt. She wore no makeup, no jewellery, and her clothes looked like they could do with a wash.

'I suppose you'd better come in,' she said with a resigned sigh, turning and shambling down the dim corridor. 'Shut the door behind you. I'll put the kettle on.'

Cross stepped into the flat and over the piles of leaflets and newspapers that lay on the floor. The carpets were threadbare, the wallpaper peeling from the walls. From another room, she could hear the faint sound of a television playing – a daytime chat show from the sounds of it.

She followed Haley into the kitchen, which was in the same state of disrepair as the hallway. The shelves and utilities looked like they'd been here since the 1970s; only the small microwave in the corner looked like a more recent addition. A large pile of dirty dishes and pans sat in the sink waiting for someone to wash them. There was a lingering smell of mould and damp, partially masked by an air freshener, but still perceptible.

'So, what's this about?' asked Haley as she filled up the kettle and switched it on.

'It's about something that happened when you were younger, fresh out of college I believe.'

'The play,' she said, without turning around.

'Yes,' said Cross, surprised that this had been her first reaction, although upon reflection, she supposed that having a colleague murdered would be a memory that most people wouldn't forget. 'I'd like to ask you a few questions about it, if you wouldn't mind?'

'Why the interest, so many years later?'

'Some new information has come to light which may help solve the murder of Oliver Wittman. We're just double-checking old witnesses.'

'I'm sure I told the police at the time everything I know.'

'That's what most people think, but sometimes when you discuss these things with others, memories come back to the surface, things you may have forgotten about for years.'

Haley gave a small shudder as Cross said this, presumably recalling something from all those years ago. Cross hated making others drudge up old memories like this, especially ones that could be so painful to relive, but she had become more accustomed to it over the years.

'Could you tell me about how you met Oliver and the others, and your relationship with them?'

Haley opened one of the cupboards, the door of which was hanging crooked on its hinges, and took out two mugs.

'Most of us were fresh out of university – English and drama graduates, hoping to make our names on the stage. Fresh faced and full of optimism.' She gave a small humourless laugh at the memory. 'Dominic and Julianne were slightly older – I think they'd graduated the previous year, done a bit of part-time acting in the meantime. I think his day job was as a barman. She worked in a sandwich shop.'

'How did you all come to meet?'

'There was an advert in a local paper. Oliver had placed it, looking for some actors to come together and put on some plays he was writing. Form a little troupe of travelling actors who could play the local venues, maybe even travel around a bit. That was the plan, anyway. Didn't quite work out for any of us. Is black okay?'

'Sorry?'

'Your coffee. I don't have any milk.'

'Black will be fine,' said Cross. 'No sugar.'

Haley took a small pot of supermarket own-brand coffee out of the cupboard, putting a teaspoonful into each of the mugs. Cross guessed that her plan to become a famous actor hadn't quite worked out.

'I believe Oliver was working on a new play with you, a modern version of something old. What can you tell me about it?'

The kettle had finished boiling, and Haley poured the hot water into the mugs, taking the time to organize her thoughts. She came over to the small table in the centre of the kitchen, sitting down on one side and placing the other mug opposite, inviting Cross to sit down. She accepted, pulling up a cheap wooden chair.

'That was when it all started to go wrong. Oliver had bought this dog-eared book from a second-hand book store in Oxford. It contained this old play, something he'd never heard of – couldn't even find any trace of it online. It was quite dry and stuffy, full of arcane language, but he thought he could take it, jazz it up and modernize it, turn it into something fresh.'

'Like people performing versions of Shakespeare set in this century, with modern language and so on?'

'Exactly.'

'Do you know what the play was called?'

She thought for a moment. *'The King in Yellow,'* she confirmed.

'Can you tell me what it was about?'

'Why so much interest in the play?'

'New information suggests it may possibly have been related to his murder, at least in some small part.'

'What, the original author wanting revenge for Oliver stealing his work or something? Let me tell you, with the age of that thing, the original author would have been long dead.'

'How do you know?'

'I studied medieval literature as part of my degree. The book wasn't *that* old, but I could tell from the bindings it probably dated back to at least the nineteenth century.'

'Are you sure?'

'Not one hundred per cent. I never read it myself – Oliver guarded it quite jealously – so I never had a chance to look inside to see if any dates were printed on it. It never concerned me at the time. But I'd say it was easily a hundred years old.'

'Wouldn't that have made it quite valuable?'

'Valuable enough to murder for? Unlikely. It wasn't in great condition, and can't have cost much. Oliver was almost as broke as we were.'

'It wasn't found after his murder though.'

'Wasn't it?' Haley shrugged. 'As I understood it, several things were taken from his flat. The burglar probably assumed it was worth something, or just picked it up with a load of other stuff.'

'So... can you remember anything about the play?'

'Not much. Oliver had only really done any serious work with Dominic and Julianne, who were going to be the two leads.' She closed her eyes, taking a sip of the coffee as she thought. Cross joined her; it was weak and bitter, not nice at all. She didn't say anything though.

'The original play was set in medieval times,' she said, 'although Oliver was obviously planning to modernize it. Dominic and Julianne were two members of a royal court, subjects of a masked king.'

'Masked? Like the *Phantom of the Opera*?'

'Yes, I suppose so. I guess he was the King in Yellow, although Oliver never told me as much.'

'And what of the plot?'

'Oliver never revealed much to me. He told me that my character, Cam-ille I think it was, was supposed to have some tragic death. Ironic, really,' she said with a little chuckle, 'given what happened to Dominic and Julianne. There was one scene later on which Oliver described as being like the witches scene in Macbeth.'

'The one set around the caldron?'

'That's the one. *Double, double toil and trouble* and so on. It was some kind of ritual thing, seemed awful to me. Very hard to make that kind of thing sound at all plausible to an audience.'

'Then you read this section?'

'No, Oliver just told me about it once. That's the only thing I remember. That and a couple of names... *Hastur* I think was one, and *Camille*, that was my character.' She seemed to give a small involuntary shrug as she re-membered these.

'Okay, so what of the book itself. Do you know who wrote it?'

'No, sorry. There was no name on the cover, just a symbol on dark vel-lum. And as I said, I never had a chance to read it myself.'

'What did this symbol on the cover look like?'

'It was a big like three question marks in a triangle, spiralling out from the middle. Here... like this,' she said, when she saw the look of confusion on Cross's face. She grabbed an old biro and drew a question mark on the back of a brown envelope. Then she turned the paper through one hundred and twenty degrees and drew another one, both of them sharing the same dot in the centre. She repeated this again, then slid the paper over the table. Cross picked it up and looked at the shape.

'Do you know what it means?' she asked.

'The symbol? Just a squiggle as far as I know. This doesn't quite do it justice though; the one on the book was more ornate. I don't know what it was about it; it just seemed slightly... macabre.'

'Do you know where he bought the book from?'

'No. I mean, he never said, but there were a couple of antique book shops that he tended to frequent.'

'Can you remember their names?'

Haley closed her eyes again for a moment. 'There was *St Julian's*, I think it was called. And *Milford Antiques* – they had a book section. Both in central Oxford.'

'Okay, thanks,' said Cross. It was unlikely they'd still have anything from that long ago, but it was still something.

'You really think he was killed for the book?'

'Probably not,' said Cross. 'But with a murder we need to ensure we've investigated all possible leads.'

Haley took another sip of her coffee and looked out the kitchen window. It opened onto a small terraced garden, overrun with weeds.

'Did you ever go to Oliver's flat after he was... well, afterwards?'

Haley shook her head. 'Why would I want to do that when he was killed there?'

'I was just wondering if you saw what was taken from his flat, or noticed anything unusual.'

She shook her head again. 'The police at the time said that his laptop was taken, his phone. Not his wallet though. They thought he'd disturbed a burglar who'd panicked and attacked him. Took what he'd already packed, but didn't stick around to go through his pockets after he'd killed him. That's just what I'd heard though.'

'Do you know where he kept the book?'

'No. And to be honest, if you're looking for it, I hope you don't find it.'

'Why would you say that?'

'If you ask me, that thing was cursed. Ever since Oliver started working on it, nothing has worked out for any of us. Especially him... and Dominic and Julianne. No one who came into contact with that book came away unaffected. I don't know what ultimately came of William and Chris. None of us could ever find any more acting work after the deaths, and we gradually drifted apart.'

'Actually, I think they're both dead too.' Haley looked at her, slightly concerned. 'It was a long time ago, both unconnected and not in suspicious circumstances,' said Cross. 'You've got nothing to worry about,' she added, not entirely convinced.

'How did they die?'

'William was killed on the way home from the pub. Staggered into the road and was hit by a passing car. There was nothing suspicious about it — the driver stopped, called the police. Post-mortem showed extremely high levels of alcohol in William's bloodstream.'

'Always did like a drink or two to calm his nerves,' muttered Haley. 'What about Chris?'

'He committed suicide about a year ago. Again, nothing suspicious — he'd been receiving counselling for depression for a while.'

Haley looked around the drab and dismal kitchen. 'Who'd have thought I was the lucky one, eh?' she said, with a small shrug.

'What do you do these days?' asked Cross.

'Me? Not a lot. I was working as a secretary, but I'm on long-term sickness now,' she said. 'Depression and anxiety,' she added by way of explanation.

Cross knew it wasn't unusual for the people around a murder victim to have lasting psychological conditions, but in this case she was wondering whether there was something to what Haley was saying. What if the contents of that book had actually affected them all?

Chapter 22.

Dartmoor University Campus, England.

The Perryman building was easy to find: well signposted and just on the edge of the campus. It was a large concrete building, a classic example of 1960s brutalist architecture, and quite the eyesore in Peter's eyes.

Upon stepping inside though, the décor was considerably more modern. It opened into an open-plan area with large sections of white marble flooring, several sets of chairs and low tables scattered around for students to congregate at. Next to the stairs at the back of the room, a large board indicated the location of the various lecture halls within the building, including room 203. Peter followed the signs, arriving at the lecture hall a few minutes later without any difficulty.

There was a set of benches in the wide corridor outside the hall, a good place to wait for the lecture to finish. He glanced at his watch; there were only five minutes until it was due to end. The case was turning into a complete non-event, but if a client was paying, he owed it both to them and his accountant to look into every possibly lead.

While he was here though, he could at least take the opportunity to try and find someone who understood the papers Jack had found. Not far along the corridor, there was a plan of the building and a map of the campus. The geology department was just upstairs, but the science faculty was in another building five minutes away, still relatively easy to find.

With a plan for what to do next, Peter took off his coat and sat down on the bench. He waited patiently, looking at the photograph and trying to memorize Dominic's face.

When the lecture ended and students came flooding out of two sets of double doors, he carefully scanned the faces, comparing them against the photo, until he finally saw a match across the crowd of people.

'Dom!' he called out, wading through the sea of students, fighting against the tide. He called again as he drew nearer, and Dominic turned his head to see Peter waving at him. He stopped and approached.

'Dom?' asked Peter as they finally faced each other.

'Yeah,' said Dominic, unsure as to whom he was talking to.

'Can we talk?'

'What about?'

'I'm a private detective. David Packham's parents hired me to look into his death,' said Peter, showing him his ID. 'I understand you were a good friend of his?'

Dominic looked at his watch, shrugged and then nodded. 'Sure. I've got a little while until my next lecture.'

Peter gestured to the bench, and they both sat down, waiting for the crowd of students to dissipate so that the noise levels returned to normal.

'So,' began Peter. 'Tell me about David in the days leading up to his death. Was he particularly upset or depressed about anything?'

Dominic shook his head. 'He wasn't the happiest guy on campus, but no, he wasn't at all depressed. I definitely wouldn't have called him suicidal – his death came completely out of the blue.'

'So you don't have a theory as to why he did it?'

Dominic shook his head. 'No idea. Sorry, mate.'

'He didn't have any messy breakups?' Another shake of the head. 'Was he taking drugs? You won't get any trouble from me if he was.'

Yet another shake of the head. 'He wasn't the type,' said Dominic.

'So do you have *any* ideas why he did it?'

'Sorry, mate, I'm afraid not. I wish I could help you. It was a terrible tragedy and all, but I'm not sure what help I can give. He was just a normal guy, a good mate. I never saw it coming.'

'Do you agree that it *was* suicide?'

Dominic considered this for a moment. 'He didn't have any enemies. I can't think of anyone who would have wanted to hurt him, let alone kill him. I wouldn't have guessed he would commit suicide, but I guess it seems more likely than the alternative. As I understand it, it's unlikely to have been an accident.'

Peter nodded. 'People don't tend to climb out of a window in the middle of the night without good reason.'

'But there was no note, right?'

'No. Contrary to popular opinion, not every suicide leaves one behind, and I can't see any reason for him to have climbed out of that window. There were no signs of forced entry into his room – or even that there had been anyone in there with him that night. The only thing that would make sense to me is if he was on some kind of bad trip – you know, imagined there was something to get away from in his room, or thought he could fly or something. But everyone I've spoken to have unanimously said that he didn't do drugs.' He sighed. This was turning into a total bust. He pulled a business card out of his pocket and handed it to Dom. 'If you think of anything, no matter how small, give me a ring or send me an email, okay?'

Dom took the card, giving it a quick glance before slipping it into his pocket. *Ten pounds says he never looks at that again*, thought Peter to himself as he stood up, preparing to leave.

Peter was putting his coat on again, when the memory of something that Cathy Hobbes had mentioned flashed into his mind. 'David hadn't been taking part in any research trials to make a bit of cash, had he?'

Dom thought for a moment. 'There was something he did a few weeks before the incident. Something for the psych department.'

Peter was suddenly attentive again. 'Do you know what it was about? Who ran it?'

'Not really. It was run by some professor in the psychology department – some kind of sleep research. David basically just got paid to sleep while they took measurements. Sounded like easy money to me.'

'Did it have any effect on him?'

'Not that I saw. Maybe a bit more tired the morning after, but he was never a morning person.'

'And you don't know who was running it?'

'Sorry, no.'

'Never mind. You've been very helpful.'

Peter now had something linking the two incidents. It could be nothing... but it could also be everything. First, however, he had to pay a trip to the geology and physics departments, to see if he could find someone who could explain the papers Jack had found.

He headed up the stairs to the geology department and walked the corridors until he found a door that identified its occupant as a geology professor and knocked on it.

'Come in,' came a deep gruff voice after a few moments' silence.

Peter opened the door to see a middle-aged man with short brown hair and round spectacles sitting behind a desk. The walls of the room were filled with bookshelves, their shelves overflowing with books and papers.

'You're not one of my students,' exclaimed the professor, slightly surprised. 'How can I help you?'

'I'm a private detective investigating a case here,' said Peter, showing him his ID. 'I was wondering if you could spare me five minutes.'

'A private detective, eh? It's not every day I get a visit from one of those. I suppose I could spare five minutes,' replied the professor with a smile.

Peter reached into his bag and pulled out a folder. He took out several of the papers that Jack had given him and showed them to him. 'Do these mean anything to you?'

'Hmmm,' muttered the professor, pouring over the sheets.

'That one there,' said Peter, gesturing to the sheet in his left hand. 'Is that a relief map of a hill or mountain?'

The professor turned the sheet around, examining the diagram carefully. 'Close,' he said. 'It's actually an underwater sonar map. This hill – or whatever it is – is underwater.'

'And those lines on the top?'

'They look like indications of buildings, remnants of a civilization.'

'Can you tell me where this is?'

'There are no coordinates on it, so not really. The most likely place would be somewhere where there used to be a settlement that's now flooded. In an artificial lake next to a hydroelectric dam, for example.'

'But wouldn't that be on lowlands though, rather than on a hill?'

The professor thought for a second and then shrugged. 'Could be a small hill with a larger valley. Unless you've discovered Atlantis, of course,' he added with a little chuckle to himself.

'What?'

'You know... a lost civilization under the sea somewhere.'

'You think...'

'No,' he said scornfully. 'Load of old tosh. This will be where they've flooded a valley somewhere, and these are the walls and remnants of an old town. There are a few examples all over... Wait. That's not right...'

'What is it?'

'These figures here.' He stabbed a finger on the side of the page. 'This says that these images are from over seven thousand metres under the surface. That's almost the limit for how far sonar mapping can go.'

'So...?'

'Well... there's no place on earth that deep which has been artificially flooded. Not even close. Everest is only nine thousand metres high for God's sake.'

'So what are you trying to tell me?'

'There are a few possibilities. Firstly, whatever you have here is faked or just plain wrong. Do you know where it came from?'

'Not really,' admitted Peter.

'Okay, so that's a definite possibility. It could just be computer generated, or the wrong figures against the data.'

'Okay. And the other possibilities?'

'This represents an area in the depths of an ocean – which are the only areas where you get water this deep. If that's the case, then either these lines and markings are naturally occurring, just giving the *appearance* of man-made structures...'

'Is that likely?'

'It's not unheard of.'

'Or else?'

'Or else this map represents some ancient civilization hidden at the bottom of the ocean.'

'So we *have* found Atlantis?'

'I think that's a little premature. Besides which, Atlantis is almost certainly fictional. But the other possibilities are much more likely.'

'What about the maps?' asked Peter, trying to bring the conversation back to normality.

The professor turned to the hand-drawn maps. 'No coordinates, no labels,' he said. 'They could be just about anywhere. There's a river, some hills judging by the relief lines, but without some more information, I can't help you.'

'What about this one,' said Peter, indicating the page with the graphs covered in wavy lines.

'Ah...,' said the professor. 'This looks to me like a ground-penetrating radar map.'

'Ground-penetrating radar?'

'It's where you use radar to map under the earth. You can use it to find things that have been buried, or natural formations under the earth.'

'So where would that normally be used?'

'In the earth sciences, you'd use it to study underwater rocks and soils. It can also be used during engineering and construction to check for pipes underwater. Archaeologists can use it to locate artefacts, and the military sometimes use it to locate mines. In rare cases, the police have used it to look for buried bodies. There's a whole range of applications.'

'I see. Is it possible to tell what it's been used for in this case?'

'I don't think so, just that it has identified something under the ground – an inconsistency in the soil density... but this isn't really my area of expertise.'

What the hell do the Brotherhood want with all of this, Peter thought to himself. 'What do you specialize in, then?' he eventually asked.

'My speciality is more to do with high-resolution stratigraphy.'

He didn't explain what this meant, and Peter didn't bother to ask. He couldn't see how it would be relevant to the case. 'Thank you for your time,' he said, standing up. 'I'm sure you're very busy.'

'Not a problem,' said the professor, handing back the papers. 'What is this case you're looking into about? I'm sure it's not every day that geology features in one of your investigations!'

'I'm afraid I can't say,' said Peter. 'But you've been very helpful.'

After leaving the geology department, Peter made his way over to the science faculty. He followed the signs to the physics department, where he set about the task of finding someone who might be able to help him. As he was looking at a board detailing all the staff members and their room numbers, he spotted someone unlocking and entering their office; the title on the door read *Head of Theoretical Physics*. *Perfect*, he thought.

The door was still open when he knocked on it and introduced himself. The professor invited him in, introducing himself as Professor Jeffrey Noakes and sitting down behind his desk. He seemed as genuinely curious about a private investigator's interest in theoretical physics as the geology professor had been.

His office was decidedly tidier than that of the geology professor. There were three chairs on either side of the room, presumably for students when they visited, and two immaculate bookcases behind his desk, each with perfectly neat rows of books on them. Scanning over them quickly, Peter noticed half a dozen with the professor's name on the spine.

'I was wondering whether any of these equations mean anything to you?' asked Peter.

The professor reached for the sheets of paper, and then took a pair of glasses from his jacket pocket, putting them on before he looked at the writing.

'Hmm,' he muttered.

'Do you recognize them?'

'Maybe,' he muttered under his breath. He stood up and picked out a book from one of the shelves behind him; *The Large Scale Structure of Space-Time* by Hawking and Ellis. He flicked through the pages until he found what he was looking for. 'Yes,' he said, 'I thought I recognized some of these formulae.'

'So what are they about?'

'These equations here,' he said, pointing to the first page of writing, 'are dealing with the curvature of space-time, and distortions created by areas of high gravity.'

'High gravity?'

'Large suns, black holes and the like.'

'Oh...'

'As this work progresses,' he continued, tapping some equations half way down the page, 'it seems to be examining how multiple distortions of space-time could overlap, and the effect that would have on both the curvature of the nearby space and the dilation of time in the immediate vicinity.'

'The dilation of time?' echoed Peter, uncertainly.

'Time dilation is where time elapses more slowly; in this case, *gravitational* time dilation, where time passes more slowly near massive bodies with a high gravitational field.'

'That sounds vaguely familiar. I think I saw a film about it.'

The professor gave an unimpressed grunt. 'There seem to be some calculations – unfinished ones as far as I can see – trying to work out what the specific effects would be for several different scenarios. I must say, this is all extremely advanced work. May I ask where you got it?'

Peter grimaced. 'I'm afraid I can't say at the moment.'

'Well, anyone who is capable of this kind of work would be extremely highly educated.'

'Degree level?'

'Probably post-doctoral.'

'Can you think of any practical use for this work?'

'Practical?'

'Something, well... something with real-world implications.'

'Hopefully not this particular world. This type of work only really has practical applications in astrophysics – modelling the behaviour of stars, particularly how multiple celestial bodies in a solar system would interact. That would be its most practical use, I suppose, modelling binary star systems, that kind of thing.'

'Binary stars?'

'Solar systems that have not one but two suns at their centre.'

'Oh. Okay...' sighed Peter, scratching his head. 'So, no earthly applications.'

'Not that I can think of.'

Peter thought for a moment. 'What about that large collider thing in Switzerland?'

'The Large Hadron Collider?'

'That's the one. Didn't people say it could possibly create a black hole?'

The professor chuckled, giving his head a little shake. 'Just the headlines of hysterical tabloids, I'm afraid. And if it did create a black hole, it would be a minute and momentary one. Nothing like what this is describing,' he said, giving the paper another tap. He looked at the pages again, a look of confusion coming over his face.

'Is there a problem?' asked Peter.

'Not a problem. I'm just struggling to understand some of these equations.'

'You don't understand the maths?'

'No, not that. I'm just not sure what quite what they're trying to model. I suppose...'

'What?'

'I said before that this might be for modelling binary star systems.'

'Yes?'

'Well, it starts off like that, but further on... I think it's trying to estimate the effects of *multiple* stars on each other.'

'Multiple, as in...?'

'Well, definitely more than two.'

'And how rare is that?'

'Not unheard of. But pretty rare.'

Peter sighed.

'Not what you wanted to hear, I assume,' said the professor with a wry grin.

'No. It's hard to see exactly how this could have a bearing on the case. But thank you anyway – you've been most helpful.'

❋ ❋ ❋

Finally, Peter turned to the psychology department. He was a little less sure about whom to ask for here, but at least it actually pertained to the case he was meant to be investigating at the university.

Upon entering the building in which most of the psychology department was housed, he consulted a chart on the wall detailing the department's staff members. The head of the department was Professor Gregory Patrick, Professor of Cognitive Neuroscience and Experimental Psychology. *If anyone knows who's conducting research trials, he ought to,* thought Peter.

'I believe a member of your staff has been running some research trials on students,' said Peter after he had introduced himself. 'I understand he had some interaction with the student in question. I'd just like to ask him a few questions.'

'Nothing untoward, I assume?' asked the professor.

'Oh no, definitely not,' replied Peter, not entirely sure about his reply. 'I've just been speaking to people who interacted with him in the days leading up to his death, checking if they'd seen any odd behaviour in him.'

'I see. Do you know which member of staff this was?'

'No, I just know that it was some kind of sleep research.'

The professor thought for a moment. 'That's most likely to be Professor Daniel Ashbrook. He's a visiting professor specializing in the psychology of sleep and dreams. I'll see if he's in.' He picked up his phone, dialled a few numbers and then waited as the phone rang. When no one answered, he hung up and tried a different number instead. 'Hi, Jeanie,' he said a few moments later. 'I'm trying to get hold of Daniel – do you know where he is?' He listened for a moment, nodding. 'Okay, thanks.'

He turned back to Peter. 'Apparently, he called in sick yesterday. He's not in today either.'

'I don't suppose you could give me his home address, so I can pop over and have a chat?'

'No,' replied the professor after a moment's thought. 'But I could get him to call you as soon we hear from him again. Do you have a card?'

'I suppose that will do,' said Peter, forcing a smile. He retrieved his wallet from his trouser pocket, extracting a slightly tatty business card. He handed it to the professor, who took it gracefully and laid it neatly on his desk.

'Now, if that's all, I've got quite a lot to be getting on with,' he said, standing up.

Peter knew when he was being dismissed. He stood up and shook the professor's hand. 'One last question – you said he was a visiting professor – where has he come from?'

'Miskatonic University in New England,' replied the professor.

'I see, thank you.'

Once he had left Professor Patrick, Peter returned to the list of staff members in the entrance. There was indeed a Professor Ashbrook listed – room 121. He headed up the stairs to the first floor, and then to room 121. When he arrived, he knocked on the door and then tried the door handle. Peter wasn't surprised when it didn't turn – the professor had obviously locked it before he left. *So much for that avenue of inquiry,* he thought. He would need to find another way to discover the man's secrets.

He turned and left, making a careful note of his surroundings as he went.

Chapter 23.

Oxford City Centre, England.

The sun was low in the sky when Detective Cross stepped out of the rain and into *Milford Antiques*. The previous antique shop, *St Julian's*, had been a bust. Unsurprisingly, the only member of staff who had been around back then couldn't remember anything from that long ago, and their paperwork only went back five years.

This shop was slightly larger, but no less claustrophobic. All the walls of the shop were covered with antique furniture and display cabinets. Several makeshift aisles had been created where additional items of furniture had been placed in rows along the shop floor. She could see several CCTV cameras over the front door, the counter and a couple of other spots – possibly useful if this had all happened yesterday, but it would be miraculous if they had recordings from all those years ago.

She made her way to the counter, past a large man in a raincoat who was examining a Victorian sideboard with obvious glee. A young man sat behind the counter, reading a well-thumbed copy of *Lord of the Rings*.

He looked up as she approached. 'Can I help you?' he asked, folding over the corner of the page he was reading and putting the book to one side.

'Probably not,' she said with a wry smile. She pulled out her warrant card, holding it out for him to see. 'I'm trying to track down an item that was sold in an antique shop several years ago. I was told it *might* have been here.'

'How long ago, exactly?'

'About ten or eleven years ago.'

The young man gave a grimace. 'I'm afraid I've only been working here for just over a year.'

'Do you keep any records?'

'Of purchases, yes. Sales... not so much. I'm not sure about that far back though.' He lifted up the counter top, beckoning Cross to come behind the counter. 'Mr Milford might be able to help you.'

'Is he the owner?'

The young man nodded. 'For at least... oh, thirty years. And his father before him. If anyone could remember what happened back then, it would be him.'

Cross stepped through and the man closed the hatch behind them, leading her into a small and cramped back room. The rear wall was covered with filing cabinets, which gave Cross some hope that they kept decent records. Most of the floor was covered in cardboard boxes, some still sealed, some partially unpacked. To her left was a window with obscure glass, through which she could just make out some bars on the outside, the setting sun barely visible behind them. To her right was a leather-topped writing desk, papers and books piled on one side.

An old man, probably in his sixties, was sitting at a sturdy wooden table in the centre of the room. He looked up as they walked in, peering up over his wire-framed glasses.

'Steven,' he said admonishingly. 'I've told you before about letting customers come back here.'

'She's not a customer,' he replied sheepishly. 'She's from the police.'

Cross fished out her warrant card again, proffering it towards the owner. He peered at it curiously and then set down the pen he was holding, closing the book that he had been writing in.

'So, Detective –' He peered again at the warrant card, '–Cross. How can I help you?'

'I'm investigating an old case from a few years ago, Mr Milford. Some new evidence has turned up, and I'm looking into a few leads. There's a particular item I'm trying to trace, which I think may have been bought from this shop. Back in December 2006, I'm afraid.'

'Call me John, but I'm afraid our records going back that far are a bit spotty. What exactly was this item?'

'A book. An old book.'

'Do you know its name?'

'*The King in Yellow*. I don't think it was written on the cover though.'

'Doesn't ring any bells, I'm afraid.'

'It was covered in dark vellum with a symbol on it.' She reached into her pocket and brought out her pen and notebook. She ripped out a page and drew the shape on it: the three interconnecting question marks. Then she slid it over the table towards him. 'Do you recognize it?'

John sat in silence for several seconds, looking at the small sheet of paper. 'You know, I do,' he said quietly. 'The book, not so much, but this...' He tapped his finger on the paper. 'Come, sit down,' he said with a quiet sigh, gesturing to the chair opposite him. Cross pulled out the chair, a solid wooden chair with an intricately carved back. *One of the perks of running an antique shop*, she guessed.

'The book was part of a lot that I think we bought at auction. I don't remember anything special about it, just some old story or something. Quite old, but not particularly valuable. It wasn't in very good condition. What I remember, though, was a man who came in after it. This was, I don't know, a week after we'd bought it. He said that it had gone to auction by mistake, and it belonged to him. Whether that was true or not I had no idea, and frankly didn't care. He didn't hold any grudge against us; he just wanted it back and was willing to pay a fair price for it. I remembered it at the time, and we looked through the shop for it, but it was nowhere to be found. I guessed one of my associates must have sold it. If it was sold for cash, we don't tend to keep a record of the sale. I never could tell him who had bought it.'

'And is that why you remember this symbol?'

John shook his head. 'After we had given up the search, he gave me a business card. Told me to call him if it turned up, or we remembered who had bought it. I thought it was odd at the time, as the card just had a phone number on one side, and that triskelion on the other.'

'The *what*? Is that what this shape's called?'

'Not that shape specifically. It means any shape like that with three symmetrical lines or curves coming out from the centre.'

'I see. When he gave you the card, did he give you a name as well?'

'If he did, I'm afraid I don't remember it.'

'What about the man himself? What do you remember about him?'

John closed his eyes, as he tried to summon up the images from the depths of his memory. 'Not much. He was white, middle-aged, average build, average height. Black hair, thinning and going grey. Spoke with an upper-class accent. The thing I remember most about him were his eyes. They were piercing, bright blue. When he looked at you, it was like he was looking into your psyche.' He gave a little shudder as he visualized it in his mind.

'Do you think you'd recognize him if you saw him again?'

'Maybe. But if you put him up against half a dozen other middle-aged men with blue eyes, I'm sure I'd have trouble picking him out.'

'What about the number? Did you ever use it?'

'Never had call to. I never saw the book again. Strange thing is, none of the staff remembered selling it either.'

Maybe Oliver had helped himself to a five-fingered discount, thought Cross. 'Did you have cameras back then?' she asked.

John gave a brief shake of his head. 'Put them in about two years ago.' He stopped suddenly, an odd look on his face.

'Are you okay?' asked Cross.

'I just...' he started, and then stood up. He walked over to the desk, pulling open one of the drawers, rifling through its contents. 'I tend never to throw anything away,' he said. 'Bit of a hoarder. I suppose it comes in useful in this business. Here we are.' He turned to face Cross, holding a small piece of cardboard in his hand. He passed it to her, and she took it, unbelievingly.

'Is this it?'

'Must be. As I said, I don't like to throw anything away.'

It was a plain white business card, crumpled and dog-eared. On it, she could see the symbol, printed in a faded butterscotch colour. She turned it over, and on the other side was a handwritten telephone number, the first digit indicating it was for a mobile. 'Can I take this?' she asked. This was starting to look more positive.

'Be my guest. No use to me anymore.'

She thought for a second. 'You said the book was part of a lot, bought at auction.'

'I think so. My memory isn't quite what it used to be but, yes, I think so. In fact, if it was, we may still have some record of it.' He shuffled over towards one of the filing cabinets at the back of the room. 'December 2006, you said?'

'Yes, or thereabouts.'

He pulled out a drawer and started fingering his way through the folders within, and then shut it, opening the drawer beneath it. He slowly made his way through the folders one by one, until he found what he was looking for and removed it. 'Yes,' he muttered under his breath. He drew out a sheet of paper, returning to the table and laying it down for Cross to see.

It was a receipt from an action house, detailing the items that had been purchased as part of a lot. It was printed on headed paper, the *Headington Auctions* logo and their contact details clearly visible at the top. Under that was the lot number and details of what it had contained, with the purchase price at the bottom of the page. She looked through the list of items, until she saw what she was after. Book: *King in Yellow; nineteenth century; bound in vellum.*

'That's it all right,' she said. She took her phone out of her pocket. 'Do you mind if I take a photo of the details?'

'Be my guest.'

She took several photos and then put her phone away again. 'This auction house. Does it still exist?'

'Certainly does, I still purchase antiques there regularly.' He looked at his watch. 'Won't be open at this time, though. I think they run from nine 'til three.'

Cross shook his hand. 'Thank you, Mr Milford. You've been extremely helpful.' She let herself out, also thanking the younger assistant on the way. When she was back in her car, she got her mobile out and called her partner.

'Dave,' she said. 'I'm not back yet, as you may have guessed.'

'I had noticed. Superintendent Reynolds was in here looking for you.'

'What did you say?'

'I said you'd popped out, that I didn't know where you were.'

'Well, if he comes looking for me again, tell him I wasn't feeling well and headed home. I'm going to be ill again tomorrow too.'

'Understood, boss,' he replied.

'One other thing. I've got a phone number. Can you run it through the system, find out anything you can about it? This was from about ten years ago.'

'I'll see what I can find.'

Cross gave him the number and hung up the phone. She would have to find a hotel for the night, ready for an early start with *Headington Auctions* in the morning.

Chapter 24.

Dartmoor University, England.

Peter White sat in his car, deep in the dark shadows under an old oak tree. He was parked close to the psychology department, and from where he was seated he could see the rows of offices where Professor Daniel Ashbrook's room was located. All the lights were out and it looked deserted. There was some activity in other parts of the building, but he guessed that wouldn't be unusual for a university campus, particularly in a faculty performing sleep research.

He pulled out a small packet from his jacket pocket, checking its contents: a set of small but very effective lock picks, as well as a micro-LED torch and head light. His phone would make do for any photographs he needed.

He'd dressed for the part: anonymous jeans and trainers and a black hoodie emblazoned with the university name and crest. To any casual observer, he'd look like any other student; the hood should hide his grey hair and other signs of his true age.

He double-checked that he'd parked legally – a parking ticket placing him at the scene would be annoying – and then strode casually towards the faculty building, a trendy backpack hung over one shoulder.

As he approached, he could see that the building foyer had its lights on, illuminating the concourse outside. Next to the main door there was a small keypad, its buttons glowing dimly in the evening light. He could see another student approaching the door from the opposite direction, a young man also in jeans and hoodie. *I'll have to time this perfectly*, he thought to himself as he slowed, taking a more leisurely approach towards the door. The student stopped, keyed a number into the keypad and then pushed the door open, stepping inside.

Peter took a quick double-step forwards, placing the toe of his shoes just over the door frame. As the door swung shut, his shoe stopped the door millimetres away from the frame, stopping it from locking shut again. The student who had just passed through turned to look over his shoulder casually but Peter ignored him, instead leaning back and typing four random digits into the keypad before pushing the door open himself. To any casual observer, it should look completely natural; indeed, the other student had carried on with his business, not paying him a second thought.

He had made note of where any security cameras were located when he had been here earlier in the day, but there were precious few; they obviously didn't expect too many major thefts. He kept his hood up and his back turned against the camera in the reception area, casually circling around and ascending the steps before heading around the corner towards room 121.

As he neared the door, he checked over his shoulder for any signs of activity but could see none. The corridor was unlit, the darkness making it easier to see that there were no lights on behind any of the doors. They obviously weren't night owls in this department – or if they were, they were busy elsewhere.

Peter drew a pair of latex gloves out of his pocket, slipping them over his hands before retrieving his lock picks. This was the dangerous part. If he was caught picking the lock, it would be pretty hard to explain. He slipped the head light over his head, the bulb sitting on his forehead and providing low-level illumination, enough so that he could just about see what he was doing without lighting up the whole area.

He crouched by the door, keeping the lock at head height so he could see more clearly, then began his work with the picks, inserting the tension wrench to apply pressure while he used the pick to lift each pin in turn. It was a long sixty seconds while he worked, but he was soon rewarded with a quiet click as the lock opened.

Now was the moment of truth; he hadn't seen any alarms in the other offices he had been in today, but this one could always be different. He pushed the door open and grimaced. There were no sirens, no beeps prompting him to enter an alarm code, no alarms unless they were silent ones, and he thought that unlikely.

He pushed the door shut quietly, and then stepped over to the window to draw the venetian blinds and mask the sight of any lights. With his privacy ensured, Peter set to searching the room. Fortunately for him, it appeared neat and tidy, with no mountains of paperwork to search through.

He started with the desk. The few papers on top seemed innocuous enough: departmental memos and lecture timetables. He turned to the desk drawers. These were either empty or filled with the usual things: packets of aspirin, tangled headphones, half-eaten packets of mints. There were some envelopes sporting the university insignia, which he leafed through. They were addressed to the professor, but not to this office. The address looked like university accommodation, presumably a temporary residence where he was staying while visiting. The letters were all of an administrative nature, confirming details of accommodation, contract terms, university contact details and so on. He hesitated for a moment, and then removed one of the letters, returning it to the drawer while pocketing the envelope that sported the professor's home address.

Peter had turned around to face the two sets of filing cabinets by the windows when an idea occurred to him. He turned back to face the desk and got on his knees, feeling the underside of the desk. Nothing. Then he pulled the drawers out, checking their undersides. The top-right drawer had what he was after and he pulled it off: a spare house key, taped to the bottom of the drawer. He slipped it into his jacket pocket.

The two filing cabinets were locked, but didn't take him long with his lock picks; they were much simpler than the door lock. Once in, he found what he was after in the second cabinet – a folder labelled *Dream Research candidates*. He leafed through the contents and confirmed what he had thought – both Melissa and David Packham had been students on the same research programme. He scanned through the others, not recognizing any names. Most of the names seemed reasonably common, probably hard to track down to a specific individual, but one name leapt out at him – Léon Descoteaux. Surely there couldn't be too many people with that name on campus. Then another entry drew his attention – this one was different from the others, named only as *Patient* X, without any date of birth. Their height and weight were given as 104 cm and 15 kg. Was this a child? Why would a university department be performing student research on a child? It could just be a person of short stature, but why then would there be no name or date of birth?

He scanned quickly through the rest of the records, but could find no actual details of the research that had been performed; presumably that was all stored elsewhere. He took out his phone, taking photographs of the list of candidates before returning them to the drawer and locking it again. When he was sure everything was as he had found it, he left, locking the door behind him.

Chapter 25.

Once he had returned to his car, Peter White started scouring social media sites for anyone called Léon Descoteaux. It didn't take him long to find someone who declared himself to be a student at the university, currently studying civil engineering. There were several photographs of him – a skinny man, with short golden hair – mostly out and about with friends. Peter was still amazed how much information people were willing to disclose about themselves these days; it certainly made his life as a private detective much easier.

He started to write him a message and then paused, wondering what approach to take. He decided on honesty, telling Léon he was a private detective investigating the death of David Packham and he would like to have a quick chat over a drink.

He had barely put his phone down and was just about to start the car when his phone gave a single silent buzz; Léon had already replied. He was happy to talk right now, if Peter was buying. He typed in a quick reply, asking where to meet and received another immediate response, naming a pub just a short drive away.

*　*　*

Peter found a parking place just a short distance from the pub. It was in the seedier side of town, the street filled with cheap shops and even cheaper flats. Most of the walls had been tagged with amateur graffiti, and there was a nasty smell of something rotten in the air.

The pub was a small establishment set on the corner of the road, and even from down the street, Peter could hear the thumping bass from its jukebox. He pushed open the doors and stepped inside. It was heaving with students, the air hot and sweaty. The jukebox was turned way up, blaring out something with a heavy drum and bass beat, the rhythm pounding into his skull. He slowly scanned everyone's faces, looking for anyone who matched the picture of Léon until he saw him standing by the bar with a group of friends. He pushed his way through the crowd and tapped him on the shoulder.

'Léon?'

Léon turned and looked him up and down. 'Are you Peter?'

Peter nodded, and handed him a business card. Léon glanced at it, and then nodded with approval, handing it back again.

'Do you want another?' asked Peter, gesturing to the empty pint glass in his hand.

'I'll have another of these,' he replied, tapping a bar pump with his glass. He had a heavy French accent, unsurprising given his name, but several pints of beer had also given his pronunciation a strong slur. Peter caught the barman's eye and ordered a pint for Léon and a lemonade for himself.

'Can we talk somewhere a bit quieter?' asked Peter as the jukebox kicked off another song, the bass even louder and more pounding this time. 'It won't take long.'

Léon nodded and leaned over to one of his friends, muttering something in his ear. Then he indicated for Peter to follow him and made his way towards the rear of the bar. Peter followed him through the crowds until they stepped through a rear door into a beer garden. Having come from the heat of the pub, the cool night air now seemed considerably colder than when he had first arrived, but Peter was just glad of the peace. There was a handful of other customers out in the garden, all of whom were smoking. Léon sat down on a bench and joined them, pulling out a rollup and small pouch of tobacco.

'So, how can I help?' asked Léon as he put the tobacco into the paper and started to roll it up. 'I never really knew David that well – I only met him a couple of times.'

'Where was that?'

'At this sleep clinic we both attended. They were doing some research into dreams and sleep.'

'What did that involve?'

Léon took out a box of matches and struck one, holding it up to the roll-up as he took a drag. 'Not much. They attached some electrodes to our heads, and then monitored us as we slept. Easiest money I've ever made.' He gave the match a quick wave to put it out, and then dropped it into an ashtray.

'Do you know what they were measuring?'

'They said they were studying the brainwaves while we slept, especially during dreaming. They did say why, but I can't really remember. It was a bit technical, went over my head.'

'And did David seem okay when you saw him?'

'He seemed fine, but we never really had any big conversations. Just idle chat, small talk, that kind of thing.'

'You didn't see anything unusual? He didn't have any fights or arguments?'

Léon just shook his head. 'I thought he killed himself – that's what I'd heard. Do you think someone killed him?'

Peter shook his head in return. 'Just dotting the Is and crossing the Ts. I'm sure it's nothing.'

Léon nodded. 'It's a shame. From what I saw of him, he seemed a nice guy. Didn't seem the type to kill himself.'

'Did you also meet a girl called Melissa Brooks when you were at the sleep clinic?'

Léon nodded again. 'Yeah, nice girl. Why?'

'She went crazy, attacked her room-mate.'

'Merde...' He sat silent for a moment, taking a long drag on his cigarette. 'Do you think there's a connection?'

Peter shrugged. 'I'm not sure. Can you tell me anything about the professor who was running the research?'

'Professor Ashbrook. Old guy. American. Struck me as kind of creepy.'

'Creepy? How?'

'Hard to say, he just seemed a little odd... He had a way of looking at you – as if he was trying to gaze into your soul.' He took another drag on his cigarette and then dropped it on the floor, stubbing it out with his shoe. Peter hated it when people did that, but tried his best to ignore it. 'He was supposed to be a big-shot professor from some East Coast college in America.'

'What about the other students? Did you ever see any children being studied?'

'Kids? No. Just other students from the university.'

They sat in silence for a moment. Peter watched Léon closely. Maybe it was just the cold – or the beer – but he seemed anxious.

'Léon?'

'Huh?'

'Was there anything odd about the sleep research you did? Anything that seems out of place now that you look back at it?'

'Well...'

Peter said nothing, waiting for Léon to break the silence.

'There was nothing odd about the research itself, as far as I'm aware. They just wired us up, let us sleep, asked us some routine questions in the morning: how did we sleep, what did we remember dreaming about...'

'But?'

Léon had started fiddling with the packet of tobacco in his hands. 'I've been having more trouble sleeping recently. I put it down to the stress of the exams I've got coming up, but... I'm not sure. I feel like I have these recurring nightmares, but I can never remember what they were about when I wake up. Several times I've woken up my girlfriend by tossing and turning in my sleep. One time, she said that I seemed to be muttering something in my sleep – something in a language she didn't understand.'

'Not French?'

Léon smiled and shook his head. 'My girlfriend is also from France.'

Peter sat back and exhaled. He would love to know what it was that Léon kept dreaming about, but given what had happened to David and Melissa, he didn't think it would be wise to try and bring those memories to the surface.

'The only thing I can remember,' he said, as if he could sense Peter's unasked question, 'is a single image: a pair of glowing red eyes, staring at me from out of the darkness.'

Peter almost dropped his glass as he recalled the sketches in David's notebook, but covered himself well. 'Eyes, you say?'

'I feel silly telling you all this,' said Léon, smiling and shaking his head. 'A grown man, afraid of his dreams. But do you think it's related to David and Melissa? Should I be worried?'

'Oh no,' lied Peter. 'I'm sure it's nothing. Just nerves, like you say.'

Once he was back in his car, Peter retrieved his phone and opened his email app. He needed to see Melissa. Something she had been through in that sleep research had changed her, and he needed to know what it was.

It was more than just David Packham now. He could feel that this was all part of something larger; he just couldn't put his finger on exactly what it was yet. Normally, he'd have no chance of gaining access to her, but this was also Cross's case, and maybe she could pull some strings on his behalf. He fired off a quick email to her police email account, asking her if she could arrange an interview for him.

When that was done, he put his phone away, only to yank it straight back out again. He'd been struck with another idea. He opened up the browser and searched for Miskatonic University, looking through their web site until he found what he was after, contact details for their psychology department. If the university here couldn't give him any contact details, he'd see whether they could be any more accommodating. He wrote them a quick email, explaining that he was trying to contact Professor Ashbrook, that he understood he was currently visiting England, and asking whether they had any contact details for him while he was here.

He checked his watch. It was late in the night, and probably past the end of the working day over there too. It might be a little while until they got back to him.

Chapter 26.

Dartmoor University Campus, England.

Peter White had been sitting in his car for over half an hour. He was parked outside Professor Ashbrook's university accommodation, observing from across the street. There had been no signs of activity, no one entering or leaving. He checked his watch again. It was almost midnight.

The building was a bungalow with a small driveway and neat garden, situated just outside the main university campus, and Peter was unsure as to whether anyone was inside. There was no car on the driveway, but that didn't necessarily mean anything. Given the proximity of the campus to his accommodation and the fact that he was visiting from America, it was quite likely he didn't have one. Peter needed answers though, and he'd waited long enough.

He remained in his car until he was sure no one was around, and then he opened the door, stepping out into the cold air. He slipped on another thin pair of latex gloves and pulled a door key from his pocket, the one he had taken from the professor's office. Casting a quick glance left and right to make sure he was alone, he strode purposefully across the road, only stopping when he reached the front door.

He checked over his shoulder again to double check no one was observing him, and then inserted the key into the lock, twisting it and pushing the door gently. It swung open to reveal a dark hallway. Peter paused momentarily, but when he heard no sound of an alarm system, he stepped inside, quietly pushing the door shut behind him.

The house was small and all at ground level. From where he stood in the hallway, Peter reckoned he could probably see every room. To his left, an open doorway led into a living room, whereas the doorway to his right opened into a compact kitchen. Another door stood closed further down the hallway, and at the end of the hallway stood a final door; from the type of lock, it looked like the bathroom. Peter quickly poked his head into the living room and kitchen to establish that no one was in them, and then quietly crept up to the closed door.

He stood motionless, listening intently for any sound from within. When he was certain there was nothing to hear, he gripped the handle and turned it, as slowly and quietly as he could. It opened into a bedroom. The curtains were drawn and it was dark, but it didn't look as if anyone was in here. There was certainly no one in the bed, which had the covers thrown back, unmade since it was last used.

The place had the feel of a hotel room, clean and well decorated but sterile and unemotional. There was a print of some modern art on one wall, but no other pretence at making it anything other than a temporary domicile.

The doors to the wardrobe were standing open, and the drawers in the chest of drawers next to it were sticking out, clothes hanging from them. Either someone had already been here and searched the place, or else Professor Ashbrook had packed and left in a hurry. Peter pulled out his torch, quickly scanning the room before deciding there was nothing of interest in here. Not anymore, anyway.

He stepped into the bathroom next. The professor's toothbrush and toothpaste were still sitting on the sink, and his electric razor was on the small counter top. There was a small mirrored cabinet on the wall above the sink and he opened it. There was nothing of interest inside, just some more toothpaste, floss, shampoo and shaving foam.

He headed back to the living room. This was tidier than the bedroom – almost obsessively tidy in fact – but it felt just as cold and clinical. There was another modern art print on the wall; it looked like this one and the one in the bedroom were part of a set. On a coffee table in the centre of the room, there was a neatly stacked pile of magazines sitting next to a solitary white mug on a coaster. A small two-seater sofa sat facing a flat-screen television. Peter checked down the side of the seats, but found nothing except an old biro.

He was about to leave when he noticed a metal bin in the corner of the room. He stepped over, picking it up and examining it. It was empty apart from a charred mess of ashes at the bottom. Someone had used it to burn some papers. He took the biro and poked around in the ashes, looking for anything of interest. At the very bottom, he found a small piece of paper that had not been completely destroyed. It was brown and brittle, and the only thing he could make out was a single word: *Pacific.*

Finally, he turned to the kitchen. There was nothing in the fridge less than two days old; it was possible no one had been back here since then. He lifted the lid off the kitchen bin and rooted around. It mostly contained empty tins and food packets, mixed in with rotting scraps of food, but underneath it all he found something more interesting. It was a discarded box from a pay-as-you-go mobile phone. Maybe the professor just wanted a cheap disposable phone while he was in the country, or maybe he wanted a burner phone, one that couldn't be traced to him. On the side of the box was a sticker with the phone's details, including its IMEI – its unique identifier. He made a note of it, also taking a photo for good measure. Maybe someone could use that to trace the professor.

Once he was certain that there was nothing more to find here, Peter did his best to place everything back as he had found it, and then left the way he had come, making sure to lock the door behind him.

Chapter 27.

April 13th, 2017. Headington, Oxfordshire, England.

It was just before nine o'clock as Detective Cross parked her car outside Headington Auctions. It was located to the east of Oxford city centre, in the leafy suburb of Headington that it was obviously named after.

She stepped out of her car and looked around. The auction house was a long, single-storey building and one of its two sets of double doors was standing open, although there were no signs of any staff or customers. She stepped through the open doorway to find an elderly gentleman in a pin-striped suit and wire-framed glasses standing behind a counter, sipping from a cup. From the little paper tag dangling down the side of the cup on a thin piece of string, she guessed it was herbal tea.

'Hello?' he said, putting down the cup as he noticed her. 'Can I help you? I'm afraid our first auction of the day isn't due for a couple of hours yet.'

'I'm not here for an auction,' said Cross, getting out her warrant card and showing it to him. 'At least, not a new one. I'm here hoping to find some details of an auction you carried out a few years ago. December 2006 to be exact.'

'Well, that's more than a few years, but we have records going back far longer than that. There's a good chance we should be able to help you,' said the man. 'Let me get Rachel; she's far better with the paperwork than I am.'

He called out her name towards the doorway at the back labelled *Private — Employees Only*, and a few moments later a young girl stepped out. She looked to be in her early twenties, wearing a minimal amount of makeup, her light brown hair cut in a bob.

'This lady is from the police,' he explained to her, 'and is enquiring about an auction from a few years ago. Be a good lass and find her any information she's after.'

Rachel looked timid and nervous. She probably wasn't used to dealing with the police, or if she was, it was probably over a minor run-in over drink or drugs as a student.

'Don't worry,' said Cross, trying to put her at ease. 'No one here's in any trouble, no one's done anything wrong. I'm just trying to establish the origin of an item that was stolen in a robbery.' The look of concern on Rachel's face lifted slightly as she heard this, although she still looked a little nervous, not wanting to look Cross directly in the eye. *Probably just natural shyness,* thought Cross, who was normally a good judge in these matters.

'Do you want to come this way?' asked Rachel, leading Cross back into the room she had come from. She was half expecting to see a room full of filing cabinets, but was relieved to instead see several desks with computers sitting on them. If the records were electronic, it would make everything much more efficient. Rachel pulled a second chair up to one of the desks, and gestured to Cross that she could sit down. Cross did so, and Rachel joined her, tapping on the keyboard and logging in to the computer. She double-clicked on an icon on the desktop, opening an application and logging into that as well. 'Do you have any details of the auction you're after?'

Cross pulled her phone out of her pocket, unlocking it and opening the photo gallery. 'I've got the lot ID right here,' she said, handing the phone over to her.

'Well, that will certainly make things easier,' said Rachel, clicking on a box and copying the numbers from the phone into the computer. She clicked a button with the mouse, and a few seconds later a window appeared showing information about the auction. 'Yes, that seems to be the one,' she said as she ran her finger down the screen, comparing the items listed there with what was on the phone. 'What information did you want about it?' she asked.

'I was wondering where the items in the auction came from,' said Cross. 'Specifically one of the books, *The King in Yellow.*'

'Let me see,' muttered Rachel, using the mouse to click on other items on the screen. 'All the items in this lot were from the same source. It says in the description here that it was from an inheritance. That's not unusual – someone inherits a whole load of items from a relative and just wants rid of them all. If they're not very good, they tend to end up in charity and second-hand shops. If they're of slightly higher quality, they often want the services of someone like us.'

'I see,' said Cross. 'And can you tell who it was that put these items up for sale?'

Rachel clicked on another button. 'Eliot Glover,' she said after a short pause. 'I'll jot down his contact details for you,' she added, pulling a small pad of paper and a pen from out of a desk drawer. She transcribed the details with painstaking precision, and then ripped the page from the pad, handing it to Cross. 'Those will be the details from the last time we had contact with him. I can't guarantee they're still accurate.'

'I understand,' said Cross.

Rachel turned back to the computer and clicked on another button. 'The lot was sold to... Milford Antiques,' she said. 'Do you need their details as well?'

'No, that's fine – they're the ones who gave me *your* details,' said Cross with a polite smile as she took out her notepad, slipping the sheet of paper into it. Then she looked back at Rachel; she was staring at the screen again, biting her lip with an expression of curiosity on her face. 'Something up?' asked Cross.

'Yes,' murmured Rachel under her breath. She was clicking on other buttons in the application, popping up other windows. 'It would appear that Mr Glover had several lots up for action – twelve in total. Normally, they'd all be auctioned on the same day, but it would appear... Yes, the lot you're interested in seems to have been done at the end of the previous day. I'm not sure why.'

Cross was about to ask for potential reasons as to why this would have happened, when she thought of a much better question. 'The other auctions – can you tell me who won those?'

Rachel bit her lip again as she resumed clicking with her mouse. Various windows popped up and disappeared again too quickly for Cross to read what was on them. 'I think... yes, they were all bought by the same individual.'

'Not Milford Antiques?'

'No. It says here it was someone called Ethan Dumen.'

'Do you have his contact details?'

'I'm afraid not. We record the name of the auction winner, but there's no real requirement to capture any additional details. Unless...' She clicked on a few more buttons and another window opened on the screen. 'No, sorry. He paid in cash. If it was by cheque or credit card, we might have still had the details. I'm afraid the name is all we have.' She grimaced slightly. 'I can't even guarantee that's his real name.'

'Do you often have buyers providing fake names?'

'Not that I'm aware of. I just mean that we don't check it. Sellers have to provide ID, just in case they try and sell dodgy or stolen items, but not buyers.'

'I see, and duly noted. You've been a great help, regardless.'

❋ ❋ ❋

Superintendent Reynolds stormed into Cross's office. His eyes darted around the room.

'Where the hell is she?'

'Eh?' muttered Dave Brooks from behind his desk.

'Detective Cross. Where is she? She was supposed to be in a departmental meeting an hour ago.'

'Oh. She's off sick,' said Brooks. 'I thought everyone knew.'

'Sick?'

'You know... not well.'

'I know what *sick* means, Brooks. I just mean that woman's never taken a sick day her entire career, except for when she's been hospitalized in the line of duty – and I'm *sure* someone would have told me about *that*.'

'No, just some bug, I'm sure.'

'Hmm,' grumbled Reynolds. He didn't seem convinced.

'Anything I can help you with?' asked Brooks.

'Not unless you can tell me what she was doing over near the New Forest the other day. That's a hell of a long way out of our region.'

'I wasn't aware that she'd been over there,' said Brooks, feigning ignorance. 'I wouldn't have thought she'd have had the time. She's been quite busy.'

'It's not like she doesn't have enough outstanding cases of her own,' continued Reynolds, ignoring him. 'What the hell's she doing sticking her nose into another force's case?'

Brooks just gave a little shrug.

'Well, if you see her, tell her to come see me straight away,' said Reynolds. He cast another glance around the room. 'And tell her to tidy up her desk – it's a bloody mess.'

❋ ❋ ❋

Back in her car, Cross retrieved her phone from her pocket and called her partner again. He picked up after two rings.

'Hello again, boss,' said Brooks as he answered the call.

'How are things back in the office?'

'Just trying to keep on top of the paperwork. Reynolds called in looking for you. Wanted to know why you were in the New Forest.'

'Shit. What did you tell him?'

'That as far as I knew, you'd never been there. He seemed pissed that you'd been wasting your time when you should have been closing some of his cases. He's always worried about his bloody numbers.'

Cross chuckled. 'It comes with the rank. But thanks for covering for me.'

'No worries.'

'I've got a couple of names for you to run down, if you've got a spare minute.'

'Sure.'

First, she gave him Eliot Glover's details as well as the name Ethan Dumen. 'Both would have been from around Oxford, about ten years ago.'

'I've got some information about that phone number,' he said. In the background, she could hear him typing into a keyboard. 'Not good news, I'm afraid. It was from a pay-as-you-go SIM with no contact details. No calls ever made or received. It was recycled about eighteen months ago and is on a new contract now.'

'I don't suppose they have any cell-tower location data.'

'Nah. I asked, but it doesn't go back that far, Normally only one to two years at most.'

'Worth a try, I suppose.'

'Before you go, I've got some initial hits on Eliot Glover. As far as I can see, he's still at that same address. Hang on a moment...' Cross could hear sounds of typing and the clicking of a mouse before he came back again. 'According to Google Maps, it looks like a nice place. Detached property with large grounds, about six miles east of Oxford.'

Not far from where I am now, thought Cross. 'Okay, thanks again.'

'Any idea when you'll be back from sick leave?'

'Hopefully tomorrow,' she said, giving a small cough before hanging up the phone.

Chapter 28.

Waterperry, Oxfordshire, England.

Detective Cross checked her GPS again as she approached Eliot Glover's house. It was set back from the road, hidden behind a dark-green hedge, and as she pulled off the main road, Cross pulled her car to a halt. She gave a low whistle as she looked down the long gravel driveway and saw the house standing at the end, set in several acres of well-manicured gardens. It was three storeys high, although not particularly wide, with a roof of slate tiles and a modern conservatory set to one side.

She drew closer, stopping the car on the drive right by the front door. As she stepped out and approached the porch, she could see that the building wasn't quite as nice as it had appeared from a distance. Several of the wooden window frames looked like they were rotting, and pieces of stonework around the edges of the walls were cracked and broken. She would bet the roof leaked when it rained too.

She stepped up to the front door, giving it a hefty bang with a sturdy brass door knocker held in a lion's mouth. Then she took a step backwards and waited. A minute later, the door opened part way to reveal a woman in her late forties. She had chestnut hair and was wearing dark trousers with knee-high boots, a tweed waistcoat sitting atop a salmon shirt.

'Can I help you?' she asked, in a crisp clear voice.

'Yes, I'm looking for Eliot Glover,' said Cross.

'I'm afraid my husband isn't in at the moment. And you are?' asked the lady, clearly not accustomed to strange women calling for her husband in the middle of the day.

Cross took out her warrant card, showing it to Mrs Glover, who bent over to peer at it closely before standing up straight again.

'What's this about?' asked Mrs Glover, concern and apprehension audible in her voice. 'Is it about those drunk teenagers again, because I haven't seen them for a while now...'

'Oh no. It's to do with a cold case I'm investigating. You're not in any trouble – I was just trying to track down the history of an item that your husband sold at auction. We're not interested in you, just the man who purchased it. I doubt your husband has much information to share about it, but we've got to ask, you know how it is.'

'Well, I suppose you'd better come in then,' said Mrs Glover, stepping back and opening the door wide. 'He's only gone to the shops, should be back any minute.'

She led Cross through the hallway into a reception room with large windows overlooking the grounds. The room was light and airy with bright sunlight flooding in from the gardens, but that only helped to highlight the aging state of the interior. The carpet looked worn, the curtains frayed, and the state of the window frames confirmed her suspicions about them being rotten.

'I'll make us both a nice cup of tea,' said Mrs Glover. She gestured towards a leather armchair, sitting in the sunlight by the window and placed to get a prime view of the grounds. 'You make yourself at home. I'll just be a minute.'

Cross ignored the chair for now, taking the opportunity to look around the room. On one wall were two floor-to-ceiling bookshelves. The books were all old, and she scanned the spines of the books, looking for anything that might be of interest. What she saw were cookery books, biographies, abridged novels and other everyday publications.

She moved over to the marble mantelpiece above the marble fireplace. A ticking antique clock stood on one side, with a few *objet d'art* scattered along its length. There were also a few photographs, some individually mounted in frames, others just propped up against the wall. She gave them a quick glance; most were either of a middle-aged man or an elderly gentle-man, sometimes both, across a period of several decades. She guessed these were probably Eliot Glover and his father.

She picked up one that showed the elderly gentleman shaking the hand of another man, while several men in the background stood solemnly in front of an old building. She turned it over to see that it was labelled as simply *unnamed* in spidery handwriting, the ink now faded to a pale brown colour. She put it back and picked up another. This was the same middle-aged man, standing in a field in front of a dense forest. He was holding a shotgun over one shoulder, a large bird hanging from his other hand and a hunting dog lying at his feet.

It was at this point that Mrs Glover returned, carrying a tray containing a china teapot and two cups, as well as a sugar bowl and small milk jug.

'How do you take it?' she asked, placing the tray down onto a small coffee table beside the chairs.

'As it is,' said Cross, and Mrs Glover poured out a cup, placing it on a coaster before making herself one with milk and two sugars.

'Are these your husband?' asked Cross, as she carefully returned the photograph she was holding to the mantelpiece.

'Yes,' said Mrs Glover. 'Either Eliot or his father, God rest his soul. We don't have many of his father – he was never really one for family photographs, although there is an oil painting of him around upstairs somewhere. Those are some of the few that Eliot found around the house after his passing.

Cross came back across the room, sitting down in the leather armchair and feeling the warmth of the sunlight on her skin. She reached out and picked up her cup of tea, taking a small sip; it was good.

'Now, how can we help?' Mrs Glover asked, once she was satisfied she had been a good hostess and that Cross was happy with her tea.

'Well, Mrs Glover...'

'Call me Helen.'

'All right, Helen. About ten years ago, your husband put up several lots for auction over in Headington.'

Helen nodded as if recalling it. 'If that was late 2006, that would have been shortly after we inherited this place from his father. There was a whole lot of clutter that Eliot just wanted shot of. We've auctioned off several bits every few years to try and pay for the upkeep of this place. It's a listed build-ing, so it costs an absolute fortune to get any work done on the exterior.' She gave a deep sigh. 'I'm afraid we'll have to sell the entire place before too long. It's quite the money pit.'

'Do you know much about the items that were sold back then?'

'Oh no, that was all Eliot's business, between him and his late father. I never really pried into any of that. He's always been the one to look after the financial affairs.'

I'm not sure you'd make a worse job of it, thought Cross, although she kept that to herself.

'Did you have any trouble with anyone about any of the items you in-herited from your father-in-law? No one demanding them from you or anything like that?'

'No...' she said, although she sounded doubtful.

'Are you sure?'

'Well, I'm sure I'd remember something like that, it's just...'

'What?'

'A short while after Dennis – my father-in-law – had passed, this house was broken into. Nothing was taken; the police thought we must have scared them away before they found anything.'

'When was this?'

'About a week after he died. The thing is, we'd already shipped the first load of items to the auction house the day before. You don't think...?'

'Oh no, I'm sure it's unrelated,' lied Cross. Presumably the auction house had better security than this old place. Easier just to buy up what they wanted at that stage.

'They broke a window to get in. Would have cost a small fortune to re-place, but luckily the insurance covered it.'

'I see.' Cross took a quick glance at her watch. 'Do you know when your husband will be home, Mrs Glover?'

'Helen.'

'Helen,' she corrected herself.

The two women turned their heads in unison as they heard a key in the front door, perfectly on cue.

'Whose car is that?' came an elderly male voice from the hallway. It sounded well educated, almost aristocratic.

'There's a lady here to see you,' said Helen. 'She's from the police, come to ask you about something you inherited from your father.'

'Really?' he replied. 'Let me just hang up my coat and I'll be right in.' A few moments later he shuffled in, a man in his early fifties sporting short grey hair with a widow's peak. He was wearing a Harris Tweed suit, although it looked worn and frayed around the edges. 'Don't get up,' he said as he noticed Cross starting to rise. He came over and shook her by the hand. 'Eliot Glover,' he said. 'I assume my wife has already introduced herself?'

'Yes,' confirmed Cross. 'I'm Detective Cross. As I explained to your wife, I'm investigating a cold case where we believe an item that used to belong to you was present. I was just trying to establish its provenance, in case it was relevant. It's unlikely, but we've got to run down every lead, you know how it is.'

Eliot gave a weak smile of acknowledgement, but still looked slightly confused. 'Well, whatever I can do to help, I suppose.' He turned to his wife. 'I could murder a cup of tea,' he said to her, and then turned back to Cross. He had an embarrassed look on his face from his choice of words in front of the detective.

Cross tried her best to ignore it, and Helen got up and took the tray back to the kitchen.

'So, Mr Glover,' she said. 'As I understand it, shortly after you inherited this house and its contents, you sold some of them through an auction house in Headington.'

'Er... yes, that sounds about right.'

'One lot in particular was a set of books. Can you remember much about them?'

'The books? Not really. I just went through the library, looking for anything that looked valuable and had no sentimental value to us.'

'What about the book *The King in Yellow*?'

'*The King in Yellow*, you say? Can't say it rings any bells, but it may have been one of them.'

Cross wasn't sure, but thought she possibly saw a glint of recognition in his eyes. She tried to gauge his body language; he looked nervous, possibly even evasive, but then again, so did most people when being questioned by the police. She tried to remind herself that he wasn't actually suspected of anything.

'What about this?' she said, pulling out the business card and showing him the three-pointed symbol on it. 'Do you recognize this?'

Eliot shook his head. 'Maybe. Hard to say. It was a long time ago.'

'Did you ever have anyone come to the house, offer to buy any of the books – or anything else – from you?'

'No,' he said, shaking his head again. He seemed more sure about this.

'But you were burgled at about the same time that you sent these books to the auction house.'

'Yes,' he confirmed. 'I think it was the day after we'd packed up several crates and the auction house had collected them. We got up in the morning to find a window smashed in the downstairs library. A fair amount of disarray, but nothing missing as far as I could tell. I couldn't be certain though, as I hadn't conducted a full audit beforehand or anything. But nothing obvious was gone.'

'And you reported this to the police?'

'Yes. They reckoned we must have disturbed the burglars when we got up in the night.'

'Did they ever find who was responsible?'

'No. It was probably just kids, or addicts looking for something they could sell. We still have problems with them occasionally, even in a quiet suburb like this. It didn't seem to be the police's most pressing problem, especially given that nothing was actually stolen.'

'Yes, I see,' said Cross, nodding in agreement. She could appreciate the sentiment.

'Do you think this had anything to do with your case?'

'Hard to say,' said Cross with a grimace, 'given that nothing was taken. It's possible, but it could also just be a coincidence.'

At that moment, Mrs Glover came back into the room carrying the same tea tray, which she gently laid back on the table. Cross waited patiently as she poured a cup of tea for her husband. 'Would you like another?' she enquired politely to Cross, who shook her head in reply.

They both waited for her to leave again before resuming.

'Mr Glover. How did your father die? If you don't mind me asking?'

'Natural causes,' he said. 'Heart attack, anyway, which at his age was fairly natural.'

'Thank you,' she said. This really didn't seem to be leading anywhere.

She stood up, putting away her pad of paper. 'Anyway, I'm sure I've taken up enough of your time,' she added.

'No, that's fine,' he said. 'Glad to help, although I'm not sure that I did.'

Cross was on her way back to the door when she had a thought. She stopped and turned back to Eliot. 'Just one more thing,' she said. 'Does the name Ethan Dumen mean anything to you?' She could see his eyes flicking about as he scanned his memory for any recollection.

'No,' he said cautiously. 'Should it?'

'No, probably not.' She thought she believed him this time. 'Many thanks for your time – and for your wife's too. Tell her thanks again for the tea.'

Cross had headed back into Oxford centre to get some lunch while she waited for her partner to call her back again. She had stopped in a cafe just outside the main city centre and ordered a light salad from the menu.

She was currently sitting at a bench in their garden, relaxing with a cup of tea in the gentle midday sun. She'd bought a newspaper from a newsagent next door, and was wiling away her time trying to finish the cryptic crossword. She was now on nine across: *Confused admirer is not alone (7)*. She looked at it for a moment, before realizing it must be an anagram of *admirer*. She wrote the letters down in the margin, mixing them around until she saw it: *married.*

As she wrote the letters back into the crossword, an idea crossed her mind. She wrote the name Ethan Dumen down in the margin, mentally rearranging the letters to see if she could make anything of it. She couldn't see anything and was about to go back to the crossword, when it suddenly appeared before her: The Unnamed. That was what had been written on the back of that photo in Eliot Glover's house; the photo of his father with a group of men. Hadn't Jack said that another name for *The King in Yellow* was *He who should not be named?*

Fuck, she thought to herself. His father must have been one of them; that was how he had got hold of the book in the first place. When he died... well, they had obviously wanted it back. That presumably meant that Eliot wasn't one of them, but surely he must have some information about them — some of their names, or where they could be found.

Her lunch hadn't arrived yet, but she didn't care. She pulled a ten pound note from her purse to pay for the meal, slipped it under her cup and hurried back to her car.

Ten minutes later, she was back at the Glover's. She banged on the door with her fist until it was wrenched open by Mrs Glover. She looked surprised to see Cross, as if she had been expecting someone else – possibly an angry man given how long and hard Cross had stood beating on the door.

'I need to see your husband,' said Cross, stepping inside and storming past Mrs Glover. 'Is he in here?' she asked, not waiting for a response, and heading straight for the reception room where they had all sat before.

Eliot Glover was sitting in the same leather armchair that she had sat in earlier. 'Who was it, dear?' he asked. 'Was it that dreadful–' He stopped mid-sentence when he saw it was Cross and not his wife. 'What are you doing back here?'

Cross fixed him with a stony glance. 'Why have you been lying to me, Mr Glover?'

'I've done no such thing,' he protested. It felt forced, like he was over-compensating.

'I've talked to many people over the years, developed quite a knack for telling when people aren't being on the level with me, Mr Glover. I was suspicious earlier, but couldn't quite put my finger on what it was.'

She stepped over to the mantelpiece, picking up the photo of his father. She turned it over again, confirming to herself that *The Unnamed* was written on the back. 'I suspect you did recognize that book, probably the symbol too.' She walked back over to him, holding the photo in front of him to see, but he didn't need to look at it to know which photo she was talking about. 'It belonged to them, didn't it?'

With this, he seemed to deflate, his will to argue leaving him. 'That bloody book,' he sighed. 'Yes, I did recognize it.'

'So why didn't you want to tell me about it?'

'I just want shot of the bloody thing. My father brought it home about a month before his death – he became obsessed with the damn thing. This was near the end, but his dementia seemed to be getting worse. He was growing more paranoid; he kept hearing noises and seeing shapes at the window. Helen thought it was just a natural progression of his deterioration, but I... I always had my suspicions. After he died, I made sure it was one of the first things I got rid of. I was tempted just to chuck it, burn the damned thing in the fireplace, but Helen convinced me that it might be worth some money. Even then I knew we'd need every penny we could get to try and keep this place in a decent condition.'

'And did it belong to them?' she asked, waving the photograph at him again.

'I don't know. Maybe. Probably. Father had been going there for a couple of years. It seemed harmless enough. I just presumed it was like the Masons or the Quakers. Are you trying to tell me that it was something more sinister?'

'I don't know yet... but maybe.'

'You don't think I had anything to do with them?'

'At this stage... probably not. The fact that they broke into your house looking for the book – as it was almost certainly them – rather than just asking you for it seems to suggest you weren't one of them.' She thought for a moment. 'And your father?'

'What about him?'

'How did he actually die?'

'He *did* die of a heart attack... It was ruled natural causes, but what really brought it on? Do you think they had something to do with it?'

Cross sighed. 'I don't know. But I do need to talk to them. She tapped on the photo. 'This building they're standing in front of – is that where they met? Do you know where it is?'

'Err...'he muttered as he racked his memory. 'I don't I think so. My father never really discussed it with me.'

'In his belongings and his papers, did you find anything with details of where this building was, where they would meet?' Eliot shook his head. 'Any maps, addresses you didn't recognize?'

Eliot started to shake his head again and then paused. 'He had a GPS in his car, one of those little boxes you could plug into a cigarette lighter.'

'Is it still in his car?'

'No. We sold it.'

'Damn it,' Cross muttered under her breath.

'No, I'm sorry – you don't understand. I sold the car, but I took the GPS out beforehand. I think it's probably still in a drawer upstairs somewhere.'

'Could you?'

'Certainly.' Eliot stood up. 'Err...make yourself at home. I may be a minute or two – I'm not quite sure exactly where it is. Would you like another cup of tea?'

'No, I'm fine,' said Cross, silently willing the man to get on with it.

He came back a couple of minutes later holding a small black box. There was a thick curly black wire hanging from it, a cigarette lighter plug dangling on the end. 'It looks like the battery is flat.'

'Do you mind if I take it?' asked Cross.

'I don't suppose so,' he said, shrugging his shoulders.

'I'll make sure I return it,' she said. 'Along with the photograph.'

Back in her car, she plugged the GPS unit into her cigarette lighter and attached the device to her windscreen. She waited patiently, and a minute later was rewarded as the screen flashed on, the device now holding enough power to start up. When it was ready, she tapped through the screens looking for any saved locations. She was grateful he hadn't used his phone like most people these days. They could encrypt all their information, hide it away behind passwords and PINs, but these simple devices were a lot more accessible.

She scrolled through the list. Most of the locations were clearly not where she was after – his house, friends and family, city car parks. Nothing was obviously the location where *The Unnamed* would meet, but there were six locations anonymously labelled with either a single letter or number. These could be either places he wanted to keep anonymous, or just the location of a single-use destination.

She went through each of these sites in turn, checking where they were. One of them was in Oxford city centre, so could probably be discounted. That left five places to check, each of which was scattered around the countryside. She jotted down the locations of each, working out an optimum route to visit all of them without too much doubling back on herself, and then set off, heading to the first location on her list.

Chapter 29.

Ashton High-security Psychiatric Hospital, Exeter, England.

Peter White sat patiently in the small interview room in Ashton High-security Psychiatric Hospital. With the assistance of Detective Brooks on behalf of Cross, he had been granted an interview with Melissa Brooks, Cathy Hobbes' room-mate, the woman who had attacked her. Brooks had warned him not to expect too much though – she had apparently suffered a severe psychotic breakdown and was under heavy medication.

The room was cold and inhospitable, with only two aluminium chairs and a metal table, which was bolted to the floor. Overhead, one of the two fluorescent tubes flickered occasionally, and in one corner sat a CCTV camera, a red light blinking on and off to indicate that it was active.

Peter's head jerked up as the door opened and two male orderlies escorted in a woman. He recognized her from that night in the dormitory, but she looked quite different now. Her skin looked pale and sallow, her eyes darting nervously around the room. Her long hair was pulled back into a ponytail but looked messy and unkempt, possibly because she would have been unable to do much with it while she was strapped into her straightjacket.

A man followed behind her into the room, Doctor Gardner, her attending physician to whom Peter had been introduced on his arrival at the hospital.

'Is the straightjacket really necessary?' asked Peter.

'I'm afraid so,' replied the doctor. 'She's been quite violent and unpredictable – even with her medication.'

The orderlies guided Melissa into the chair and then left again. Doctor Gardner moved into the corner of the room, standing with his hands behind his back and taking a watching brief.

'Hello, Melissa,' said Peter, in what he hoped was a calm and relaxing tone. 'Do you recognize me?'

A small snarl grew on her lips and she uttered a low grunt. It was hard to know if this meant yes or no.

'Do you know why you're here?' asked Peter, but he wasn't sure she was listening to him. Her eyes were darting around the room, as if trying to follow something he couldn't see. He decided to try again. 'I'm here because I want to try and help you,' he said. 'I want to try and understand why you did what you did. Can you remember what you did?'

Peter jumped as she flicked her head back violently and started laughing at the ceiling. 'None of this matters,' she muttered between laughs. 'Soon he will be free, and all of this...' She twisted her head around to indicate her surroundings, 'all of this will be no more.'

'Who? Who are you talking about? Was there someone who put you up to this, told you to attack Cathy?'

Melissa slowly lowered her head until she was looking directly at Peter, holding his gaze without blinking. 'You can't understand,' she said slowly. 'You haven't seen...'

'I want to understand,' said Peter calmly. 'Can you show me? Can you explain it to me?'

Melissa was still staring at him, and now she tilted her head slightly, as if looking at something she didn't quite understand. It was quite unnerving. 'You'll see before long... You all will. When the stars are aligned, he will walk free once again–'

'–What did you say?'

She stopped, and a humourless smile spread across her lips. 'When the stars have all been gathered and aligned, he will be released to walk upon the Earth once more, and none of this will matter. Your life as you know it is over... you just don't realize it yet.'

A dread chill had come over Peter. This all sounded too familiar. 'Melissa,' he said calmly. 'Who told you this? Who have you been talking with?'

Melissa continued to stare at him in silence, before closing her eyes and dropping her head down, looking into her lap. 'You know, don't you?' she said eventually, raising her head slightly. 'Not like *these*,' she whispered conspiratorially towards Peter, with a flick of her head towards the doctor in the corner of the room. '*They* tell me it's all a delusion, but *we* know better, don't we? Only...' She stopped and then muttered something under her breath, something inaudible.

'What?' urged Peter, leaning towards her.

With unexpected speed, Melissa lunged forwards out of her chair, leaping over the table and hurtling towards Peter. He saw the doctor freeze momentarily in shock as she barrelled into him, knocking him backwards to the floor. He was still sitting in his chair even as it smacked into the ground. He could see a vicious snarl of rage across her face as she landed on him, her head approaching his at speed. He tried to roll to one side, but forgot that he was entangled in his chair; he managed to move a small distance, but not enough. Their heads collided, her forehead smashing into the side of his temple, stunning him.

From somewhere beyond his feet, he could hear movement and a door opening. Her face swam into focus in front of his, her eyes wide and darting, saliva dripping from her lips. She opened her mouth wide, her teeth digging into his cheek, then suddenly flew backwards, hauled off him by the two orderlies who had originally brought her into the room.

'Take her back to her room!' barked the doctor, still standing in the corner of the room, shocked into motionlessness. 'And increase her sedation,' he added as an afterthought.

'You'll see! You'll all see!' she screamed as she was dragged backwards out of the room, struggling violently despite her small stature and straightjacket.

Peter ran his fingers over his cheek. He could feel indentations from her teeth still present in his skin, but he didn't think she had actually managed to bite a chunk out of him.

'Soon he will sleep no more, and then the end will be upon us all!' he heard Melissa scream from the corridor outside.

Peter stepped out of the hospital reception and into the car park, having brushed off the apologies from the staff over the attack. His heart was still beating fast, and he was glad to be outside again. He was heading back to his car when his phone beeped. He pulled it from his pocket, unlocking it when he saw he had a new text message. It was from Dave Brooks, replying to his query about Professor Ashbrook's phone.

Phone went dark 12 hours ago. Last seen at GPS coordinates 50.897, -1.668 – Langley Woods. HTH Dave.

He sat down in his car and then opened the GPS app in his phone before entering the coordinates. As Dave had said, the location was shown as Langley Woods, on the outskirts of the New Forest. Looking for someone there would be like looking for a needle in the proverbial haystack, but he wasn't sure what else he could do at this point. He started the engine and set off.

Chapter 30.

Cairo International Airport, Egypt.

Jack and Jennifer disembarked from the airplane and headed straight for passport control. They'd decided to pack light, simply bringing a well-stocked backpack each, small enough to fit into hand luggage.

They passed through passport control and customs without problem and entered the large lobby, which was bustling with people. Jennifer spotted several people holding out cards bearing names, and they headed towards those until Jack spotted a card bearing the name *Jack Night. Close enough*, he thought, heading towards the man who held it.

The card's owner was dark skinned and well built, with short black hair and a thin moustache, dressed in black trousers and a white shirt. As they approached, the man seemed to recognize Jack, dropping the card and holding out a hand. 'Jack Night?'

'That's me, and this is my wife, Jennifer.'

The man nodded. 'Peter sent me a picture of you,' he said, in English that was clear but with a heavy Egyptian accent. 'My name is Al-amir, but you can call me Al. Do you have any bags?'

'Just these,' said Jack, gesturing to their backpacks.

'Very good. Follow me,' said Al, leading them through the crowds towards the exit.

'Did Peter tell you where we need to go?'

'Yes,' said Al, 'he gave me GPS coordinates of an area west of Samalut. Said I was to give you whatever assistance I could.'

'Do you know how long it will take to get there?' asked Jennifer, as they made their way out of the terminal building into the scorching mid-afternoon air.

'It is about a three-hour drive south, and then probably half an hour across the desert.'

'Across the desert? Will that be okay?' asked Jack.

'I have come prepared,' said Al, stopping before a large Toyota Hilux parked illegally in front of the building. It appeared to have larger than normal tyres and suspension, modified for desert conditions. 'Please, jump in the back,' he said as he ripped a piece of card from under the windscreen wipers, something Egyptian printed on one side.

Jack opened the door for Jennifer, and she climbed in, Jack following close behind. Al climbed into the driver's seat, setting up his phone with a sat-nav app on the dashboard.

'Do you want to head straight to the desert,' asked Al, 'or head to a hotel first?'

'Straight there,' said Jennifer. 'Time may be of the essence.'

'Good, good. I understand. Make yourself comfortable,' he said. 'I will go as fast as I can, but we will have a few hours to kill. There is water and food back there for you. If you want to have a nap, now is the time, while we are on the good roads.'

Al started the engine, indicating and then pulling out. The traffic was relatively light and they made good progress getting out of the airport complex and onto the main roads.

'Did Peter tell you why we're here?' asked Jack, after they reached the main road south, which ran parallel to the Nile, and Al had relaxed into a steady cruise.

'He did not say, and I do not need to ask,' said Al. 'We have worked together several times and I trust him implicitly. If he says you are friends to be trusted, that is good enough for me.'

'Okay,' said Jack. 'It could be nothing, but it's also possible that there may be trouble when we arrive. The men there could be dangerous.'

Al chuckled. 'Do not worry about me, my friend.' He reached down under his seat, and when he pulled his hand out he was holding an automatic pistol. 'I can take care of myself.' He looked at Jack in the rear-view mirror, noting the look of surprise on his face. 'You need one too?' he asked. He placed the gun on the passenger seat, and leaned over, opening the glove box. When he sat back up, he was holding a revolver. 'Here,' he said, passing it back to Jack, who took hold of it. Al reached over again, this time to re-trieve a small box, which he again passed back to Jack. 'Ammunition,' he said. 'The gun is not loaded.'

Jack opened his backpack, slipping the gun and bullets inside. 'You know how to shoot, yes?' asked Al.

'I do,' said Jack. 'I learned... well, a long time ago. But it's been a little while since I last used one.' Jennifer brought her hand up to her cheek as he said this, feeling the faint scar that she still bore from their encounter with Silas in the Necropolis.

'Ah, no worries,' said Al. 'It's like riding a bike. A couple of shots and... Boom! It'll all come back to you.'

'Well, let's hope it doesn't come to that,' said Jennifer, forcing a polite smile.

Al looked disappointed at the idea that there might not be a gunfight. 'Maybe,' he said. 'But it is best to be prepared, yes?'

'Yes,' agreed Jack and Jennifer together.

'Now, get some rest, my friends. You are in safe hands.'

Chapter 31.

Langley Woods, Buckinghamshire, England.

Peter White pulled into a small car park on the edge of Langley Woods. This was as close as he could get by car, about a mile away from where the professor's phone was last seen.

As he was about to step out of the car, he noticed his phone. He had put it on silent but it was buzzing away in his pocket. He pulled it out and glanced at the screen; Jack Knight was calling.

'Hello,' he said, accepting the call.

'Peter,' said Jack. 'Just thought I'd check in, see if there any updates.' It sounded noisy in the background, like they were driving through a busy street. The signal kept breaking up but he wasn't sure if it was his end or theirs – there was barely any phone signal out here on the edge of the woods. 'We've landed in Cairo and met up with Al,' Jack continued. 'We're heading towards the dig site now and thought we'd check with you while it's quiet, see how you're getting on.'

'I've got more questions than answers, I'm afraid,' replied Peter. 'Those notes you found... Some of them relate to underwater and underground imaging, and the maths is to do with astrophysics.'

'Hmm,' replied Jack. 'It's hard to think of two fields that are less related.'

'Quite. What interest they are to the Brotherhood is anyone's guess.'

'Okay, I can take a better look when we get back. Our expedition could be interesting... we'll let you know what we find. But you take care of yourself.'

'Will do,' replied Peter. He hung up the phone and double-checked it was still on silent mode. The reception icon of his phone was wavering between one bar and no signal. The professor's phone could be turned off, or the battery flat... or there could just be a complete lack of reception out here.

Peter checked his bearings, using a map and the compass on his phone. There was a dirt track leading in roughly the right direction, and he decided to take it. With any luck, the professor had done so too; he had no reason to believe otherwise just yet.

He set off along the trail, heading deep into the woods. He was using the GPS on his phone to try and head to the professor's last known location, picking whatever route looked most direct whenever the path forked. Before long, any signs of civilization were gone and he was ascending a winding path up a hill, the slope steep on either side. His trek took him deeper and deeper into the woods, further and further from the well-worn paths, until the ground beneath him was less of a footpath and more of a groove worn into the grass.

He was beginning to wish he'd planned a bit more before setting out. He was getting thirsty and hadn't brought any water with him. He wasn't planning on getting lost out here, but people had gone missing before in smaller forests than this. He checked his phone again; that at least had lots of battery left, and he should be able to rely on that to get him back to his car.

As he put his phone back into his pocket, he looked across the woods and just for a moment thought he saw a flash of sunlight reflecting off something through the trees. It could just be some rubbish, something glass or metal left behind by another visitor to the forest, but as he looked closer, straining to see through the trees, he saw it again; there seemed to be something large back there.

He set off through the undergrowth, taking a direct path towards whatever it was. As he approached, the shape became clearer: an old log cabin covered in leaves and creepers, almost perfectly camouflaged. The sunlight had been reflecting off one of its small windows. If hadn't been for the reflection, he would never have spotted it.

As he drew closer to the cabin, he started to pick out voices within – at least two people arguing with raised voices. He approached the cabin slowly, using the trees and bushes as cover. One side of the cabin had a door but no windows, and he circled around to come in from that direction, where his approach couldn't be seen by anyone within.

He inched closer, out of the foliage and into a clearing. He was halfway to the cabin when the door burst open and a man strode out. He was tall and muscular with short dark hair and stubble, clothed in a dark jacket and blue jeans. As he saw Peter he stopped, momentarily shocked.

Peter had barely any time to react before the man started to reach into his jacket. He rushed towards him, closing the distance rapidly even as he saw the man withdraw his hand, a pistol clenched in his fist.

He crashed headfirst into the man, knocking him into the doorframe and both of them crumpled to the ground from the impact. Peter rolled away, quickly picking himself up as he clambered back to his feet. The man had managed to keep hold of the gun, but as he climbed to his knees, Peter kicked at it. His foot collided with the gun, and it flew through the air, bouncing off the wall of the cabin and landing on the ground several feet away.

With his other hand, the man grabbed at Peter's leg. He yanked on it, unbalancing him and sending him flying backwards, landing on his back on the soft grass. The man looked at the gun on the floor, then over at Peter and then back towards the gun again. He started to shuffle over towards the pistol on his hands and knees, and Peter rolled over, pulling himself to his knees. Next to him on the floor was a thick section of tree branch, damp and covered in moss but a good three inches across. He grabbed hold of it as he pulled himself to his feet, then turned to see the man reaching for the gun.

He bolted towards him, swinging the branch above his head. As he brought it down over the man's back, it simply shattered into dozens of pieces, the wood damp and rotten.

The man seemed unaffected by the blow, but his attention had at least been drawn away from the gun. Instead, he pounced upwards. Peter stepped back and to the side, the man's lunge narrowly missing him. He stumbled on for a few feet before he stopped and turned back to face him.

The two men were ten feet apart now, the gun lying on the floor behind Peter. They circled each other, each man weighing up the other, looking for weaknesses. Peter turned to look for the gun on the floor, and as he did so the other man charged, hurtling towards him at full speed. As he came within reach, Peter grabbed hold of him with both hands, one knee bent out in front of him. He threw him over his knee, using the man's own momentum to spin him around and throw him to the floor, where he collapsed with a cry.

Peter dived for the gun, grabbing it with both hands as he hit the floor, turning and rolling in a fluid motion until he was facing the man. He wasn't moving; he was motionless on the floor, his body lying at an awkward angle.

With the gun trained on him, Peter cautiously approached and gave his leg a sharp kick. When there was no response, he slowly knelt down and rolled the body over. In the middle of his chest was a large bloody wound. He had fallen onto the sharp stub of a branch, which rose vertically from a fallen tree trunk.

There was nothing he could do for him. Instead, Peter turned his attention to whoever still remained in the cabin. He had heard at least two voices arguing.

He looked down at the gun in his hand. It was a Glock automatic, highly functional and very reliable. After checking the safety, he ejected the cartridge, made sure it was loaded and then slotted it back into place. He stepped towards the cabin, stopped next to the open door and listened; apart from some distant bird-song and the gentle whistle of the wind through the trees, it was silent.

'Is there anyone in there?' he called out. There was no reply. 'Professor Ashbrook,' he called out again. 'If you're in there, I'm not here to hurt you.' Again, no reply.

Okay, thought Peter to himself. *This is where it gets dicey.* He crouched down so that his head wasn't at normal head height and then very briefly peered around the door frame, scanning the room for a split second before pulling his head back again. The inside of the cabin was a single empty room, with no obvious occupants and no one shooting at him. He chanced another look, longer this time. He still couldn't see anyone. There were no signs of movement, just furniture and a glowing fire in the corner.

He stood up again. He held the gun down low by his waist, his left arm held out before him. This way, if anyone jumped him they wouldn't be able to easily knock the gun away; he could block with his left arm and still get a clean shot. He took a deep breath and then stepped inside, quickly moving sideways so that he wasn't cleanly silhouetted against the light of the doorway.

The cabin was a single large room. An oak table sat in the centre with six wooden chairs placed around it. Some bare cabinets sat around the walls. There was a wooden burner stove in one corner, a dull fire glowing within. There were papers scattered all over the table with several lying haphazardly on the floor. The one thing that wasn't present was any people. Then he noticed the window at the rear of the room lying open, a chair resting underneath. *Shit.*

He dashed over and stopped next to the window. He twisted, quickly peering through the window before pulling his head back again almost instantly. He saw no one in his brief glimpse, and no shots rang out. He looked again, longer this time. The amount of vegetation and cover out there worried him – plenty of cover for anyone with a gun – but it didn't look like anyone was lying in wait.

Then he saw him. In the distance, just visible through the foliage, was a man. He was at least a hundred yards away and running through the undergrowth; a significant head-start in this terrain. He thumbed the safety on the pistol and stuffed it into his jacket pocket.

He was about to give chase when he noticed the stove. The door was open and several half-burnt sheets of paper were protruding. Someone had been trying to burn some of the papers, get rid of the evidence. He darted over to the stove and grabbed the edge of the few papers that weren't completely destroyed. He yanked them out, ignoring the heat, and beat their smouldering edges against his trousers, sparks and ashes flying all around his feet. When he was sure they were no longer alight, he threw them onto the table next to the other papers and then hastily made his way back to the chair. He leapt onto it and grabbed hold of the top of the window frame, swinging through the open window in a single fluid motion.

The man was no longer visible, but Peter was confident of his last location and he started to give chase. From his last known direction, he thought the man was heading back in the direction Peter had originally come from. He ploughed on through the undergrowth, and before long he was back on the dirt trail that had brought him to the cabin. It looked like the man was sticking to the trail, making it much easier to follow him.

Peter ran as fast as he dared on the uneven terrain, occasionally stumbling but never quite tripping. He was faster than his prey and slowly gaining on him.

'Stop!' he yelled as the man darted around a twist in the path, momentarily out of sight. He charged round the bend to see the man still running. He was only fifty feet away now, the dirt path straight for another hundred. He stopped and pulled the pistol from his pocket, thumbed the safety off and then fired a single shot into the air. 'Stop or I shoot!' he yelled as the retort of the gunshot rang out.

The man slowed down and then stopped, leaning forwards and resting his hands on his thighs, taking in huge breaths of air. They were standing on a path along the side of a hill, the woods steeply ascending on one side and descending on the other.

Peter advanced slowly, holding the gun in front of him with both hands but pointed down towards the floor between them. 'Turn around, slowly,' he said as he neared.

The man did so, and Peter could see he was a middle-aged man, probably in his fifties, his grey hair tousled and messy. His face was bright red and he was panting hard. 'Who are you?' Peter demanded.

'Daniel Ashbrook,' stammered the man in a strong Boston accent.

'Professor Ashbrook?' replied Peter. 'You're a hard man to get hold of.'

'Who are you?' stammered the professor. 'What do you want with me?'

'David Packham. Melissa Brooks. Do those names mean something to you?' As he talked, he kept the gun trained on the professor, ready to shoot at a moment's notice; he still wasn't sure whether the professor was an innocent party in all this.

The professor gave a subdued nod. 'It wasn't my fault,' he muttered. 'They made me do it.' His shoulders seemed to slump, as if his will to fight was leaving him.

'Who did?' asked Peter.

'Those men. The ones who kidnapped me, brought me here.'

'And who are they?'

'I don't know. The man at the cabin... Did you kill him?'

'I think so.'

The professor stood there panting, trying to get his breath back, until he decided to break the silence. 'Who exactly are you then? Assuming you're not one of *them*?'

'I'm not one of them. I'm a private detective. Peter White.'

Professor Ashbrook raised an eyebrow in surprise. 'In which case, do you mind lowering the gun, Peter? I think I've had about as much adventure as I care for at my age.'

Peter lowered the gun slowly. He was still holding it in both hands, ready to fire, but now aimed it towards the ground midway between them. He took a couple of steps forwards.

'Okay, Professor, time to start talking. And start at the beginning.'

'I suppose the beginning was about two weeks ago. I arrived home to find two men in my house – or at least the house I'm staying at while I'm visiting. They were armed. They made me sit down, and they explained the situation to me.'

'Which was?'

'They needed access to my research. You know about my research?'

'I know about the trials you were running for the university. Some kind of dream research? And I believe there was more to it than would first appear. I think it drove both David Packham and Melissa Brooks mad... and maybe others, I'm not sure.'

Professor Ashbrook nodded and swallowed. 'I'm so sorry,' he said. 'I never believed anything like that would ever happen. But they had my children; I had to do what they said.'

'So what did they want with your research?'

'I was studying how different brain wave patterns affect dreaming. Others have performed research to try and correlate different brain waves and how they correspond to different dream states; my work was basically a continuation of that. The problem was that they wanted to go further than I had planned. They wanted to try and set up a resonant frequency when the subjects were asleep, trying to alter the brain waves to *initiate* certain dreams.'

'They were trying to make people dream. Why?'

'It was more than that. As the experiments went on, they started to show signs of success.'

'So they made them dream. I still don't understand why.'

'It was more than just making them dream. The subjects would experience lucid dreams – lucid nightmares really – and they were all the same.'

'You're telling me that they all shared the same dream?'

'Yes. Well, kind of.' He hesitated for a moment, as if unsure of what to say next.

'Go on, Professor,' said Peter, 'no matter how mad it might sound.'

'I don't think they were just sharing a dream. I think they were all *receiving* the same dream. That was the point of trying to alter the brain waves... it was like trying to tune in an old-fashioned radio, trying to pick up a particularly faint and distant signal. Several of the better subjects – including David and Melissa – would almost seem awake when they were in the height of it – although they never remembered much when they woke up in the morning.'

'What did they see, Professor?'

'My god, those poor students,' he muttered. Peter could see tears in the corner of his eyes. 'I don't know exactly, but it was enough to scare them to the very depths of their souls. God forgive me for what I've done. But please understand, they have my children. They still do. They're adults now, but still... no man wants to outlive his children. I've got to get them back. Can you help me?'

'Maybe,' said Peter. 'Where are they?'

'America. Providence. Or they were when I last saw them.'

Peter sighed. He realized he was still gripping the gun tightly and he relaxed his arms. He put the safety on and slipped it into the belt of his trousers. 'I'll see what I can do, but we're going to need a plan.'

As he let go of the gun, he felt his phone vibrate briefly in his pocket: an incoming message. They were close to the car park now, on the edge of civilization where there was some reception again. He slipped it out of his pocket and unlocked it; he had a new email, a reply to his enquiry from Miskatonic University.

'Ah,' he said to the professor, holding up the phone. 'Your old university in America. Maybe they can help us.' He opened the email, scanning it briefly and then he froze. *Mr White*, it began. *Thank you for your recent correspondence, but I am very sad to inform you that Professor Ashbrook passed away in a car crash shortly before he was due to travel to England to perform his duties there...*

He stopped reading as a hand grabbed the gun from his waist, deftly taking the safety off and twisting it back around to point at him in one fluid motion.

'Who are you?' asked Peter, slowly raising his hands, the phone still in his hand. 'Who are you really?'

'One of the Brotherhood,' replied the imposter, his voice switching to a British accent. 'We needed access to the professor's resources, all that technical hardware and all those students willing to be guinea pigs. He wasn't willing to play ball, and there was no easy way to pressure him. In the end, it was easier just to kill him and replace him. His visiting England where no one really knew him made it quite simple in the end. I was picked as I looked most like him.'

'What about his children? Do you have them hostage?'

The man sneered back at him. 'He doesn't even *have* any children.'

'Is anything you told me true?' sighed Peter.

The man shrugged. 'Most of it. It was easier than trying to come up with a consistent lie while you were pointing a gun at me.' He waved the gun threateningly towards Peter. 'So who knows that you're here? Who have you talked to about us?'

Peter smiled. 'This ain't the first time someone's pointed a gun at me,' he said. 'Not even close. And it doesn't usually work out too well for the other guy.'

'Well, you'll have to make an exception this time, won't you? Who have you told?' he barked at him, more forcefully than before.

Peter weighed up his options. Keeping the man talking and hoping for an opportunity was the only thing that came to mind. 'I haven't reported any of this back to David's parents yet,' he said. 'They don't know anything.'

The man eyed Peter curiously, trying to decide if he was telling the truth or not. He seemed to decide that he was. 'Good,' he said, and raised the gun.

'There is someone I *have* told, though,' said Peter. 'An old friend. Jack Knight.' The man's mouth opened slightly as he took in this new information. 'You recognize *that* name, don't you?' said Peter. 'He killed your old leader... and I'm sure he'd be willing to do it again.'

The man nodded his head slowly. 'And you... you were one of his cadre, weren't you?'

Peter gave a brief smile to confirm. 'The police also know I'm here. They're the ones that gave me your location here in the woods.'

'How?'

'Your burner phone. I found the box in your bin. It's all over now.'

The man shook his head. 'It is all over, but not how you think. I've concluded our research; we now know what we need.'

'Which is...?'

'As our god sleeps, he dreams. Particularly sensitive individuals have sometimes been able to grasp snippets of those dreams – have been able to see beyond what mortal man is meant to comprehend. With my work, and the help of the boy, we have been able to see so much more... to understand so much more.'

'The boy?' asked Peter. This must have been the mysterious *Patient X* in the research.

'The son of your friend,' sneered the man. 'Bill Knight. I'm sure you're aware of the *special circumstances* of his conception. He is more connected to the dreams than any I've ever come across. I was able to use him as a reference, as a tuning fork if you like, by which the others could be attuned.' He gave Peter a scornful look. 'Your friend's son will be the downfall of your civilization. Now that we know, the day of his release is fast approaching. When that day comes, life on this world will become so much more... *interesting*. Not for you, of course, as you'll be long dead.'

As he said this, he began to raise the gun and Peter knew he had to act now. He was still holding his phone in his hand, and he threw it hard with a snap of his wrist, aiming for the man's head. The man fired the gun as he instinctively raised his other arm to protect his face, but his shot went wide and high. He wasn't a real university professor, but Peter was gambling on him being as out of shape as most academics of his age that he'd met.

Peter wasn't a young man anymore either, but he still had a few years on the imposter and had kept himself in good shape. He moved quickly towards the man, trying to close the ground before he could compose himself and fire another shot. He was aiming towards Peter again, holding the pistol out in front of him, but that only brought the gun closer to him, exposed and undefended.

There was another loud bang as Peter collided with the man, knocking his arms sideways as he tried to grab the gun. He felt an intense burning pain in his side as they both collapsed to the floor, their arms outstretched and grappling for the gun. They hit the floor together and Peter's momentum carried them backwards, rolling over the edge of the path. They tumbled over the edge of the slope, the two men intertwined and gathering speed as they rolled down the hill. Then the man was wrenched from Peter's hands as he slammed hard into the base of a tree. A couple of seconds later he heard the deafening crack of another gun shot, and then silence.

Peter was lying on the mossy undergrowth against the tree trunk, his back aching from where he had smashed into it. He put his hand to the side of his chest where the bullet had hit him and was relieved when it came away with only a modest amount of blood on it; he was lucky enough to only have been grazed. He tried to pull himself to his feet and stumbled, falling back to his knees. He had hit his head on the way down and his vision was blurred, his ears ringing.

Slowly, he clambered back to his feet, leaning against the tree trunk for balance, and looked around. The path was about fifty feet up the hill. He turned and looked down the slope, where he could see the man lying face down on the floor. He was lying against a large tree branch on the floor and didn't seem to be moving.

He staggered towards him, his legs shaking with every step, and then dropped to his knees. With both hands he gave the body a push, rolling him over. The gun was lying underneath him, and from the state of his torso he had clearly shot himself when he crashed to a halt.

Peter rolled him back over again and pulled himself back to his feet. His vision was starting to clear, although he still had the ringing in his ears, and he started the slow trek back up the slope again. This man wasn't going to give him any more information, but maybe there was something of interest left in the cabin.

He lumbered up the hill, staggering from tree to tree for support, eventually dragging himself over the crest. As he started to near the cabin again, he realized he wasn't going to find any information there any more. Dark black smoke was rising above the tree line in front of him. He picked up speed, jogging as fast as his aching muscles would let him, but as he drew close, he could see that the cabin was well and truly ablaze. *Shit*, he thought. *I should have spent more time putting out that fire.*

Chapter 32.

Samalut, Egypt.

Jennifer awoke with a jolt as the pickup truck bounced over a large bump in the dunes. 'What?' she muttered with a shake of her head.

'Don't worry,' said Jack, 'we've just gone off road, heading towards the dig site.'

'How long have I been asleep?'

'A couple of hours.'

Jennifer rubbed her eyes and gave a brief yawn. 'How long until we get there?'

'Twenty to thirty minutes,' said Al. 'Can we just drive up, or do we need to go in slowly, lights off?'

Jack looked at Jennifer for confirmation, and then back to Al. 'Slow and quiet, I reckon. If you can drop us off a short distance away, that would be ideal. We can sneak in on foot.' He glanced towards Jennifer, and she nodded in agreement.

'Do you need me to go around, flank them?' asked Al.

'No, no, I don't think that will be necessary,' said Jack. Al's eagerness for action was starting to get on his nerves. 'We're hoping to avoid conflict if at all possible. If you could stay with the car that would be best – be ready for a quick escape if necessary.'

'Very good,' replied Al, but Jack could tell he was a little disappointed. They drove on in silence until Al started to slow the car down twenty minutes later, the noise of the engine dropping as the speed decreased. 'We are close now,' he said.

Jack looked at Jennifer. 'Can you drop us say... five hundred metres away?' Jennifer shrugged in agreement.

'Very good,' said Al. He drove on for a few more minutes before pulling to a gradual halt. 'I'll stop over there,' he said, gesturing to an outcrop of rocks in front of them. 'This should provide good cover for the car, as well as being a landmark for you to aim for on your return. You should try and make good note of your surroundings as you approach,' he added. 'It can be easy to lose your bearings out here in the desert.'

Jack and Jennifer approached the dig site slowly. They had both taken torches and held them in their hands, Al's revolver tucked securely into Jack's belt. He had loaded five bullets into the gun, leaving the chamber under the trigger empty for safety. They had left their bags in the truck for now.

Before them lay a shallow valley, a long expanse of sand bordered left and right by low hills. By the light of the moon, they could see several trenches cut through the ground where excavation had begun, and a scattering of large tents had been erected around edges of the site. In the centre, a large round area had been cleared, but it was impossible to see what had been unearthed from this distance.

The whole area was silent, with no signs of any activity. As they drew closer, they stopped at a rope cordon that had been erected around the site, attached to metal stakes every few metres. Plastic signs hung from the ropes, warning trespassers to keep out in both English and Egyptian, but these were merely a polite request and would prove no impediment to entry.

'Where do we begin?' whispered Jack.

Jennifer nodded towards one of the large tents nearest to them. 'How about there?'

They ducked under the rope and made their way towards the tent. They moved slowly and cautiously, unnerved by the stillness of their surroundings.

Jack pulled the cloth doorway open, stepping into the dark interior and then holding it for Jennifer to follow.

The inside of the tent was dirty and chaotic. Jack and Jennifer turned on their torches and scanned their surroundings. Crates were scattered all around, some open, others still closed. Jack peered into one to find a collection of digging tools: shovels, forks and trowels of differing sizes. Another contained assorted packets of food and bottles of water.

'Here, look at this,' called Jennifer softly. She was standing by a table in the centre of the room and Jack came over to see what she was looking at.

There were several items on the table: a lantern, a black combat knife with a four-inch blade and several bottles of water. It was a map that had caught her attention, however, a map of the site, or at least the parts that had been identified. There were underground rooms marked on either side of the valley, built into the hills and labelled as burial chambers. Tunnels and passageways linked the two sides, with dozens of small rooms scattered along them. The round area that they had seen uncovered was simply labelled as *The Seal.*

'Where first?' ask Jennifer. 'One of the burial chambers? Isn't that where the goodies are traditionally stored?'

'I was going to suggest The Seal myself,' said Jack. 'I was thinking–' Whatever he was about to say was cut short when a loud muffled bang reverberated up from somewhere nearby. It felt like it came from under the ground.

'What the hell was that?' hissed Jennifer.

'I think it was an explosion, somewhere underground,' replied Jack. 'Someone's here, and they're excavating in a hurry.' He rushed over to the tent entrance and pulled back the cloth covering the doorway. Across the other side of the site, he could see a cloud of dust and sand that was hanging in the air, thrown upwards by the explosion and illuminated by the moonlight. 'Over there!' he exclaimed as he set off. 'Follow me.'

Jennifer grabbed the knife from the table, slipping it into her belt and following him across the sand, crossing over the centre of the dig site towards the dust cloud. They were roughly halfway across when Jennifer grabbed Jack's hand, pulling him to a stop.

'What?' he whispered.

'The Seal,' she said, gesturing with her hand. Jack looked to his left and saw the circular area that had been excavated. It was a circular stone disk, easily thirty feet across and set two feet beneath ground level. Eight concentric circles were carved around the centre at irregular intervals, each circle bearing a single circular marking. Around the circumference were a series of symbols, each a collection of points connected by lines.

'What the hell is that?' asked Jack.

Jennifer stepped closer and then climbed down onto the stone circle to take a closer look.

'Are those...?' she muttered.

'What?'

'That one...' she said, pointing her torch at the one closest to her. 'And that one,' she added, pointing to one a few feet further away. 'Don't they look like constellations to you? That one could be Orion. And that one over there that's vaguely V-shaped could be Pisces.'

'And that one shaped like an M — that could be Cassiopeia,' said Jack. He had jumped down to join Jennifer and was walking around the edge examining the symbols. 'And there's the Big Dipper.'

'Ursa Major,' Jennifer corrected. 'But what the hell does it mean?'

'Some kind of star chart?' pondered Jack. 'Or some kind of map?'

'Maybe... but we need to keep going,' sighed Jennifer.

They hurried on towards the site of the explosion, where the clouds of dust were now starting to settle. They slowed as they approached, taking in what they could see before them. They had seen the trenches dug into the ground from afar, but now realized they were corridors that had been excavated, their stone floors and walls exposed to the air after hundreds, possibly thousands of years. At irregular intervals, doorways were built into the walls, some of which had been cleared out, others full of dirt and yet to be emptied. In front of one of the open doorways was a blast pattern of dust and debris, clearly the location of the explosion.

Jack cautiously lowered himself down into the stone passageway and then reached up, grabbing Jennifer by the waist as she sat on the edge, helping her down. Jack held his torch out in front of him and stepped through the doorway. The air in the room was still full of dust, and he struggled not to cough, placing his left arm over his mouth to keep out the sand.

Jennifer joined him in the room as he shone his torch around the walls. They were standing in a plain stone chamber over twenty feet in either direction, a flat low ceiling overhead. In the centre sat a plinth; if there had been a coffin or sarcophagus there at any point, it had already been removed. The walls of the room were made from large sandstone bricks, but Jack's torch illuminated a gaping hole in the rear wall. Rubble had been strewn around the room, but the majority was on the other side of the wall. At least it seemed to be someone trying to break their way in, rather than *something* trying to break out.

Jack strode purposefully across the room, stopping when he reached the threshold. The light from his torch revealed a rough stone corridor extending away from them, gradually descending as it disappeared into darkness. From far away, they could just make out voices, retreating into the distance.

'A hidden passageway?' exclaimed Jack.

'Let's go,' said Jennifer, taking the lead as she ducked through the hole and stepped into the passageway beyond.

They found themselves walking down a long corridor, lined with worked stone on either side and with an arched ceiling overhead. The floor was rough stone, littered with small pieces of masonry, parts of the ceiling that had collapsed. They hurried down the passageway until it reached a crossroads, splitting into three.

Jennifer stopped, contemplating which path to take. She listened for a moment and then cast her torch on the floor. A trail of footprints was clearly visible in the dust and dirt, disturbed for the first time in millennia.

'Forwards,' she said, taking the lead once more.

They pushed on again, only slowing once a room became visible in the darkness: a doorway fifty feet away, illuminated by a flickering light. They could hear a low rumbling sound from within, the noise of stone grating against stone. As the noise stuttered and then stopped, they could hear the voices again, louder than before.

They both turned their torches off, not wanting to announce their presence. Jennifer stayed in front as they advanced along the corridor, desperate for any chance to get a clue to Bill's whereabouts.

As they neared the doorway, they realized the room beyond was unoccupied; there were no signs of movement within, and the voices, while louder than before, still sounded a little way off. The room itself was illuminated with four burning torches, one on each wall, casting flickering shadows around a chamber that was cluttered with objects. Jennifer stepped inside and realized with astonishment what they were — an archaeologist's dream come true. In the centre of the room sat a stone sarcophagus sur-rounded by burial treasures: canopic jars, stone boxes, bowls and pottery, tools and weapons, some remnants that might have once been cloth. In one corner lay several skeletons draped in tattered remains, possibly the servants of whoever had been buried here. Another doorway led from the far side of the chamber into a narrow corridor.

'This stuff must be worth a fortune,' muttered Jack.

'A king's ransom,' replied Jennifer.

'But whatever they're after, it wasn't any of this,' said Jack.

Their attention was drawn to the far side of the room as the low rum-bling sound resumed, louder than before. They could see the doorway narrowing, a stone wall sliding across to cover it once more.

Jack and Jennifer glanced at each other wordlessly and then sprinted for the corridor, the doorway slowly narrowing even as they looked at it.

As he darted across the crowded room with Jennifer just behind him, Jack noticed movement out of the corner of his eye but it was too late. From behind a tall sarcophagus flew a man, crashing into Jack and knocking him to the floor.

Jack scrambled to his feet to see that his assailant was already back on his own. He was dressed in brown trousers and white shirt, a turban wrapped around his head and face. In one hand, he held a curved knife, brandishing it menacingly before him.

Jennifer's momentum had carried her beyond the two men and she skidded to a halt, feet away from the doorway. It was barely two feet wide. She turned to face Jack.

'Go!' cried Jack with a wave of his arm. 'I'll be right behind you.'

Jennifer nodded, and stepped gingerly through the doorway, desperate not to lose their quarry.

Jack looked at the man standing between him and the ever-narrowing doorway, and then took a step backwards. The turbaned man advanced, passing the knife from hand to hand threateningly. As he drew closer, Jack suddenly remembered what Al had given him. He was holding his torch in his right hand and he lifted it up, throwing it at the man. He instinctively raised an arm to protect his face, and as he did this Jack reached for the revolver tucked into his belt, pulling it out and aiming it towards the man in a single fluid motion. He just had time to see the man bearing down on him as he pulled the trigger.

He had expected a deafening roar in the small confines of the room, but instead... nothing; just a dull click. *Shit.* He'd left the first chamber empty. It was too late for another shot. The man had swung his leg around in a wide roundhouse kick, neatly making contact with Jack's hand and sending the gun clattering into a dark corner of the room. Then the man spun again, his outstretched leg sweeping low as he crouched, knocking Jack's legs away from underneath him. He fell backwards onto the floor with a crash, landing on a piece of pottery and sending shattered shards flying – a priceless item of antiquity rendered into pieces.

The man stepped closer, brandishing his knife and ready to pounce. Jack grabbed a small clay pot from the floor, throwing it at the man's head. The man instinctively brought his hands up to protect himself, surprised by the attack. The pot collided with his forearm, shattering into fragments, and the knife fell from his hands, tumbling to the floor.

Jack scrambled to his feet as the man collected himself. The dagger lay on the floor between them, but the attacker spared it barely a glance, instead advancing towards Jack, his eyes focused solely on his prey. Behind him, Jack could see that the doorway was now only a foot across.

Jack held his hands up, ready to either defend or attack, but the man sprung forwards with lightning reflexes, aiming a fist towards his head. It was too fast to dodge, and the blow struck cleanly on the side of his temple, sending him staggering backwards. He dropped to his knees from the force of the blow, the room swinging before his eyes. He tried to stand up, but a savage kick caught him in the side, knocking him over and onto the floor.

Jack was seeing double, and he scuttled away from both his attackers, rolling over and crawling along the floor, any rational plan of attack now gone. Another kick caught him in the ribs, rolling him over, and he looked up at the blurred outlines of his attacker. He had retrieved his knife, and now he bent down, grabbing Jack by the collar and pulling him from the floor.

As he was lifted up, Jack flailed about with his hands, desperately trying to find anything to defend himself with. His fingers wrapped around something cold and solid, and he grabbed it, frantically swinging it in a wild arc towards his attacker. The thick clay pot smashed against the side of the man's head, shattering into a myriad of pieces from the force of the blow. The attacker stumbled, momentarily stunned, letting go of Jack and falling to his hands and knees.

Jack seized his moment of advantage, rolling away from the man and then pulling himself up onto unsteady feet. He reached for the first item that came to hand and found a canopic jar. He lifted it up and then brought it down with as much strength as he could muster, just as his attacker started to raise himself up off the floor. It collided with his head with a dull thud and the man collapsed back down again. This was followed by another loud crash as the door finished its slow crawl across the passageway and the low rumbling ceased.

Jack dropped to his knees as his legs buckled underneath him, then onto his hands. His head was still ringing, his vision blurred, and his side was killing him; he wondered whether the attacker had broken one of his ribs.

Using a large stone container for support, he pulled himself up off the floor and then kicked the man gently, prodding him to see if he moved. When he remained perfectly still, Jack squatted down next to him and rolled him over onto his back. He was still breathing, slow shallow breaths. He removed the man's belt and then rolled him over onto his front again, pulling his arms tight behind his back and using the belt to tie them there. With the man restrained, he picked up his torch, then the knife, and then located the revolver in the corner of the room. He stowed the gun in his pocket and the knife in his belt, and held the torch in his hand.

He staggered over to the wall, which now covered the passageway, shining his torch onto it. The surface of the stone was covered in carvings, ancient Egyptian hieroglyphics as well as many other glyphs that looked vaguely familiar, probably from one of the many occult tomes he had studied over the years in the course of their adventures. In the centre of the door were four concentric circles, each with a different set of inscriptions on them. The outer circle contained the same constellation-like patterns that they had seen around the Seal, about twenty in total. The next ring contained hieroglyphics, then one that looked like it depicted phases of the moon. In the centre was a final circle containing ten sets of dots representing the numbers from one to ten.

Jack ran his fingers over the circles and then tried twisting the outer one. As he gave it a firm push, the circle twisted around, rotating enough to move the constellations by one position before stopping with a loud click; it appeared to be an ancient combination lock. He tried moving the dial back to the previous position, but nothing happened. He tried pushing in the centre, in case that was a button to trigger anything; again nothing. Whatever combination the others had used, it had presumably reset itself. He performed some quick calculations in his head, looking at the number of symbols on each wheel, and quickly realized that there would be hundreds of thousands of combinations; guessing was going to get him nowhere. Realistically, he had only one way to open this door.

He stumbled back over to where he had left his attacker lying face down on the floor. He rolled him over onto his back and gave him a hard slap across the face. His head snapped to the side with the force of the blow but his eyes stayed shut, his breathing remaining slow and regular. He would have to wait until the man awoke of his own accord.

Chapter 33.

Jennifer headed off down the dark passageway, her torch the only illumination. The tunnel had been carved out of the rock, the walls and floor rough and uneven. She thought of how much manpower it would have taken to do all this by hand thousands of years ago, digging through the rock with nothing but hand tools. Then she thought of the pyramids; this would have been trivial by comparison.

It was quiet up ahead now, with no sounds of speech or movement. She moved as quickly as she dared while trying to keep her own noise to a minimum. She really didn't want to walk into another ambush.

It didn't take her long to reach the end of the corridor. In front of her, Jennifer could see the passageway opening into a large room. She approached cautiously, switching off her torch as she realized that dull illumination was coming from within, an eerie yellow-green light spilling out into the tunnel. As she reached the doorway and peered through, she could see an ornate room. The walls and floor directly in front of her were constructed from worked stone, bricks and tiles made from a rough off-white rock. The other side of the room, however, was far more ornate. Near the rear of the chamber, the wall on the left contained two huge stone arms made from a smooth midnight-black stone. This in turn extended into the body of a naked woman overhead, before two legs returned to the floor on the other side; the crude image of a woman bent over backwards across the room. Two passageways exited the room: one between her arms, the other between her legs. The far wall, situated under the huge black torso, was covered in hundreds of small hieroglyphs. Standing in front of it was a rough stone altar, a couple of large glow sticks lying on its surface, the source of the ghostly emerald light that illuminated the room. Everything in the room was covered in a thick layer of dust and dirt. Through this, she could see a trail of footprints leading across the room and then out between the colossal stone arms.

Jennifer slowly followed the footprints, their outlines becoming clearer as she moved across the room. It was hard to be sure, but they looked like several different trails – definitely more than one person. Standing underneath the huge carving, she shone her torch upwards, and in its light she could see that the body of the woman was covered with hundreds of little stars, small flecks of bright white stone embedded in the black onyx. She turned the torch off again and stepped into the passageway, inching her way slowly towards another room less than twenty feet away, illuminated in the same sickly yellow-green light.

This room was smaller than the last, filled with four rows of stone benches and two wide stone columns in the centre. She ducked into the room, crouching down behind the nearest bench and hoping her entrance hadn't been noted.

Muttered words drifted across from the far side of the room. She remained silent, hunched behind the pillar, until she was sure that no one had spotted her. Slowly, she peered out, keeping low on her hands and knees. By the light of more glow sticks, she could see Randolph standing on the far side of the room. He was standing close to the wall, inspecting it closely and running his hands over the stone as if trying to find something.

To his side stood an olive-skinned woman with dark hair. She was older now, but Jennifer thought she recognized her; she was the woman who had whisked Randolph away from the dreamlands after they had left Aloysius's temple. She was squatting down, looking through a large notebook that lay on the floor. Jennifer couldn't see what was written within but the book looked old, the large pages aged and worn.

Randolph stepped back from the wall and bent over, pulling a glass bottle from his backpack before removing the cork and taking a swig from it.

He offered it to his companion who accepted gracefully, taking a mouthful of the clear liquid before handing it back. Randolph re-inserted the cork and placed it back in his backpack.

'What do you think?' asked Randolph. 'Is this the place?' The woman said nothing for a moment, obviously deep in thought. 'Well?' added Randolph, clearly impatient.

'Yes,' said the woman eventually. 'I believe it is.' She had a Mediterranean accent that Jennifer couldn't quite place. 'You should look for a sequence of hieroglyphs that look like...' She consulted the book again. 'First, a line with a bump. Then a human face above an oval mouth, a lion lying down and two reed leaves. Then a semi-circle over an incomplete rectangle. Finally, a loaf of bread on a mat with a semi-circle and square underneath.'

Randolph started scouring the wall, trying to find the symbols. 'I can't see it,' he muttered, more to himself than to his companion. The woman appeared to be scribbling something on a piece of paper.

Jennifer decided to get closer, slowly crawling forwards towards the next stone bench. She inched towards it with painstaking slowness until she finally arrived, Randolph and his associate still oblivious to her presence. She took shelter behind the bench, but as she put her weight against it, part of the desiccated stone crumbled away, falling to the floor. There was a muffled crack as it hit the ground and broke into several pieces.

Randolph and the woman whirled around. 'Who's there?' shouted Randolph. 'Show yourself.'

Fuck it, thought Jennifer. She drew the knife from her belt and stood up, stepping out of the shadows to confront the pair of them. 'Where is he, you bastard?' she growled.

'Who?' replied Randolph, looking left and right, genuine confusion clearly visible on his face.

'Bill, who else?' she replied.

Randolph smiled, a look of realization spread wide across his face as he composed himself. 'He's not here. If you've come looking for him, I'm afraid this has all been a bit of a wild goose chase.'

'Where is he?' she growled.

'Somewhere quite safe, I assure you – and a long way from here.'

'If you've hurt him in any way...'

'Oh, we've no interest in harming him. He's been quite useful to us in our research. You, on the other hand, have been a constant thorn in our side.'

'So what?' spat Jennifer. 'You're not going to kill me. There's no use pretending. You need me alive for your previous prophecies about Bill to come true.'

'No, your destiny lies elsewhere, it's true,' said Randolph. A thin smile had formed on his lips. 'But that doesn't mean we can't hurt you, imprison you.' He turned and looked at his partner.

'Can I?' she asked demurely.

'Be my guest.'

The dark haired woman advanced towards Jennifer, pushing her sleeves up her arms as if to prepare for physical exertion.

Jennifer held the knife out in front of her, waving it back and forth to show she meant business. The woman continued towards her, only stopping when she was four feet away. She stood hunched, her legs spread apart and bent, ready to pounce. She was staring intently at Jennifer, as if trying to size her up.

'You come any closer and I'll kill you,' muttered Jennifer. 'Just ask Randolph. He knows I'm capable of it.'

'Oh yes, quite capable,' chuckled Randolph's voice from the back of the room.

The woman just smiled though, a thin steady smile. She took a sudden step forwards, and when Jennifer reacted to this, she moved back again, stepping gracefully to the side and twisting around to face her again.

She took another lunge forwards, feinting with her other foot this time, before stepping back and twisting around again. Slowly, she started to circle around Jennifer, never taking her eyes from her.

'Stop playing with your food, my dear,' called Randolph. 'We've got work to do.'

She lunged forwards again with her left leg, Jennifer taking a counter-step and raising her arm to defend herself again, but this time the woman didn't step back. Instead, she brought her right leg forwards, sweeping it in a fast, low arc.

Jennifer saw it coming, but couldn't react fast enough. She took half a step backwards, managing to take most of her weight off her foot before it was knocked away from underneath her. She still stumbled back, barely managing not to fall. As she swayed precariously, the woman pounced with panther-like reflexes. She grabbed her arm and twisted it back, forcing her to relinquish her grip on the knife. It fell to the floor with a clatter, and as it did so, her other fist flew rapidly through the air. It connected hard with the side of her head and Jennifer reeled. She could see stars in front of her eyes and the whole room was spinning before her. She tried to face her opponent but could no longer focus on her. She felt as if she was about to collapse when the woman's foot struck her stomach, sending her flying backwards across the room and into the wall, where she fell to the floor like a rag doll.

Jack was sitting on the floor next to his unconscious attacker, patiently waiting for him to regain consciousness. But as the minutes dragged on, it became clear that he was unlikely to wake of his own accord any time soon. Jack was growing restless. He hated waiting here, powerless, while anything could be happening to Jennifer.

He stood up and started to pace up and down the room, but that was achieving nothing. He needed to *do* something. Then he had an idea. He checked the restraints on the turbaned man, then turned and left the room, backtracking until he reached the surface. Once there, he headed back to the large stone disk known only as *The Seal.*

As he reached it he stopped, looking down at the huge stone circle and the inscriptions carved into it. He quickly rifled through his pockets, and found a half-chewed plastic biro. Then he checked his pockets for something to write on, considering some of the notes in his wallet before deciding to simply use the back of his hand.

He scratched away on his skin, making a crude representation of the symbols that were carved into the stone. Surely these must be related to the constellations present on the locked doorway – some kind of key or primer.

When he was sure he'd done the best he could, he scrambled back to the tomb, clambering back along the passages as fast as he could manage with the pain still aching in his head and ribs.

But as he arrived back at the room, he stopped short in shock. The doorway stood open and three figures were standing before him: Randolph,

Jennifer and another woman. Jennifer's hands were tied behind her back and a strip of cloth was stretched across her mouth, tied tightly behind her head to gag her.

Randolph was holding an automatic pistol in his hand, casually aimed in the direction of Jack. The woman was holding Jennifer's upper arm in one hand, Jennifer's knife in the other.

'Ah, Mr Knight,' said Randolph. 'We were beginning to wonder where you'd got to. I didn't think you were the type to abandon your wife in her hour of need.'

'Are you okay?' Jack called out to Jennifer, ignoring Randolph for now. Jennifer nodded her head, grunting something angrily through the gag.

'Your gun, if you will,' said Randolph, gesturing towards the gun, which protruded from Jack's belt. 'And the knife. Throw them towards me, on the floor. *Slowly...*'

Jack did as he was asked, pulling out the gun and throwing it to the floor, quickly followed by the knife. Randolph looked towards his partner, giving her a brief nod. She let go of Jennifer before stepping over and collecting the weapons. She placed them both in her backpack, keeping Jennifer's knife in her hands.

'I have a little job for you,' said Randolph.

'Why should I help you?' spat Jack.

'Because I'm the one with the gun,' replied Randolph simply. 'And your wife as a hostage. Come now.'

Randolph led Jack through the doorway and then back to the room where Jennifer had been captured. There was now a dark doorway open in the rear wall, a hidden passageway that had been revealed. Randolph waved his gun, gesturing for Jack to proceed. Jack did as he was directed, crossing over to the far side of the room, and the others followed. He stopped in the doorway and shone his torch into the darkness. The walls were sandstone bricks, thick with cobwebs, and the floor was covered in a deep layer of sand and dust. God knows when anyone had last been down there. Randolph's partner pulled Jennifer to a halt next to one of the pillars, and then stood next to her, holding the knife to her side.

'What now?' said Jack, fearing the worst.

'What we're after is down that tunnel somewhere,' said Randolph. 'You will fetch them for us. You know what they are.'

'The orbs,' said Jack. 'The *Aztria*.'

Randolph gave a little nod of acknowledgement. 'You *have* been doing your homework, haven't you? Yes, according to our research, there are two stored down here.'

'So what? You need someone else to do the dirty work for you?' Randolph gave him a little shrug. 'What if I refuse?'

Randolph lifted up the gun, pointing it at Jack.

'I'm guessing that whoever goes stands a good chance of not coming back – otherwise you'd be doing it yourself. So why should I? What's to stop you killing me anyway when I bring them out?'

'Maybe I will, maybe I won't,' said Randolph. 'But if you do bring them out, I promise to leave your wife alone.'

They both turned to look back at Jennifer. Randolph's partner was still holding the knife to her ribs.

'You're bluffing,' said Jack. 'I know you won't kill her.'

Randolph gave a quick nod to his partner. She grabbed Jennifer roughly, twisting her around to face the other way. Jack could hear a muffled cry, Jennifer calling his name through her gag.

'You're right, of course. She cannot die just yet, and not at my hands. But I could still make life very *unpleasant* for her. Show him an example, Ania,' he said, nodding again to his partner.

Ania pushed Jennifer against the stone column, holding her firmly in place with her free hand. She took the knife and started to drag the tip along the length of Jennifer's forearm, the blade ripping effortlessly through the skin. Jennifer gave a muffled scream as the blood ran down her arm, dripping into a small puddle on the floor.

'Stop it!' shouted Jack.

'Enough,' said Randolph, and Ania stopped, removing the knife. 'I think I have made my point? Or do we need another demonstration?'

Jack shook his head. 'No, I'll go.'

'Excellent.'

'Any clues as to what I might expect? Are we talking Tutankhamun's curse, or Indiana Jones-style adventures?'

Randolph used his gun to point to the floor next to Jack, and Jack turned to look. A large notebook sat on the floor, open on a page full of hieroglyphics. 'That may help,' said Randolph. 'It got us this far.'

Jack knelt down and picked up the book. It was old and bound in scruffy leather, many of its yellowing pages separated from the spine. He flicked through it quickly, page after page of faded spidery handwriting with the occasional hand-drawn illustration. 'This is meant to help?'

'Maybe, maybe not. Take it or leave it – I care not. I care only for the *Aztria.*'

Jack sighed and stood up, holding the book to his chest. 'I don't suppose it can hurt,' he muttered, before turning and stepping into the dark passage-way.

'Before I go,' said Jack, 'What about Bill? Where is he?'

'Somewhere quite safe, far, far from here,' said Randolph. 'He's in no imminent danger... unlike the two of you. He wouldn't be my immediate concern, if I were you.'

'You obviously don't have children of your own,' muttered Jack.

Randolph gave a small mirthless laugh. 'No. And if you ever want yours to see you again, I'd get going.'

Chapter 34.

Jack cautiously made his way down the corridor, the light of the torch his only illumination. The pain in his head and ribs was slowly subsiding. Hopefully they weren't broken after all.

The floor was made of uneven stones, slippery from the dust and sand. He peered into the darkness and could just see the corridor make a right-angled turn to the right. By the light of his torch, he could see several small dark spots on the wall ahead, but from this distance was unable to clearly distinguish what they were.

He advanced along the bumpy floor, his torch in one hand and the book clasped against his chest in the other. Then, as he stepped on a raised stone, he felt it depress as his weight pressed down upon it. A loud click echoed through the dark tunnel and then there was a sudden brief swoosh. Jack saw a blur of movement through the shadows and felt a blow push hard against him. He looked down to see an arrow sticking out of the book he was holding. He threw himself against the wall, pressing himself flat against it in case of any further arrows.

After several seconds of waiting, he decided it was over. He crouched down and took a good look at the arrow. It looked crude and ancient, more of a bolt than a true arrow: a sharpened metal stake about a foot long. It had been fired with enough force to pierce the back cover and travel through all the pages, the very tip of the metal barely visible as it poked through the leather front. Jack grabbed hold of it, twisting and pulling it out of the book, laying it on the floor next to the wall.

He resumed his quest, now proceeding more carefully towards the bend in the corridor, tentatively tapping the floor before him with his foot. He stood flat against the wall, shuffling along sideways with the painstaking slowness of a man trying to edge his way through a minefield. When he reached the end without incident, he carefully examined the wall; the dark spots were small holes in the wall, pipes through which the bolt had been fired. He didn't know why only one of the bolts had been fired. Maybe it had broken over the centuries; maybe they were triggered by different stones or had simply fired already. Regardless, it didn't really seem to matter anymore.

He shone his torch around the bend in the corridor and saw that it continued a short distance before opening into a dark chamber. He slowly shuffled sideways along the corridor, staying flat against the wall until he reached the doorway and peered inside.

It opened into a circular chamber forty feet across. Evenly distributed around the room were seven arched stone doorways, each containing a solid stone door: eight exits from the room if you included the passageway he was standing in.

Cautiously, he took a step inside. Then another, and then another, until he was standing in the centre. By the light of his torch, he could see a large cartouche on the floor containing two hieroglyphs:

He continued to cast the torch around the room, and the light picked out a single hieroglyph carved into each of the doors. There were seven in total, each depicting a different type of man:

He stepped towards one to examine it more closely. Each hieroglyph was a foot high, standing above a hole almost four inches across. He tried peering down the hole with the help of his torch, but found it difficult to make anything out. It was about two feet deep and there was definitely *something* at the end, but he couldn't tell what.

One by one, he examined all the doorways; they were all the same except that each bore a different symbol. To progress, he presumably had to pick one; but what did they mean?

He opened the notebook that Randolph had given him and was flicking through the book when several sheets dropped out. They were loose, inserted in the back cover, and he picked them up, unfolding them. They were photocopied pages, copied from something called *Gardiner's Sign List*. Jack scanned through the sheets before realizing they were a list of hieroglyphs and their common meanings.

He scanned through the list, looking for the two symbols on the floor. The fact they were in a cartouche meant that they represented a royal name, and it didn't take Jack long to find a meaning he could relate to: the *Black Pharaoh*. According to Silas, this had been a name by which Nyarlathotep had been known in ancient Egyptian times.

Next he searched through the list for each of the symbols on the doors. It took a little while, but he eventually established that each was a different type of profession: God, Ruler, Servant, King, Guard, Soldier and Ambassador.

Okay, he thought to himself. *If this is a temple to Nyarlathotep, then god is presumably the correct symbol to his treasures.* The door with the *god* symbol stood opposite the entrance. He approached it cautiously and crouched down to peer into the hole. Once again, he shone the torch into the opening, squinting and straining his eyes to try and discern exactly what was in there, but all he could make out was some kind of thin metal bar lying horizontally across the end of the shaft. With increasing trepidation, he started to insert his hand into the hole, slowly pushing it deeper and deeper until his arm was inserted almost up to his shoulder.

He could feel the bar at the end now, a cold metal pole about an inch in diameter. He pondered what to do with it. He tried pushing it, then slipping his fingers around it and pulling: nothing. Then he thought to twist it. He held it tight and tried to twist it clockwise. It was stiff, untouched for God knows how long, but with a creak and a groan it started to move.

As he strained, using all his strength to rotate the bar, a memory surfaced of something that Silas had told Jennifer; Nyarlathotep was a servant of the outer gods, a messenger. He let go of the pole, yanking his hand violently from the hole. He pulled so hard that he stumbled over backwards onto the floor, a sound of metal scraping on stone echoing from the hole as he fell away. He sat up again suddenly, looking at his forearm. There was a shallow cut across his arm, halfway between the wrist and elbow. It had been a close call; if he had been a split second later, would he have lost his arm?

He took a minute to regain his composure, and then looked for the door bearing the symbol that mean *servant*. This was two doors along, on the right-hand side from where he had entered.

Jack wiped the sweat from his brow and then slid his hand into this door's hole until he could again grasp the lever at the end. His arm was once more deep into the hole, almost up to the shoulder. He prayed that he was right this time and grasped the lever hard, twisting it firmly. As the lever started to move, he felt something tighten around his wrist, but it felt unlike the previous occasion. This was the moment of truth. Ignoring the constricting pressure, which felt as if it was going to swallow his arm, he gave the lever a firm final twist.

A deep click reverberated from inside the wall, and the force on his arm lessened. From somewhere behind the wall came the sound of a deep thud followed by a low rumble. He pulled his arm out, visually inspecting it to ensure it was okay, as the wall in the doorway gradually started to rise up and into the ceiling.

Jack looked down at the torch in his hand. Maybe it was just nerves, but he was sure that its light wasn't as bright as before. If the batteries were dying, he needed to get a move on before he became lost down here in the darkness.

He stepped through the doorway and down a short uneven stone corridor into another chamber. This one was smaller again, only fifteen feet across. On the far side was a statue of black stone standing eight feet tall. It was an Egyptian pharaoh, towering over Jack with his two hands held out flat before him. There was something creepy about the statue that Jack couldn't quite put his finger on, but his attention was drawn towards its outstretched hands; resting on either palm was a metallic orb about three inches across. This was what he was after… what Randolph was after.

Jack shone the torch around the room, looking into the dark recesses for anything untoward but saw nothing. Cautiously, he took a tentative step forwards towards the statue. Then another. He kept the torch aimed towards the floor as he went, carefully examining the stone tiles for any signs of traps.

Once he had halved the distance to the statue, he looked up at it again, using his torch to illuminate its face. Now it was clearer as to why it had unnerved him. The statue itself was detailed and ornate with intricate details on its headdress and robe, but the face itself was blank. It had not been removed or defaced, but was deliberately smooth and featureless, devoid of any eyes, nose or mouth. This was surely a temple belonging to *The Faceless*, then. Despite the lack of eyes, Jack felt uncannily like it was watching him. He kept averting his own eyes from that face and instead focused on the outstretched hands and the orbs that sat upon them.

He inched closer, until the statue's hands were within reaching distance, and then stopped. It was too quiet. It all seemed too easy. He looked around again, checking for any signs of movement but saw none. His exit seemed clear behind him. The light from his torch was definitely dimming though; he was sure of it now.

Hesitantly, he raised his right hand and reached out to touch the orb in the statue's left. As his finger made contact and brushed against the smooth metal surface, he felt a small jolt of electricity. He instinctively snatched his hand back, but when nothing else happened he reached forwards again, slipping his fingers over the orb and wrapping his fist around it.

The metal of the orb seemed warm to the touch and impossibly smooth. It felt as though it were covered in oil, but when he brought back his arm and opened his fist, he could see that it was perfectly dry. Its surface was covered in minute runes and symbols, intricately carved into every inch of the surface. As he focused on the surface of the orb, he seemed drawn to those patterns etched on its surface. The rest of the room seemed to fade away into shadow, and his own breathing seemed impossibly loud, the sound of his heartbeat echoing heavily in his head.

From the darkness of the shadows, he could start to hear whispers. Low, dry murmurs with the intonation of a human voice, but not in any language he could recognize. Out of the corners of his vision, the shadows started to move, swirling and fading as if whatever lurked within them were no more substantial than smoke. His eyes flicked back and forth, but as he looked towards the shadows, the movement seemed to fade away, as if it had all just been an illusion.

His heart was racing now, the beating sound thumping in his head, and under it, the growing sound of the whispers, growing not in volume but in number. From behind him, the sounds seemed to increase as if drawing nearer, a thousand voices whispering in some forgotten tongue, and as they did so the fear at the back of his mind began to grow in unison. He span around to face the corridor, so his back was now to the statue, but still the voices grew, and still they came from behind him, accompanied by an increase in the flittering movements in the shadows. An unnerving dread was steadily building from the pit of his stomach, threatening to overwhelm him. He felt like he was going to throw up.

Jack span back round again, slamming the orb back onto the pharaoh's outstretched hand. As he did so, the room flashed back to normality; it was as if someone had flicked on a light switch, the light banishing the shadows to oblivion.

The feeling of fear and dread slowly dissipated and he could feel his heartbeat decreasing, its volume fading away as the room returned to normal. He wiped his brow with his forearm and it came away damp with sweat. He needed a plan.

He looked down at his torch, the light growing dimmer still; it was now a dull yellow. 'Grab them and run like hell,' he muttered to himself. 'How's that for a plan?'

He turned back around so he was facing the Black Pharaoh again, gazing up into his featureless face. He took the torch, placing it between his teeth so that both hands were free, and then reached out towards the statue. He held both his hands above the orbs, closed his eyes and began to count. When he reached four, he grabbed an orb in each hand.

The jolt this time was stronger, making his hands clench tighter and his arms jerk backwards. He span around to face the exit as the shadows seemed to come alive, as if darkness itself were oozing out of the walls. He stumbled towards the corridor as the voices rose up from the depths of the earth, like a huge crowd audible from miles away, but drawing closer with every breath.

A black mist was descending all around, obscuring the walls of the room as he staggered back into the circular chamber with the seven doorways. He paused momentarily to catch his breath, which was proving awkward with the torch in his mouth. Out of the corners of his vision he could swear that the ebony mist was forming shapes, stretching into twisted and contorted faces. The voices were louder now, a rising cacophony of whispered cries, dry and hoarse.

The mist was concealing the exits from the room so that he could no longer see where the exit was, but he could remember its location: two doors to his left, a ninety-degree path. He closed his eyes to ignore the churning shapes all around him, growing more distinct with every passing moment. He moved quickly, doing his best to ignore the sensations he felt on his body, as if he were being stroked by something immensely light and delicate.

He opened his eyes to confirm he was now standing in front of an empty passageway. From right behind him, he could hear a faint voice whispering, calling out to him. Instinctively, unable to stop himself, he twisted his neck to peer behind.

From out of the seething blackness, now more like thick smoke than a mist, a face formed – a screaming corpse-like visage baring his teeth from within his blackened eyeless skull.

Jack screamed as he felt silky hands brushing his limbs, and the torch fell from his mouth, clattering to the floor where it rolled away into the darkness. He ran blindly down the corridor, bouncing off the walls. One arm smashed into the wall as he reached the turn in the corridor, but he ignored the pain, stumbling along as fast as he could.

Ahead through the roiling darkness, he thought he could now see light; it was as if he were looking though a thick woollen mask, the light blurred and obscured. Despite his rising levels of panic, he could now make out individual voices from among the crowd. The words were foreign and indistinct with one exception; they were all calling his name.

As he lurched forwards, he tripped, stumbling and falling to the ground. His arms smacked the cold stone of the floor and the orbs fell from his grasp. As they rolled away along the floor, the darkness faded, bringing with it the flickering torchlight of the room where he had left Randolph. With a final ghostly cry of his name, the voices died away, as if banished by the light.

Chapter 35.

Oxfordshire, England.

The sun was setting below the horizon as Cross pulled her car to a halt by the side of the road. She was now at the final location on her list. She was tired, weary from spending all afternoon driving around the Oxfordshire countryside, but as she lifted up the photograph and compared it to the profile of the estate standing in front of her, her spirits lifted. This looked like it might be the place.

The building was set well back from the road, down a wide gravel path lined with tall silver birch trees on either side. She slowly drove the car down the driveway as quietly as she could before pulling over and stopping next to another parked car.

She turned off the engine and stepped out. The structure in front her was a wide brown-brick building with a triangular peaked roof on either side. A large solid set of double doors stood in the centre. It was dark, with no signs of life inside, and she pulled out her torch. First she went to the car parked next to hers. Its bonnet was still warm; whoever it belonged to couldn't have arrived long ago. She took out her notepad, jotting down its registration, before heading towards the front door.

She scanned the front of the building with her torch, the light eventually stopping above the door. There was a decorative bas-relief there, an arch patterned with circles and triangles, but in the centre was the same triskelion that had been on the book and business card. This was the place. She was expecting to find the door locked, but tried the handle anyway. To her surprise, it turned, the door swinging inwards with a low creak.

'Hello?' she called as she stepped inside, but there was no reply. She felt stupid announcing her presence, but she had to remind herself she wasn't on official police business. She had no probable cause, no search warrant. Hell, she could probably get suspended just for being in here.

The inside of the building was all white marble, apart from the floor, which was tiled with black and white squares, like a chessboard stretching off in all directions. On the far side of the room, a stone staircase ascended away from her, reaching a landing before splitting left and right, both sets of steps leading up to a balcony on the floor above. To either side of the staircase stood wooden double doors, both shut. On the rear wall, hanging above the stairs, was a large painting. It depicted a man wrapped in a faded yellow cloak sitting upon a throne, his face hidden by a grotesque wooden mask. Cross approached carefully, letting the light of her torch fall upon a small brass plaque mounted on the wooden frame. It was titled *The King in Yellow.*

This was definitely the place.

She knew she ought to leave, maybe find some reason to call for official backup, or at least call Jack and Jennifer to search the place together. She turned back towards the front door, but before she could take a step towards it, a scream echoed through the quiet air from somewhere beneath her. It was muffled but still rang out in the darkness, stopping as suddenly as it had started.

She passed the torch into her left hand and drew her telescopic truncheon, extending it to its full length with a flick of her wrist. There was someone here, and they sounded like they needed help. She just hoped she would be able to help without falling victim to the same fate as them.

She stepped back down the stairs and tried the doorway to her left, looking for a way down to wherever that scream had come from. The door opened into another large room, some kind of auditorium. The centre of the room was tiled with the same black and white marble squares, but to her left and right were rows of seats upholstered in a red velvet cloth; they rose up as they neared the walls, to give those at the rear a better view of whatever took place in this room. Two large chandeliers hung from the ceiling, but there were also sconces set along the wall, each of them holding remnants of large red candles.

At the far end of the room was a stage. A large crimson curtain hung from the ceiling, stretching the entire width of the room and obscuring whatever lay beyond. In front of the stage an aisle ran across the room, doors on either side.

She crept along the centre of the room until she reached the stage. Curiosity getting the better of her, she reached out, taking hold of the curtain. It felt soft in her hand and she was just about to lift it up to see what lay beyond when there was another scream, louder this time. It came from somewhere behind the door to her left. She let go of the curtain; it would have to wait.

As she approached the door, she slowed, carefully taking hold of the handle. She could hear nothing on the other side and she twisted it slowly, trying to make as little noise as possible.

The door opened into an office. Four groups of desks were positioned around the corners of the room, each of them clean and tidy with just a dark computer screen and keyboard sitting next to an angle-poise lamp.

In the middle of the room was a wide space. A sizable Persian carpet had been hastily rolled up, shoved to one side between two floor-standing gothic candle holders, each made of solid iron and over four feet tall. Where the rug had been was now bare floor, revealing an open trap door.

Cross crept across the room until she could peer down through the hole in the floor; a set of wooden steps descended steeply into the darkness. From somewhere far below, she could see a faint flicker of light and hear muffled voices, too faint to clearly understand. With her truncheon held firmly in one hand and her torch in the other, she took a couple of tentative steps down. When nothing untoward happened, she continued, descending under the ground.

The steps descended for twenty feet before levelling out into a short corridor, which then opened into a circular chamber. This room was almost fifty feet across with a low domed ceiling, four arched corridors leading off from each side. Between each corridor a set of rusty manacles hung from the wall. They were thankfully empty, but it was what Cross saw in the middle of the room that unsettled her the most.

An eight-foot-tall obsidian statue was standing on a plinth. It was clearly the same robed figure as the portrait in the lobby, but whereas the painting had looked almost regal, the statue before her was the stuff of nightmares. The hooded figure's face was obscured, but from under the hood slid thin wispy tentacles. These were accompanied by thicker tentacles flowing out from under the base of the billowing robe, winding around the pedestal and falling to the floor. One hand of the creature was outstretched towards her, beckoning her into the room, while the other held a metal sword, the tip of which rested on the pedestal between his feet. On the top of his head sat a dark metal crown, its viciously sharp points making it look more like a weapon than regalia of state.

Apart from the metal sword and crown, the statue was made of stone and extremely detailed. It looked incredibly realistic, as if it could come to life at any instant. The portrait upstairs was obviously the public façade of this monster, whereas this was its true identity. Cross gave it a wide berth as she tiptoed into the room. Despite not being able to see its face, she felt as if the statue was watching her, tracking her movements through its place of worship.

Another low cry made her stop in her tracks — more of a wail than a scream this time. It was from the corridor opposite, and when she turned off her torch, returning it to her pocket, she could see dim illumination from the other end of the passage.

She crept slowly down the passageway towards the light and sounds, not wanting to leave the statue directly behind her but without any real alternative. She could hear voices now, distant, but just about intelligible.

'Just tell us where they are,' came a man's voice from the darkness. 'Then I can leave and this will all be over.'

'They're not here,' whimpered another man.

'But we all know that's not true,' came the first voice again. 'They're here, and one of you will tell me exactly where.' There was something about that voice that bothered Cross. It seemed familiar. She felt like she ought to be able to place it, but despite racking her brain, mentally flicking through all the criminals and low lifes she could think of, she still came up drawing a blank.

'I can't,' came another sobbing voice. 'I don't know where they are, *honestly.*'

'Then you are of no further interest to me,' said the first man. Cross jumped as a deafening boom rang out in the narrow tunnel, the roar of a gunshot from close by. Suddenly, she was feeling decidedly underprepared. Another scream rang out. Cross couldn't tell if it was from someone who had been shot or a witness who knew that they might be next. She stopped in her tracks, listening intently, not sure what to do next.

'Okay, okay,' she heard one of the men plead from out of the darkness. 'I'll tell you whatever you need to know. Just... just put down the gun.'

'Tell me now and I'll have no more use for the gun,' he replied in a calm, low voice. 'Where are the orbs?'

'In the statue,' whimpered the man, all the fight gone from him now. 'Grasp his hand and twist it firmly.'

This is my chance, thought Cross. *If I can get to them first, maybe we can stop them, prevent whatever they're trying to do.* She took a couple of steps backwards before turning and hurrying back to the statue as quickly and quietly as she could. She crossed over the room and turned back to face it. She closed her eyes, grasping the cold stone hand in hers, holding it tight, but when she tried to twist it nothing happened. She cursed silently, and then tried again, trying to twist the other way this time. There was a tiny sensation of movement this time. It felt like it was meant to move, but was stuck or rusted shut through disuse. She tried again, harder this time, putting all her might into it. She felt something slip, and then it was loose, the hand of the statue rotating freely.

A grating noise came from the pedestal of the statue, but this was masked by the deafening sound of two more gunshots. *Shit*, thought Cross. *They're eliminating any witnesses.* She knelt down, placing her truncheon on the floor and examining the base of the statue; she could see where two of the tentacles had moved aside, exposing a dark recess. She knew she had no time to waste and she thrust both hands into the dark space, her fingers groping around inside. Her fingertips could feel something in there and she thrust her arms deeper, grabbing them and yanking them out. As she withdrew her hands, she could see that they held two metal spheres, each about three inches in diameter and covered in intricate markings. They felt warm in her hands, unnaturally heavy, and as she knelt there, she felt a calmness rush over her. The world around her seemed faded and muted, as if nothing was real now apart from her and the orbs she held in the palms of her hands.

She was suddenly brought back to reality as another deafening gunshot rang out. But this one was closer than before. A man was standing in the corridor opposite, aiming a gun at her. She reacted instinctively, throwing one of the orbs at the man, aiming for his head. She hoped that an instinct for self-defence, coupled with his desire for the orbs would distract him long enough for her to get away.

Without waiting to see if her aim had been true, she turned and ran, grasping the second orb in her hand and leaving her truncheon on the floor. She ran for the steps, bounding up them two at a time. From somewhere behind her another shot rang out, but it hadn't hit her and she ignored it, running as fast as she could. As she emerged into the near darkness of the room above, she turned and slammed the trap door shut. There was no lock or bolt on it, so instead she grabbed hold of one of the solid iron candle holders, tipping it over and toppling it on top of the trap door. Then she ran, sprinting back to the car as fast as her legs would carry her, never slowing to look back.

As she neared the front door, she reached into her pockets, fishing out her car keys. She burst through the door and was heading for her car when she paused momentarily. On her keyring hung a small penknife, and she fumbled it open, her other hand still grasping the orb.

When she reached the space between her car and the one parked next it, she bent over and stabbed the knife into the side of the other car's front tyre. She was rewarded by a loud hiss, the wheel instantly deflating.

She unlocked her car, yanking the door open and diving inside. Not bothering with the seat belt, she threw the orb into the passenger footwell, jamming the key into the ignition. The engine burst to life and she floored the accelerator, the car flying backwards in a shower of gravel.

As she shot backwards, she looked up and saw a man emerging from the doorway, his face cloaked in shadows. As he raised the gun, she yanked the steering wheel, sending the car sideways. Midway through the turn, she stabbed on the brakes and clutch, spinning the car around. She heard another loud bang from the gun, but ignored it, focusing on the road ahead as it span through her vision. She slipped the car into first gear, jabbing the accelerator again as the car lined itself up again and gunned it, accelerating forwards now, away from the building.

There was another bang and the back window of the car exploded, fragments of glass flying everywhere, but she did her best to ignore it. The car burst onto the main road, which was thankfully free of traffic, and Cross turned hard right, skidding the car perfectly onto the middle of the road. She accelerated hard. She knew the man wouldn't be able to give chase, not with a puncture, but she still wanted to put a significant distance between them before he could get any backup.

Chapter 36.

Dig site, ten miles west of Samalut, Egypt.

Jack looked up to see Randolph sitting on a stone bench. He was holding the pistol in his hand, casually aiming it in Jack's general direction.

'What... What the...' spluttered Jack. Randolph merely gave him a quizzical look. 'What the fuck was that?' Jack finally managed.

Randolph gave him a humourless grin. 'I think you may have been in contact with the dead.'

'Ghosts?' spat Jack incredulously.

Randolph grimaced. 'More like a soul's distant echo across space and time.'

'Well, they didn't seem very happy.'

'This whole area was built on the back of slave labour,' said Randolph. 'Thousands, maybe millions must have died over the millennia at the hands of heartless pharaohs. I'm sure you'd be unhappy too if you'd been in their place.' He withdrew a velvet cloth from his pocket, carefully picking up one of the orbs with it, being careful not to touch the surface. He dropped it into his bag before doing the same with the other.

Jack slowly dragged himself up off the floor until he was standing again. He looked around the room. 'Where's Jennifer? You said you'd let her go once I returned with the orbs.'

'Ah... About that,' started Randolph. 'There's been a slight complication.'

'What do you mean,' growled Jack, taking a couple of steps towards Randolph, stopping as the gun was raised to point directly at him.

'It would appear that someone has stolen another of the *Aztria* from us. The description was a little vague, but I have a hard time believing it wasn't one of your... companions.'

'I don't know anything about that,' said Jack, with a certain degree of honesty.

'Nevertheless,' said Randolph. 'Before you get your wife back, I want *it* back.'

'But I don't know—'

'—Then find out,' snapped Randolph. 'Find your comrades, retrieve the *Aztria* from them and then we will talk again.' He looked at his watch. 'You have thirty-six hours. You'll need to make haste to get back to England.' When Jack just stood there, he raised his voice, waving the gun towards him. 'Go… if you want to see your precious wife again!'

Jack took a burning torch from the wall and set off, retracing his steps back to the camp once more. Only when he had reached the cool air of the surface did he stop and think. The tome that Randolph had given him, the one that had taken the impact of the arrow: what secrets could it hold? Would there be anything he could use to help get Jennifer or Bill back again?

He crept his way back down into the tomb, taking particular care as he neared the chamber where he had left Randolph, but the room was dark and silent now. He looked around the room by the light of his torch, and saw that on a far wall was another inscription of a doorway, hastily drawn in chalk. This was presumably how Randolph had left. He gently ran his hand across it but simply felt the solid cold stone; it was no longer operational.

He left it and headed back to the room where he had dropped the book. It was still there, lying on the floor, and he bent down to pick it up. He carried it back to the room with the gateway, and then used his torch to light the other torches that were dotted around the chamber, banishing the shadows from the room. Then he took a seat on one of the cold stone benches under a torch and started to flick through the pages of the book.

It was written in a mixture of Latin and archaic English and most of it made no sense to him, but as he reached a point just over halfway through, he spotted something he recognized. It was a sketch of a doorway, the inscriptions uncannily similar to the ones on the wall before him.

He looked at the Latin words and phrases underneath it, wracking his brain for their meaning. Then it came to him; these were the incantations to activate the doorway. He started slowly reciting the passages to himself, silently at first and then out loud as the words started to flow more easily from his lips. When he heard the words aloud, he stopped, surprised at their familiarity. He had heard these words before when he was leaving the Brotherhood's lair... and he had recorded them.

He fished his phone out of his pocket and checked the battery; there was still a little life in it. He found the video he had recorded of the cultist activating the gateway and played it back, following the words on the page as he listened; they were indeed the same.

Buoyed by the knowledge that he was on the right track, he moved over to stand in front of the doorway and recited the passage again, clumsily at first. Then he repeated himself, speaking along to the sound of the recording, trying to match the metre and rhythm like someone using an audio course to learn a new language. Again and again he repeated the words, steadily growing more fluent until suddenly the chalk lines on the wall burst into life, a flash of bright white light, as the doorway in between took on a dull glow.

With a grin on his face, Jack took a step forwards into the doorway... and smacked into the stone wall. He reached out his hand and pressed against the glowing light before him, but it felt solid, cold and unyielding. Something was different, something was wrong. Had he not been accurate enough?

He picked up the book again, scanning through the text below the passage, trying madly to discern any meaning despite his haphazard knowledge of the language. Then he hit a section he thought he understood. It talked about a *clavis* – a *key* – and described how these doorways could be locked. He slammed his hand against the wall in disgust. Without the key, he would be unable to follow Randolph; he would have to make his way back to England the old-fashioned way.

Chapter 37.

April 14th, 2017. Matford, Exeter, England.

Detective Cross drove through the night, not stopping until she skidded to a halt outside her house back in Matford. She glanced at the clock on her dashboard; it was 12:03. Slowly, she reached over and picked up the orb from the passenger footwell where it still lay.

She was tired – exhausted – but as she sat there with the orb in the palm of her hand, it seemed to be calling to her. The world outside seemed to fade away, so there was only her and the orb, drawing her in with an almost hypnotic power. She had been tired as she drove home, but she had also been pumped with adrenaline. Now, as she stared at the orb, she felt completely calm and peaceful. Her eyelids were oh so heavy, almost impossible to keep open. She could just rest here. There was nothing important she needed to do, all her worries were just fading away. The metal orb seemed to be growing warmer and heavier in her hand, almost pulsing with energy. Her eyelids drifted shut.

She jolted awake as a car door slammed nearby. Looking left and right she turned and saw two young adults climbing out of a beat-up old Peugeot. They were giggling and laughing, their hands all over each other. They walked towards one of the houses, stopping to kiss passionately on the driveway.

She turned back, and was suddenly struck by a dull ache from her left hand. The muscles were strained, her fingers clamped firmly around the orb. Slowly, she forced her hand to relax and then flexed her fingers. She reached for her handbag, opening it with her other hand and then dropped the orb gently into it. There was a dull red mark on the palm of her hand where the orb had been resting and she gave it a gentle rub. It wasn't painful, just slightly tender. She shook her hand, trying to get the blood flowing and to restore some kind of normality back to it.

The clock on her dashboard read 12:29 – it had been almost half an hour since she had arrived. Had she fallen asleep? If not, what exactly had just happened to her?

It could wait, she decided. She opened the car door and stepped out into the cold night air, clutching her handbag tightly. The two lovers seemed to have disappeared, and she made her way to her front door, unlocking it and stepping inside. The house was just as it had been when she had left it, and she turned the hallway light on. She was unnerved by what had just happened, and the bright light and relative warmth helped to calm her nerves. She stepped into the living room, turning on the lights and walking over to her drinks cabinet, where she took out a crystal glass and a bottle of single malt scotch, pouring herself a large measure. She took a deep whiff of the golden-brown liquid before taking a large sip to steady her nerves, and then set it down on the counter.

She wondered what to do with the orb and decided to hide it somewhere for now, somewhere safe until she could meet up with Jack and Jennifer. She scanned the room, searching for a hiding place until the saw a box in the drinks cabinet. It was from a bottle of scotch, a dark brown circular tube that looked to be about the right size. She opened it up and slipped the orb inside. It was a perfect snug fit, and she gently placed the box back, hiding it behind the bottles.

With the orb hidden for now, she stepped over to the desk in the corner of the room where her laptop sat. She hung her handbag over the corner of the chair and sat down, opening the laptop and tapping her fingers on the desk while it started up. When it was ready, she typed in her username and password and then stood up again, wandering across the room to retrieve her scotch, bringing it back to the desk and taking another long sip.

She started the secure networking software to connect her to the police network and logged into that as well. While it was connecting she pulled her notebook from her handbag, opening it to the page where she had written the number plate of the car from *The Unnamed*'s headquarters. She opened the vehicle registration database, carefully transcribed the details, and then clicked the button to start the search. While she waited, she took another sip of the whisky.

There was a quiet ping from her computer a few seconds later as it returned the vehicle details. *This couldn't be right*, she thought, as she looked at the information on the screen. The make and model were correct, but according to the information in front of her, it belonged to Exeter police force – *her* police force. What the hell did this mean? Was it one of their unmarked pool cars? She would need to find out who had checked it out.

Before she had a chance to do that, however, a quiet tune began to echo from the laptop's speakers; someone was trying to Skype her. Looking at the small window that popped up, she could see it was Peter White, and she clicked on the button to accept the call.

'Hi there, Peter,' she said towards the laptop, as a picture of Peter's face appeared in a window. 'Can you hear me okay?'

'I can see and hear you fine,' he said. 'I hope it's okay to call you at this time of night – I saw that you'd just come online.'

'Not a problem, how can I help?'

'I've got some good news and some bad news. The good news is that I have at least confirmed that the Brotherhood did take Jack and Jennifer's son.'

'I'm not sure that's great news.'

'We do at least know for certain we're on the right track now. They were using him for some kind of dream research. Unfortunately most of the evidence was destroyed.'

'Damn. If that's the good news, what's the bad news?'

'I just received a phone call from Jack. He's still in Egypt, but is making his way back as fast as he can... on his own.'

'What happened to Jennifer?'

'The Brotherhood have her.'

'Fuck.'

'Quite. They think one of us has one of the orbs and want to do an exchange. I had to tell him that it wasn't me. Please tell me it's you, or else it could be bad news for Jennifer.'

'Doesn't news travel fast!' she exclaimed. 'Yes, it's me. I managed to track down the set guarded by the *Subjects of Yellow*. I got away with one of them, but not without almost having my head blown off.'

'Well, that's something, at least,' said Peter. 'I know Jack was hoping to trade them for Bill... I suppose we'll see now just how good a negotiator he is.'

'Do you think he can trade it for both of them?'

'If they're that important to them... then possibly.'

'But we don't really know what they are though, do we? What the hell are we giving them? What are they going to do with them?'

'All good questions. Maybe Jack will have some more answers when he gets back, which will be... well, I suppose it's later this morning now. I'm going to meet him at his house as soon as he gets back.'

Cross nodded, taking another sip of the whisky. A high-pitched clink rang out from behind the kitchen door and she jumped, almost spilling her drink. *What the hell was that?* she thought. 'Give me a second,' she said into the laptop. 'I'll be right back.'

'Not a problem,' said Peter.

She stood up and walked over to the kitchen door, opening it and stepping through. It was dark and she flicked the light switch on.

'Jesus!' she exclaimed as she caught sight of someone standing on the far side of the room. He was in front of the rear door, which now stood ajar, the window in it broken. She relaxed slightly as she realized it was Superintendent Reynolds.

'Oh, it's you,' she said in puzzlement. 'What are *you* doing here?' Then she saw the gun he was holding in his right hand. A gun he was pointing towards her, a silencer on its end. 'What the fuck?' she muttered under her breath.

'Where is it?' he asked slowly.

'Where's what?' she replied. This wasn't making any sense to her.

'Don't play the fucking idiot with me,' he growled. 'The orb. The *Aztria*.'

Gradually, realization begun to dawn on her. 'It was you,' she said. 'This evening in Oxfordshire. You were the one who shot at me.' When he said nothing in return, she slowly began to raise her hands, taking a step backwards towards the doorway.

'Stop!' he ordered, and she did. 'Don't move any further. I don't want to shoot you, but I will if I have to.'

'And how are you going to explain that,' she said. 'Me, shot with your gun, your DNA all over the crime scene?'

'This isn't *my* gun,' he chuckled. 'It's taken from the evidence lockers. And as for your DNA... well, once I hear about your tragic death, I'll be sure to want to come and see for myself. No one would be surprised about my presence here... or any trace DNA.'

'I've hidden it well, though,' she said. 'Kill me, and you'll never find it.' She just hoped he couldn't see through her bluff.

'So where is it?' he spat. 'You haven't had enough time to take it any-where safe. It must be somewhere in this house. If you don't tell me, I'm sure it won't take me long to find it. I'll rip this place apart if I have to.'

Cross sighed, her shoulders slumping. 'It's in the living room,' she said, tipping her head backwards to indicate the room behind her. 'Shall I?' she said, taking another slow step backwards.

'Slowly,' he said. 'No sudden movements or they'll be your last.'

Slowly and deliberately, Cross took several steps backwards until she was standing in the middle of the room. Reynolds followed her as she went, keeping his distance. Calmly, she took a few more steps back, until she was standing next to the wall with Reynolds in the centre of the room.

'Okay, where is it?' he said, casting quick glances around the room, never taking his eyes off her for more than a moment.

'And if I give it to you? What then? I'm supposed to believe you'll just let me walk away?'

Reynolds smiled a humourless smile. 'No, you're right,' he said. 'You know too much now. But I can make it quick and painless. Or I can shoot you in the guts, leave you to bleed out with your stomach acid leaking all over your internal organs. Before the end, you'd be begging me to put you out of your misery.'

'So you're going to kill me either way.' It was a statement, not a question.

'I should have killed you a long time ago. You were always far too in-quisitive, sticking your nose in where it didn't belong. I wanted you dead, but they said you could be useful, and your death could create too much un-wanted attention.'

'And *they* are... the Brotherhood?' Reynolds nodded. 'So you're one of them?' Reynolds gave a small nod of acknowledgement. Cross thought for a second. 'So you're the reason the Lamarre massacre was hushed up. You're the reason from my demotion.'

'I wanted you dead, but had to settle for that instead. There's something you should know about me, though,' he added.

'What's that?'

'In the end, I *always* get what I want.'

'So, I give you the orb, and then you kill me anyway and then just carry on, business as usual?'

'Yep, and there's nothing you can do about it.' He raised the gun, aiming directly at her head. 'Now,' he said slowly and patiently, 'Give me the orb.' It was as if he were addressing a small child, or in his case a junior police officer.

'No,' she said, just as slowly and patiently. 'I think you're done here.'

'What?' he said. He seemed genuinely mystified.

'Have you got all that,' Cross called across the room.

'Pretty much,' came Peter's voice from the laptop. 'I started recording as soon as I realized you were in trouble. All recorded in crystal clear audio and full HD. I've also alerted your partner. You should have some friendly backup there shortly.'

Reynolds' face was growing bright red with rage. 'You stupid bitch,' he cried. 'And as for you...' He turned the gun to shoot at the laptop and as he did so, Cross lunged towards him. A shot rang out, but due to the weapon's silencer it was more of a muffled crack than the usual deafening bang.

The two of them flew to the floor, Reynolds' hand slamming into the polished floorboards, but still managing to hold on to the gun. Cross lay on top of him, pinning his arm to the floor, but it was her left arm against his much stronger right arm, and he started to lift it up. With all her strength, she pulled back her right arm, punching him as hard as she could in the side of the head.

His head snapped back, hitting the wooden floor, but it only seemed to make him angrier. He snarled, baring his teeth, and he pushed back against her, rolling her off him and pushing her to the side.

He tried to bring the gun around, but she grabbed hold of his arm with both hands this time, fighting to keep it pointing away from her. Somewhere in the distance she could hear Peter calling out, but his words were lost, drowned out in the heat of battle.

Reynolds was moving now, clambering on top of her, pinning her to the ground. The gun was getting closer and closer and she desperately tried to wrestle it away from him, but to no avail. He brought his head closer to hers, sneering at her. She brought her head back and then snapped it forwards, trying to head-butt him, but she couldn't get any force into it and ended up bashing it ineffectually against his cheek.

'You stupid bitch,' he whispered at her, his face just inches away from hers. 'I knew I should have killed you years ago.' There was another muffled crack as he squeezed the trigger of the gun, and then an explosion of pain in Cross's side as the bullet tore through her. Her grip on his arm disappeared, her arms falling limply to her side.

He pulled himself upwards, kneeling above her now. A crimson circle was starting to form on the floor underneath her.

'I *always* get what I want,' he spat at her again.

Cross whispered something back at him, her voice too weak for him to hear. 'What?' he whispered back, leaning forwards over her again, genuinely intrigued as to what her final words might be. Again, she whispered something, and he leant right forwards, holding his ear above her mouth. 'What?'

'Not this time,' she wheezed in his ear before swinging her hand around towards his head. She had reached into her pocket and withdrawn her pock-et-knife, and she now slashed out at him with her last ounce of strength. With his head held sideways above hers, his neck was exposed and she aimed the blade straight at it. The knife dug deeply into his flesh and she slashed it across his throat. Blood gushed from the wound, spraying across Cross, although she barely noticed. He rolled off her, desperately clutching at his throat as the blood poured through his fingers until he collapsed on the floor next to her, his legs convulsing involuntarily.

'For God's sake, hold on,' came Peter's voice through the computer's speakers. 'Help is on its way.'

'The whisky box...' groaned Cross in a low cry, before collapsing into unconsciousness.

Chapter 38.

Peter pulled up in Cross's street thirty minutes later. The road in front of her house was closed, the street full of police cars and ambulances. He climbed out and looked around through the mass of people milling around until he saw who he was after.

'Dave!' he called out. 'Detective Brooks!'

Detective Brooks was standing behind a cordon talking to a uniformed police officer, but turned his head as Peter called him. Slowly, he traipsed over.

'I'm Peter White,' said Peter. 'I don't think we've ever been properly introduced.' He held out his hand and Detective Brooks shook it firmly. 'How's she doing?'

'Not well. It looks touch and go as to whether she'll pull through.'

'And Superintendent Reynolds?'

'Dead. Bled to death on the floor.'

Peter held out his hand and opened it; in it was a small memory stick. 'I've got the whole thing on here – she was Skyping me just before it all kicked off and I managed to record almost all of it.'

Brooks gave him a nod, pocketing the stick. 'I'll make sure it gets to the right people; you can depend on it.'

'Can you get me inside?' asked Peter. 'Cross had something she desperately needed to get to a friend of mine. I think her last words to me were where she had hidden it.'

Brooks sighed. 'I suppose it's important?'

Peter nodded solemnly. 'The lives of a good woman and her son may depend on it. It's what Cross had risked everything for.'

'Okay, come with me.' Brooks lifted up the police tape and ushered Peter through.

Chapter 39.

Ash House, Dartmoor, England.

Peter White was sitting in the long dusk shadows of the porch when Jack stepped out of his car, his feet crunching noisily on the gravel driveway. Peter stood up, stretching with a stifled yawn, and Jack silently unlocked the front door.

Jack stepped inside, and Peter followed him into the kitchen. Jack took the heavy tome from Egypt out of his bag and laid it on the centre of the kitchen table, before adding the copies of the notes and photographs he had taken from the Brotherhood.

'So what's the plan?' asked Peter. He placed his own bag on the table, and opened it to show the orb within. 'Are you going to trade this for Jennifer and Bill?'

Jack gave a resigned sigh. 'That's one option... but I don't trust Randolph. Especially not to give up Bill now that he's also got Jennifer to bargain with. We still don't know what their master plan is.'

'We have these papers of mathematics,' said Peter, leafing through the sheets on the table until he found the ones he was referring to. They're something to do with areas of high gravity if I remember correctly... how multiple stars or black holes would interact. Do you think this has something to do with the other planet where you saw them?'

Jack thought for a moment. 'No, I think it's more direct than that. When Jennifer spoke to Silas, he told her that some believed these orbs contained the spark of a dying sun. He also said that collecting all the orbs together would be like creating a small star or black hole here on Earth.'

'Then you think that's what the mathematics is about?'

'It would certainly explain their interest in it,' said Jack. 'I think they're trying to understand what would happen if they brought all eight orbs together. If that's the case and they're planning to use them to destroy the world, I'm not sure we should even consider giving it to them.'

'I don't think that's their plan,' said Peter. 'I think it's more likely that they're planning to somehow try and use them to release their god from wherever he's imprisoned. I heard that from both Melissa Brooks and the professor.'

'That also fits in with what I heard from Randolph. So *how* is he imprisoned? Do you know?'

Peter shook his head. 'He's supposed to be somewhere outside of space and time as we know it, somewhere that can only be unlocked when *the stars are right.*'

Jack looked at the orb sitting on the table in front of them. 'But these surely must be part of their plan. If they contain the spark of a dying sun, however figuratively, could *they* be the stars, rather than stars in the heavens?'

Peter shrugged. 'It's always possible. We've got no idea *what* they are.'

'And even if they're not planning to destroy the planet, but only want to release their master... is that still a fair price to pay for Jennifer and Bill? How much death and destruction might that unleash upon the world?'

'Unknown. Maybe none. Maybe their plan won't even work. But worst case? I wouldn't like to guess.'

'So we need another plan,' said Jack

'Could we destroy it? The orb?'

'They're meant to be indestructible.'

'But have you tried?'

Jack shook his head. 'No.' He stood up. 'I'll be back in a moment.' He stepped out of the room and re-entered a few minutes later carrying a metal sledge hammer.

'Are you sure?' asked Peter. 'If you do destroy it, you might be giving up any chance of getting back Jennifer and Bill.'

'If it's what it's supposed to be... then I won't succeed anyway,' said Jack. He brought the hammer up above his head, bringing it down onto the orb with all his might. The hammer bounced off it with a quiet ring, smacking into the table and creating a large dent in its polished surface.

Jack put the hammer down on the floor, and he and Peter leaned over the orb, inspecting it closely.

'Not even a scratch,' said Peter.

'Okay, we can't destroy it, at least not easily,' said Jack.

'How about hiding it?'

'Where? It'll only be delaying the inevitable, as sooner or later they'll track it down.'

'But maybe too late for their current plans.'

'And too late for Jennifer and Bill too. If we want to stop their plans permanently, then we'd somehow need to get rid of all of them. We need a solution that would give me at least a chance of getting my wife and child back.'

Peter sat back down at the table and leafed through the other sheets. 'So we've got these maps of underwater terrain, these numbers and that tome,' he said, gesturing to the book on the table. 'What does it all mean?' He picked up the book and started to leaf through the pages. 'Have you learned anything from this?'

'Something,' said Jack. 'It has the ritual for opening their gates, and I think the ritual for creating one too. But when I tried to use a gate that Randolph had created, it didn't work.'

'Do you know why?'

'I think when you create a gateway, you can create it so that it needs a key – to keep out undesirables like you and me.'

'Then how did you get through the gate from the sanatorium to their base – and back again?'

Jack fell silent for a moment, and then put a hand up to his neck. 'Hold on a moment.' He stood up and stepped out of the room. He returned a moment later holding the pendant he had found on the body under the sanatorium. 'I was wearing this around my neck all those times I successfully used any of their gates. This *has* to be it.'

Peter nodded back at him in agreement.

Jack's phone buzzed, and he pulled it out of his pocket. 'It's a message,' he said, unlocking the phone. 'From the Brotherhood.' He scanned through the text of the message twice and then looked at his watch. 'It's details of where and when to meet up for the exchange. We've got less than twenty-four hours to figure this all out.'

Chapter 40.

April 15th, 2017. Imber Village, Wiltshire, England.

Jack arrived at the rendezvous point just after the crack of dawn. It was a deserted village deep in the Salisbury plains, now owned by the army for training purposes. Peter had been able to use his military contacts to get a map of the site and then help sneak Jack in under the cover of darkness. Jack knew that once the proceedings started he wouldn't have much time, and he wanted to be prepared. He explored the area around the meeting place, examining the ruined and abandoned buildings until he found what he was looking for. Inside one of the houses, on a wall in a dark corridor was a faint outline of a doorway, drawn in chalk on the wall. They still didn't know that he understood their trick, their secret mode of transport. Or at least he hoped they didn't – everything rode on that.

Now that he had found where they would come from, he strode out into the courtyard outside, scanning the horizon until he saw what he was looking for. Then he sat down on the grass and waited.

It was just over thirty minutes later when two men strode out of the ruins, just where Jack had expected them to come from. He looked at his watch; they were two minutes early, as eager as he was to get this over and done with.

The men were wearing full-length black robes with hoods to mask their faces, and they drew to a halt ten feet from him. The first man slipped his hand out of his robes, revealing a handgun, which he coolly levelled at Jack. Jack remained sitting nonchalantly on the floor, as if this was just a normal Saturday morning. The second man circled around them, looking high and low as if searching for something. 'You came alone?' he barked at Jack.

'Of course,' said Jack. 'That was the deal, right?'

'You have the orb?' asked the first man from within the depths of the robe. Jack didn't think he recognized the voice. 'That was also the deal, unless I'm very much mistaken.'

'I have it,' said Jack, holding up a small backpack.

'Then hand it over.'

'First show me Jennifer. I want to know she's safe.'

'That isn't part of the deal. Give us the orb, and when this is over, Randolph will let her go.'

'Where is she?' said Jack.

'Not here.'

'Then take me to her.'

The first man cast a glance over at his partner. This obviously wasn't running to their script. 'I can't do that. You have to give me the orb. I'll give it to Randolph, and then *he'll* let her go.'

'Then take me to Randolph.'

'I can't.'

'Can't... or won't?'

The man ignored him. 'We're wasting time here. Do you have the orb or not?'

'Of course I have. Do you think I'd risk my wife's life?'

'Then hand it over.' He was getting annoyed now.

Jack started to climb to his feet.

'Slowly,' said the man with the gun. 'No fast moves.'

Jack nodded. 'Are you going to take me to Randolph or not?'

'Just waste the fucker,' said the second man. He was clearly nervous and agitated. 'Let's just take the orb and get the fuck out of here.'

The first man raised the gun, pointing it at Jack's head.

'That'll be a no, then?' asked Jack. Slowly, he raised one hand in the air, holding up three fingers.

'What the...' started the first man. He was cut short as a sudden loud crack rang out and he fell backwards, a crimson spray exploding from his back. From the tree line several hundred metres away, Peter White readjusted his sights down the sniper rifle.

The second man just had time to look down and see the red dot on his chest. 'Oh, fuck,' he muttered, and then he too collapsed backwards as a bullet impacted with his chest.

'I guess I'm going to have to do this myself then,' sighed Jack, stepping into the building from whence they came.

Inside the dark room Jack muttered the incantations, reciting the words in the low guttural language of the Old Gods. As he finished, the doorway lit up and bathed the area in a white glow. He closed his eyes as he stepped into the light, bracing himself for the feeling of exhaustion and disorientation he associated with travelling through these gates, but as he arrived on the other side, he felt better than he had expected. Maybe he was starting to become less affected by the process; he didn't know whether that was a good thing or a bad thing. Maybe it didn't matter anymore.

He was standing in the circular room again, illuminated only by the glow of the doorway behind him, the eleven other portals standing dormant before him. He drew a torch out of his bag, turning it on before the light from behind him went out.

He looked at the other doorways, examining each in turn until, with a sigh of relief, he found what he was after. This was a doorway that had been blank before, but the recent markings on the wall matched what he had hoped to find. Scrawled in chalk as part of the elaborate patterns were four numbers – 49, 9, 126 and 43 – what he now knew were in fact coordinates of latitude and longitude – 47°9' South, 126°43' West. A place somewhere in the middle of the Pacific Ocean, hopefully an island.

He slipped the backpack off his shoulder, reaching inside to grab hold of the orb he had placed within. As he held it in the palm of his hand, he felt calm, focused and confident.

Reluctantly, he let go, removing his hand from the bag, slinging it back over his shoulder. He spoke those guttural words again, activating the second doorway. This was where he would find him. It was time to finish Randolph's game once and forever.

Chapter 41.

47°9' South, 126°43' West: a small island in the Pacific Ocean.

Jack found himself standing on flat black rock, looking out over an ocean. Before him stood a stony shore of smooth oily-black pebbles, and beyond that was deep green sea, as far as the eye could see. To his left and right were black cliffs and mountains, towering imposingly over him. Behind him was the base of a sheer cliff face, a glowing doorway flickering on its surface. Everything was dark, cold and wet, much of the floor covered with dark-green algae.

Standing before him was Randolph. He was holding a gun outstretched, aimed directly at him. He didn't look entirely surprised to see him.

'Where are we?' asked Jack.

'My master's resting place,' replied Randolph with a grin. He waited for a moment, until the doorway behind Jack turned dark and lifeless. 'I'm assuming that the men who were sent to meet you won't be joining us?' Jack gave a brief shake of his head. 'Well, then you'll have to take their place. Together, we're going to set my master free.'

'What makes you think I'm going to help you do anything?'

Randolph waved the gun casually. 'I would have no qualms about killing you. Or hurting your lovely wife and son.'

'You're not going to kill either of them.'

'True. Their destiny lies elsewhere. But I could make life very unpleasant for either of them. *Extremely* unpleasant. So, Mr Knight, give me the orb.'

'I need to know you're going to let Jennifer go first.'

'You're in no position to demand anything, Mr Knight. I could just shoot you and take it from you.'

'Then why don't you?'

'Because you may come in useful. The journey ahead of me is not without some peril, and now that you are here, I may as well put you to some use. If you do what I say and help me, I promise I will let your wife go unharmed after this is finished.'

'And I'm just supposed to trust you?'

'Have I ever lied to you, Mr Knight? I may not have always told you everything, I may have withheld information from you, but have I ever actually *lied* to you? Ever broken a promise I made to you?'

'No,' muttered Jack reluctantly.

'Unlike your good selves, I might add. Your wife will be released, unharmed, if you do everything I say.'

'And what's to come of me?'

'Let's just hope you've made a will. Once this is all over, I've got no particular interest in killing you myself, you understand, but it remains to be seen whether either of us will make it off this island alive. If memory serves, you've been willing to risk your life for your dear wife before. Trade your life, even. Now... Give. Me. The. Orb.'

Jack slung the backpack off his shoulders, placing it on the floor. He carefully unzipped it and reached inside.

'Slowly, Mr Knight. No surprises.' He gave the gun another quick shake to remind Jack of its presence.

'If we're going to die here together, then you may as well call me Jack,' said Jack, withdrawing the orb from the bag. The world outside him and Randolph seemed dull and muted as he held it in his hands, the clouds and waves moving just that little bit more slowly out of the corner of his vision.

'Very well, Jack. Throw it towards me.'

Jack threw the orb onto the floor before him. It rolled across the black stone towards Randolph until he brought his foot down on it, stopping its movement. Once Jack had let go, the world seemed to pop into life around him again, the colours and sounds flooding back.

Randolph crouched down, picking up the orb in his left hand, never taking his eyes or his gun from Jack. Jack could hear him muttering something under his breath as he held it in his hand, before he slipped it into his jacket pocket.

'Very good,' he said. 'Let's go. We have a bit of a trek before us.' He motioned towards Jack's right with his gun, away from the sea and towards the centre of the island. Jack could see a narrow path between the rocks and headed for it.

They walked in near silence for several minutes across the desolate wasteland, Randolph just giving occasional directions. The landscape was barren black rock, slippery and slimy as if it had recently been underwater. As they journeyed further inland, so their elevation rose, gentle slopes that soon became rocky hills that they were forced to climb up on hands and feet.

As they reached the top of a particularly steep incline, Jack stopped, standing on a plateau of coal-black rocks. In front of him stood a narrow crevasse between two sheer cliffs, a narrow and winding passage leading off before them. He leaned forwards, his arms resting on his thighs as he tried to get his breath back. The air here was stale despite the strong breeze, a fetid odour of rot and decay.

'So,' he said in between deep breaths, 'what exactly are these orbs then?'

'Relics from a bygone era,' said Randolph. 'Fragments of a god, from before mankind was born. From before even this world was born.'

'You truly believe that?'

'I wouldn't be here if I didn't'

'And where exactly is *here?*'

Randolph waited a short while before he answered, as if deciding how much to tell him. 'An ancient place. A sacred city built before mankind had ever walked on this Earth. This was the home to the Great Old Ones who once ruled over this world. It has lain at the bottom of the Pacific Ocean for aeons. When the conditions are right, and with the right rituals, it is possible to raise it to the surface, so that the likes of you and I can visit.' Randolph cast a glance at his watch. 'I've cut the timing a bit fine, but we still have plenty of time to get there.'

'To where exactly?'

'To the ancient prison where my master lies sleeping... dreaming... and waiting for his release.'

'If he's so powerful, why does he need you to release him?'

Randolph smiled politely. 'The vault where he is interred is accessible via the nearby city, but it is not truly here in any physical sense. The doorway lies here, but is merely a gateway to a place outside normal space and time, a pocket of reality divorced from our own, where space and time are not as they are here.'

'And you alone can unlock this door?'

'*Unlock* may not quite be the right word. The doorway can only be opened when the stars are aligned, but luckily for me, I've brought along my own stars.'

Jack stood up straight again and turned to face Randolph. 'The *Aztria*.'

Randolph raised an eyebrow in surprise and gave a little smile. 'I see you know a little more about these orbs than you've been letting on. Yes, I believe these will let me... well, not necessarily unlock the door, but tunnel through it.'

'To distort and bend space enough for someone to slip through. Or something...'

The smile widened on Randolph's face. 'My, my, you have been doing your homework, haven't you?' he said. He looked around as if to gauge their exact position. 'We should get going,' he said, motioning for Jack to continue.

Jack peered down the crevasse. It was narrow and looked tight but passable. He could feel a stiff breeze of the foul-smelling air blowing towards him from whatever lay on the other side. 'Are you sure about this?'

'Quite sure,' said Randolph, waving his gun once again.

Jack took a few tentative steps forwards. The floor was thick and sticky here, a viscous ebony goo. He started down the narrow passageway, his boots squelching as he stepped. He felt like he was walking through tar. 'You keep talking about this being a city, but all I've seen so far is rock. Rock, stone...' He looked down at his boots, covered in the slimy black mud that they were walking through. 'And this... *ooze*.'

'Keep going,' said Randolph. 'Not much further now.'

With a deep sigh, Jack resumed his trek. True to Randolph's words, it didn't take long. It only took a few more twists and turns before the crevasse opened up, revealing a massive valley floor below them. Laid out before them, spreading off into the distance were the remains of an ancient city, the ruins of a bygone civilization.

Jack stumbled and almost collapsed as he realized that he knew this place. He had been here before. That first dream he had had in Ash House, all those years ago. A dream of a vast underwater city, the colossal ruins of an ancient civilization. He shuddered as he remembered how the dream had ended, that *thing* that had been imprisoned within, waiting for him.

'You see,' said Randolph. 'Behold the sacred city of R'lyeh, where my master lies sleeping, awaiting our arrival.'

Jack was staring at the city before him. The vast cyclopean structures appeared to be almost moving before his eyes, buildings impossibly twisted and angled, like a construction from one of M.C. Escher's most fevered imaginings. The other side of the valley seemed to twist upwards in defiance of Euclidean geometry, and as he looked up, the tops of the mountains they had passed between seemed to leer impossibly overhead and in front of them.

'What the hell is going on?' he muttered, closing his eyes to stop himself feeling dizzy. He felt like he had just stepped off a particularly savage roller-coaster.

'My master is imprisoned... well, you can think of it as an isolated pock-et of space-time, cut off from our own dimensions. He is confined in a space which is not really a space, at least not in our universe – in a time where no time passes as far as he is concerned. We're close now. It really plays hell with the local geometry,' he added with a grin. He looked at Jack, who was leaning forwards and looked like he might throw up. 'The feeling of nausea will pass before long.'

Jack gave it a moment or two and then opened his eyes. He did feel slightly better. He could see a rocky pass leading down before him, down to-wards where a huge set of stone doors was set into the floor.

'Time to go,' said Randolph. 'My master awaits.'

Jack stepped forwards. As he took a first step down the rocky path, he stumbled, his feet not meeting the rocky step where his eyes told him it would be.

'You should be careful,' said Randolph.

'Yeah, thanks,' replied Jack sarcastically. He set off again, more carefully this time, feeling with his feet as he went. The path was straight, leading dir-ectly towards the doors, but as he approached their location kept moving, twisting around to his left even as he walked directly towards them. In the distance, the buildings and mountains seemed to shift and move as he walked, as if he were suffering from severe vertigo. It was as if the space here had been stretched and bent, twisted around and onto itself.

As he reached the bottom of the slope, he realized that, impossibly, the two doors were in fact set into the cliff face at the bottom of the mountains. As he looked up while facing the doors, he could see the crevasse far above him.

Jack drew to a halt about fifty feet — or what felt like fifty feet, he could no longer be sure — from the stone doors. From here, he could see patterns all over them. Some of the symbols he recognized, sigils and glyphs from long-dead languages only recorded in a few secret tomes; others were a mystery to him. A circle was inscribed around the perimeter of the doors, and positioned around its circumference were eight circular indentations. Curved lines — or were they straight? He was finding it hard to tell — swept away from these depressions, intersecting as they carved out a particular path. The whole pattern seemed to sway before his eyes; the lines appeared to bend and twist, but if he focused on any particular area, it seemed fixed. It was making his head ache, and he closed his eyes before turning around to face Randolph.

'What the hell are those markings?' he enquired.

'They describe the movement of certain stars through the heavens,' replied Randolph. 'A journey of centuries. Eons, really. We're fortunate that I've brought my own, so we don't have to wait quite so long.' He took his bag from his shoulders, throwing it onto the floor by Jack's feet. 'Take those and the others, and place them into the depressions in the door.'

'Others?'

'My colleagues have been kind enough to bring the others for us. We've just been waiting for you to bring the final one.' He motioned towards the door.

As Jack looked again, he could see three small wooden boxes. Two were either side of the door, roughly the same distance from it as he was. The third was the same distance again, but above it.

'How am I meant to get to that?' he asked.

'Take these over and you'll see,' grinned Randolph.

Jack knelt down and reached into the bag. He pulled out the two orbs, one in each hand. He felt calmer as he held them, time seeming imperceptibly slower. Randolph seemed distant now, as if he wasn't really standing twenty feet from him, but was instead some kind of projection, not real at all.

'So is your master behind this door?' asked Jack.

'In some sense, maybe. But in a more real sense, he is not even in our universe. He exists outside of our space and time, able to communicate only through the power of dreams. Traditionally only a one-way communication, but with the help of your son and some other guinea pigs, we've been able to establish... well, a more direct line of communication.'

Jack nodded, thinking of what Peter had told him of the students who had been involved in the dream research – and what had become of them.

'Only very rarely do the stars align correctly so that my master can be released, but we're not willing to wait that long. *I'm* not willing to wait that long. Instead, we're going to break him out. Use the power of our own stars to bend and distort the walls of his prison. Distort the very fabric of space and time enough for him to tunnel his way through.'

'You're mad,' muttered Jack. 'And if I don't help you?' He looked down at the orbs in his hands, where he could feel little sparks of electricity jumping between them.

'Then you will die, and your wife shall live a life of perpetual torture... all the way until her untimely death.'

'You're not giving me much of a choice are you?'

'No, Mr Knight, I'm not.'

'I thought you were going to call me Jack?'

Randolph smiled a sickly smile. 'No, *Jack*,' he corrected.

Jack took a few tentative steps towards the door. The feeling of vertigo was even more pronounced now and grew stronger as he neared the epi-centre. As he inched his way closer, the world seemed to slowly rotate before him, the vertical doors in the cliff face becoming huge trap doors in the floor again. As he reached their edge, he could now see that each of the three wooden boxes was in fact lying on the floor, each on a different side. He turned, looking back at Randolph, who now appeared to be looking down at him from above. He still held the pistol in his hands, but Jack wondered whether he would stand any chance of hitting him here. Hell, he could probably stand five feet from him and the bullet would fly off in a curve somewhere. He wasn't sure he wanted to chance it, though.

He knelt down, placing the two orbs on the floor next to the door. The ground consisted of fine, slightly damp black sand, and they sunk in deeper than their weight would have suggested. He would gather all the orbs first, and then perform the final stage of inserting them into their final resting places.

Jack stood up again, stumbling towards the first box, the world seeming to twist under his feet with every step. He knelt down, cautiously opening the lid with trembling fingers. Inside were two similar orbs lying on a bed of purple velvet. He took a deep breath and then grasped them both, holding one in each hand. The world seemed to fade away again, dull and muted. It was almost peaceful, tranquil.

He took a few steps back towards the doorway, and then fell to his knees as a tremendous pain seared through his head. He could feel the orbs tingling in his hands, but could also sense another force, a lurking presence of great power watching over him. He tried to ignore it, taking the final few steps towards the door, and placing the two orbs on the dark sand.

He stood again and headed towards the second box. He seemed to be working against an unseen force, pulling him back as if he were walking up a steep incline. He moved step by step, slow painful strides, the pain between his temples growing with every footstep. He stopped when the box was in reach, collapsing to his knees before lifting the lid. There seemed to be small sparks of electricity between these two even before he reached in and picked them up. As he touched them, he was jolted as if being electrocuted. He instinctively pulled his arms back in reaction to the shock, and then tried again. The shock was smaller the second time, and he managed to retain hold of them, although he could feel the power surging up his arms.

He struggled back towards the door, the orbs seeming heavier with every step. The pain in his head was thumping now, beating out an ancient primal rhythm. The outside world seemed impossibly slow, Randolph barely moving at all. As he dropped the orbs into the ebony sand, lightning erupted in the sky, striking down at the tops of the mountains that surrounded him but it was impossibly slow, disproving everything he thought he knew about relativity. It was as if he was watching a video from an ultrahigh-speed camera; he could see the lines of light descending through the sky, forking and splitting as it headed towards its target. If there was any thunder, he couldn't hear it.

His legs heavy, the pain in his head almost impossible to bear, he headed for the final box. He could see now why Randolph had wanted Jack to perform this for him. As he picked up the final two orbs, his head snapped backwards with pain. He could sense the Great Old One now, feel him waking from his eternal slumber. In his mind, he could see his eyes opening, gargantuan red orbs in the darkness. It was aware of him, and he felt humbled in his presence, an inconsequential being of no long-term importance. If he ever slept again, he felt as if those eyes would be forever in his dreams, seeking him out, pulling him towards them until he could take it no longer. Everything made sense now. He could see his place in the universe, and how utterly insignificant it was. How insignificant *everyone* was. This was the end of days and he felt powerless to stop it, even as he carried the final orbs towards the door. He knew that mankind had been the keeper of this planet for too long, and now it was time for the ancient ones to return.

He collapsed as he dropped the final two orbs next to the door. He was impossibly tired, all of his energy spent, but he was feeling compelled to continue, drawn in by those dark red eyes, bottomless pools of evil that burrowed into the very depths of his mind.

But he knew now what he had to do. Maybe Randolph would make Jennifer's life a living hell, but that would be no different to what might happen if this creature – for he was loath to call it a god – was set free upon the world. He would try his best to save her, but he knew now that some sacrifices might have to be made – and he knew too that she would agree with him.

From out of his pocket, he drew a pen, a fat permanent marker from which he removed the lid. Then, he knelt down, the pain pounding in his head, and crawled on his hands and knees to the centre of the doors.

Strangely, as he neared the centre, the pain in his head seemed to subdue slightly. Sparks were jumping from the eight orbs, leaping through the air from one to another, but as he knelt in the space between them all, positioned in the eye of the storm, their effects seemed lessened as if cancelling out – or maybe balancing – each other.

With great care, he started to draw on the high stone doors, inscribing his own gate, just as he had seen on all those gates he had stepped through and in the tome he had brought back from Egypt. But this was a doorway to a place of his own choosing, a place far away from here and far away from any life as he knew it. He inscribed the necessary signs and symbols, all the while muttering the necessary incantations under his breath. He just hoped he had got this right; he might only have one chance. He looked over his shoulder as he did so, glancing at Randolph. He was moving so slowly that he almost looked frozen in time, but he could occasionally see minute signs of movement. He wondered how he might look to him, would he appear to be moving at impossible speeds, or would he also seem unmoving?

As he continued to utter the words required to give power to this portal, he saw a huge flash of light. For a moment, he thought it was another flash of the lightning that occasionally lit up the sky overhead, but then he realized it was Randolph. He had fired his gun, the normally instantaneous flash of muzzle flare appearing to last well over a second.

He could see the bullet moving through the air towards him, impossibly slowly, almost hanging in the air. He tried to ignore it, desperately trying to finish the ritual, but it was like trying to ignore a deadly animal lurking just behind you. Every time he looked, the bullet seemed to be moving faster, speeding up as it grew closer, synchronizing with his space and time.

As he drew to the end of the spell, he removed his jacket, placing it in the centre of the gate. Then he stepped away from it, moving sideways and out of the path of the bullet. It was now about a third of the way between Randolph and himself and moving at a walking pace. As he spoke the final words, there was a brief glow from the doorway, a small whoosh, and then another sudden bang as the bullet flew past, making a crack as it travelled faster than the speed of sound.

Jack headed to the nearest set of orbs. He knelt down, the pain in his head and the ache in his bones growing again as he did so. He picked up each orb in turn, gently throwing them onto his jacket, which lay in the centre of the gate.

He stumbled around the huge stone doors, taking a circular route to the next set of orbs. He could see another flash from Randolph now, another bullet being fired. He ignored it, kneeling down and throwing the next two orbs onto his jacket. As they landed next to the others, he heard a deep *thump* as if from a far-off explosion, and felt a force push him back as if being hit by a blast wave from an explosion.

He crumpled to his knees, screaming in pain as the feeling in his head intensified. He could sense the creature in his mind again, feel those eyes seeking him out, and it was *pissed*. He was doing something right then.

Something was running down his chin and he brought a hand up, wiping his nose. It was blood, dripping from one of his nostrils. He wiped it with his sleeve, trying his best to ignore it as he crawled on his hands and knees to the third set of orbs.

He heard the bang as the second bullet flew past him, and saw another extended flash from Randolph's gun. Surely by now he must realize how futile that was? He picked up the next two orbs, one in each hand. They felt incredibly heavy now; either that or he was becoming increasingly weak. Or maybe it was both. He threw them towards the middle with what little strength he had left, but it didn't seem to matter. As they approached the others, they almost seemed to be sucked in, drawn towards their brothers. The sound and force wave were even greater this time, his arms and legs collapsing even as he knelt on the ground, his face hitting the soft black sand.

He was so tired. He didn't know if he could make it to the last two orbs. He could feel the pull of the six orbs in the centre, trying to draw him in. He crawled on his belly towards the last pair, but it felt like he was climbing a near-vertical wall. The pain in his head was almost unbearable, his vision blurring and his ears ringing.

As he finally drew within reach of the final two orbs, he stopped. He lifted the first with one hand, finding only enough strength to lift it a couple of inches from the floor. It was enough, though. He lifted it up above the edge of the stone door, giving it only a feeble push, but it was enough. The orb rolled towards the centre, accelerating towards the others until it rested next to them. He repeated this with the final orb, too tired to watch as it rolled away.

Then, everything changed. Jack rolled over onto his back. He was looking up at the sky, but it seemed to be shrinking. The mountains on either side of this city seemed to be stretching, growing closer together, until he realized what was happening. The space around him was curling up, closing in on itself. Everything outside his immediate surroundings was growing darker and less distinct, as the pull from the orbs seemed to intensify. He was forced to grab hold of the ground to stop himself being pulled closer, sinking his fingers into the black sand to find solid rock underneath. *So this must be what it feels like to be near a black hole*, he thought to himself.

He was spent, exhausted, barely able to move his limbs, but he was so close now, so close to ending this. He pulled one hand from the sand, struggling to reach inside his shirt where he grabbed the pendant that was hanging around his neck on its leather thong. He ripped it from his neck, the leather thong snapping, and held it up in the air. Then he let go.

The talisman flew through the air, pulled in towards the orbs. As it struck them, stopping just above the inscriptions on the stone, the gateway activated, the black markings bursting into bright white light. With a blazing flash, the orbs dropped through the gate. They had been sent to the heavens, to a place between the stars, maybe even to whence they came.

There was a sudden silence, then an explosion of light and noise as the universe uncurled itself, dimensions unfolding and restoring themselves. Jack felt his body being thrown through the air before he landed, collapsing into the soft black sand, and unconsciousness finally descended over him.

Chapter 42.

Jack awoke with a start. He was aching, his head throbbing and his ears ringing, but miraculously he still seemed to be alive. He was lying face down in the black sand not thirty feet from the huge stone doorway, which to his great relief was still firmly shut.

He pulled himself to his feet, wiping his nose on his sleeve again. It left a long red smear on his arm, but the worst of the bleeding seemed to have stopped. He felt unsteady, wobbling on his feet until he realized it wasn't his legs that were wobbling – it was the ground. It was shaking and vibrating; maybe it was about to begin its descent again, returning to the depths of the Pacific until such time as the actual stars were right again.

He looked around, scanning the horizon, and spotted movement. Randolph was running up the hill, back towards the crevasse, back towards their arrival point. He too had realized that the island was about to sink, and would be making his way towards the gate they had arrived through. Jack instinctively reached for the pendant, which had until recently hung from his neck. It was gone now, gone with the orbs, and so was his chance of getting off this island – unless he could catch Randolph before he left.

He set off, sprinting after him, his legs weak but growing stronger with every step. If Randolph made it back first, not only would Jack be left here, consigned to a watery grave, but Randolph would have Jennifer, and Jack didn't want him to make good on his promise.

By the time he was halfway up the hill, he had already lost sight of Randolph who had disappeared into the fissure between the two mountains, but he didn't give up, didn't slow down. He scrambled up the rest of the hill using his hands as much as his feet, until he crested the top and stood before the narrow crevasse. The ground was still shaking, small rocks and stones tumbling down from the mountains overhead, but he couldn't worry about that now. He charged on, oblivious to the debris plunging down all around him. If he was struck by rubble as he clambered along the narrow passageway, jumping and climbing over any obstructions in his way, he didn't even notice, such was his single-minded determination to catch up with Randolph.

When he emerged from the other side of the crevasse, Randolph became visible again. He was at the bottom of the rocky slope before him, closer than he had originally been but still hundreds of feet away. Jack set off, scrambling and sliding down the rocky slopes, almost out of control. As he reached the bottom, he managed to translate his downward momentum into a horizontal sprint. He could see that Randolph was closer now; he appeared to be limping slightly and Jack was gaining on him.

Jack ran on, the muscles in his legs burning with pain, but he could see the end ahead of him: the cliff wall where the doorway was inscribed. He was still a hundred feet away as Randolph reached it. Jack could hear him calling out the words to activate it.

He pushed himself into a final desperate sprint, and as the doorway burst into life with a flash of white light, Jack threw himself at Randolph, grabbing at him and hoping to tackle him to the ground. Instead, they both flew forwards, carried on by Jack's momentum, and stumbled through the doorway as one.

They arrived with a flash, landing on the floor of the circular antechamber, still wrapped around each other. Randolph rolled from underneath Jack, turning to face him and kicking him away.

Jack grabbed at Randolph's feet as they flailed towards his face, trying both to protect himself and to stop Randolph getting away. One of the feet got past his defences, knocking him backwards, and Randolph scrambled backwards on his hands and feet before rolling over and climbing to his knees.

Jack climbed to his own feet and charged at Randolph. Randolph tried to side-step his attack, but was too slow. Jack barrelled into him, knocking him over and falling down on top of him again. He had started to rain a barrage of blows upon him with his fists when a gunshot rang out, an almighty blast in the enclosed chamber.

Jack looked up to see Sebastian standing ten feet away, holding an old revolver, which was aimed at the ceiling. Then he lowered his hand, moving his aim to point towards Jennifer. She was standing next to him, Bill by her side.

'Step away, slowly,' said Sebastian, loudly and clearly. 'You don't want anyone to get hurt.'

Randolph crawled backwards from Jack, climbing to his feet and wiping blood from his nose. He spat a mouthful of blood and saliva onto the floor.

Jack dutifully took a step back, putting his hands up. 'Okay,' he said. 'Just don't hurt them.'

'Don't worry about me,' cried Jennifer. 'They won't kill me; they're too concerned about their precious fucking prophecy.'

A look of realization spread across Jack's face, but it was too late. Sebastian had already retrained the pistol onto him. 'True,' he said with a shrug. 'But there's nothing to stop me killing you.' He carefully aimed the gun at Jack's head, slowly starting to squeeze the trigger.

'No!' cried Randolph.

'What?' exclaimed Sebastian.

'I'm going to kill this fucker myself,' growled Randolph, wiping more blood from his face as he stepped over to Sebastian, grabbing the gun from his grasp. He took a couple of steps back towards Jack. 'I should have done this a long time ago,' he spat. 'You've interfered with my plans for the last time.' He raised the gun, and Jack closed his eyes, waiting for the inevitable gunshot.

But it didn't come. Instead, Jack heard a scream. He opened his eyes to see Jennifer grabbing Sebastian from behind, her hands wrapped around his head, her fingers gouging into his eyes. Randolph glanced to his side to see what was going on, and that was all the opportunity Jack required. He lunged forwards, grabbing Randolph's hand with his own, and the gun was sent flying, skidding along the stone floor into the darkness.

Randolph swung his now-empty hand towards Jack, his fist connecting with the side of his head. Jack responded with a punch of his own, hitting Randolph in the side of his gut, partially winding him and sending him staggering back.

Jack's head was spinning from the blow, but he stepped forwards, taking another swing at Randolph. His aim was true, but Randolph twisted to the side at the last moment and Jack's fist carried on past his face. Randolph reached up to grab Jack's outstretched arm, trying to push him away. With his right arm tightly gripped by Randolph, Jack desperately tried to kick him with his left foot but was unable to get any real power into it. Unbalanced and on only one leg, he toppled to the ground as Randolph twisted his arm, pushing him sideways.

Then Randolph was on top of him. He felt a stunning blow to his kidneys, then another sharp jab on the other side of his body. A punch caught him on the cheek and his head snapped sideways, hitting the floor. Stars were spinning before his eyes and he could taste blood in his mouth.

Randolph was about to take another swing at Jack when a shot ran out. Both men turned to see Jennifer standing in the shadows and aiming a gun at Randolph. Bill was cowering behind her, his hands over his ears. Sebastian was lying on the floor, not moving.

'Let him go,' she shouted and Randolph complied, raising his hands and getting to his feet. Behind him, Jack slowly picked himself up from the floor, wiping the blood from his face.

'You can kill me, but another will simply take my place,' spat Randolph. 'Your boy still belongs to us, and we are legion.'

'Go stand with your father,' said Jennifer. 'Close your eyes, and promise me you won't open them until we tell you to.'

'Okay,' said Bill, hesitantly.

'Promise me,' she insisted.

'I promise,' he said in a nervous whisper, taking a few hesitant steps towards Jack. As he drew close, Jack grabbed hold of him, pulling him close, and Bill clung onto his leg, gripping hard and closing his eyes.

Jack and Jennifer looked at each other across the dark room. Jennifer took a hesitant step towards her husband, stepping out of the shadows and into the flickering torchlight.

'I understand now,' she said in a quiet and emotionless voice. 'I can see how this has to end.'

Jack looked at her as she slowly raised her hand; in it she held the old revolver.

'Jennifer, what are you doing?' His voice was wavering and unsteady, the concern clearly audible in his tone.

'Only what needs to be done for our son.' In contrast to her husband, her voice was calm and even.

Jack took a step forwards and then stopped as she raised the gun higher. 'It doesn't need to be like this,' he pleaded gently. 'We can find another way.'

Jennifer could see a tear in his eye, and she shook her head slowly, looking down at his feet to avoid his gaze. 'This is the only way out for him. I can see that now. I wish there was another way, but...' She stopped, letting the words trail off into silence.

Jack dropped to his knees before her, his tears now starting to flow freely. 'At least look me in the eyes one last time.'

Jennifer lifted her head slightly, so she was looking directly at him, their eyes meeting again across the room.

'I love you,' he said softly.

'I know,' she replied almost inaudibly, as she lifted the gun and took aim. 'That's what makes this so hard.'

'Please don't,' he implored her, his eyes wet and his hands clasped together in supplication.

With a tear in her eye and a lump in her throat, she took a deep breath. For a moment, Jack thought she wasn't going to go through with it, and then she closed her eyes.

'I love you, and I'm sorry,' she whispered as she pulled the trigger. There was a deafening crack as the sound of the gunshot echoed in the small chamber, then the soft thump of a body hitting the floor.

Jennifer collapsed backwards to the ground, the gun falling from her grip. She fell on her back, her dead eyes staring at the ceiling, sparing Jack the sight of the large hole in the back of her head.

'No!' screamed Jack.

'Dad!' shouted Bill.

'Don't open your eyes,' cried Jack. 'Keep them closed. Can you do that for me?'

'I... Yes. Yes I can,' he sobbed, tears running down his cheeks.

Jack knelt down, holding him tight. 'It'll be okay. Trust me, Bill,' he said.

Randolph looked at Jennifer where she had fallen, and then at Jack. He looked speechless. When he found his voice, he replied with a single word. 'Go,' he said.

'*What?*' exclaimed Jack.

'He is not who we thought he was. We will have no more need of him.'

'But?'

'He is not the one Aloysius spoke of, for he cannot now kill his mother.' His eyes were darting around feverishly, his mind trying to make sense of all the repercussions. 'Go now, before I change my mind.' He closed his eyes, slumping forwards and dropping to his knees. 'You will not hear from us again,' he muttered in a low voice.

Jack stepped over to the body of Jennifer, who was now lying in a pool of her own blood, leading Bill with his left hand. He knelt down, picking up the gun from where it lay on the floor. He turned to face Randolph, pain and rage visible in Jack's eyes in equal measure.

Randolph put his hands up, holding them in the air before him. 'I know how you must feel,' he said, slowly and calmly, 'but if you kill me now, no one will know the truth. No one will know that your son is not the prophesized one after all.' He looked up at Jack, looking him directly in the eyes. 'If you kill me, this will not be over. You need me as a witness.'

Jack clenched the gun tightly, still aiming it at Randolph with shaking hands. He didn't care anymore. After all that Randolph and the Brotherhood had put him through, he didn't deserve to live. He placed his finger on the trigger.

'Dad?' asked Bill in a timid voice.

'Y...Yes,' stammered Jack, distracted from his rage.

'Please... let's just go,' he pleaded gently.

Jack looked at Bill, at the small hand tightly gripping his own. He turned back to look at Randolph, then sighed deeply and slipped the gun into his belt. He span around, quickly examining the doorways until he spotted the one he wanted, the one he had come through to get here. 'Okay, son,' he said, 'Let's go.' They walked hand in hand over to the doorway, stopping just in front of the door. 'Stay there for one moment,' he said, letting go of his hand.

'Dad?' cried Bill, the fear clear in his voice.

'Don't worry, Bill,' replied Jack. 'Keep your eyes closed. I'll just be a moment, and then we'll be out of here.' He stepped over to where Sebastian lay on the floor, kneeling down and pulling a pendant on a chain from around the corpse's neck. Then he pulled the gun from his belt and stepped back over to Randolph, pointing the gun directly at him. As he drew close, his hands were no longer shaking.

He stopped two feet away, the gun pointed directly at his chest. 'If I ever see you again, I *will* kill you,' he whispered, too quietly for Bill to hear. Randolph nodded silently, a broken man. Then Jack reached forwards, grabbing the pendant that hung from Randolph's neck, snapping the leather thong and ripping it from his chest. 'I'm sure someone will be along soon enough to find you.'

He walked solemnly over to Jennifer's corpse, picking her up and heaving her over his shoulder, ignoring the blood that had congealed over her head and torso. He couldn't just leave her here. Bill was still standing in front of the doorway with his eyes closed, and Jack staggered back over to him, slipping Sebastian's pendant over his head before taking hold of his hand, Randolph's pendant clasped tightly in his fist. Quietly, he muttered the incantations, and together they walked through the doorway and out of the Brotherhood's life forever.

Epilogue.

Three years later.

Jack and Bill walked along the gravel path, the fresh summer breeze blowing lightly on their faces. It was the beginning of spring, the first flowers appearing in the long grass to accompany the ones standing in nearby pots and vases.

They silently walked hand in hand down a well-trodden path, one that no child that young should ever have to walk. When they reached their destination, Jack knelt down on the damp grass, Bill leaning over to place a handful of flowers on the gravestone before them. Once more, he read the inscription that was engraved there.

Jennifer Knight 1970 – 2017
Beloved wife and mother
Vita Mutatur Non Tollitur

Bill sat down on the grass and looked up at Jack, who was wiping a tear from his eye. 'Tell me about her,' he said. 'About mother.'

Jack gave a little smile. 'She was the bravest person I ever met.'

'Remind me again what she looked like.'

'She was beautiful, possibly the most beautiful woman I've ever met. She had this long black hair and the most piercing blue eyes. When she looked me in the eye and smiled, it was as if we were the only two people in the world.'

Bill looked away in concentration, as if trying to recall something from the depths of his memory.

'She gave her life so that you could have yours,' said Jack. He gave Bill's hair a little tousle, making him squirm.

'But you won't tell me how she died?'

'One day,' he said. 'One day, when you're older. I think it's fair to say that it's a long story, not all of it pleasant.'

'I asked Aunt Betty,' nodded Bill. 'She said it was complicated.'

'That's a bit of an understatement,' said Jack. 'You do deserve to know everything, and I will tell you, just...'

'Just not today.'

Jack nodded, looking up and letting the warm sunlight fall onto his face. 'Today, we have each other, and for that we should be eternally grateful.'

www.ingramcontent.com/pod-product-compliance
Lightning Source LLC
Chambersburg PA
CBHW071236190726
48292CB00007B/2310